# A PROVOCATIVE FLIRTATION

This would not do, Lord Gaventry lamented. He had his own purposes in coming to the Pump Room, which had nothing to do with either taking the waters or flirting with the lady before him. But, the moment he had caught sight of Miss Sarah across the room, he seemed to have had no other object in mind but to flirt with her . . . again.

So, here he was teasing her and tormenting her, whispering in her ear when he should not, taking steps toward her so that she had to back away if she meant to keep a maidenly distance between them. In other words, he was engaging her in a quite serious and quite provocative flirtation. Worse, still, she seemed to be responding, or so the curling smile on her lips would indicate and the glow of her lovely brown eyes.

He drew in a long, slow breath as he let his gaze take in every feature. She was lovely, there could be no two opinions on that score.

# BOOK YOUR PLACE ON OUR WEBSITE AND MAKE THE READING CONNECTION!

We've created a customized website just for our very special readers, where you can get the inside scoop on everything that's going on with Zebra, Pinnacle and Kensington books.

When you come online, you'll have the exciting opportunity to:

- View covers of upcoming books
- Read sample chapters
- Learn about our future publishing schedule (listed by publication month *and author*)
- Find out when your favorite authors will be visiting a city near you
- Search for and order backlist books from our online catalog
- Check out author bios and background information
- Send e-mail to your favorite authors
- Meet the Kensington staff online
- Join us in weekly chats with authors, readers and other guests
- Get writing guidelines
- AND MUCH MORE!

**Visit our website at
http://www.kensingtonbooks.com**

# A ROGUE'S REVENGE

*Valerie King*

## ZEBRA BOOKS
## KENSINGTON PUBLISHING CORP.
http://www.kensingtonbooks.com

ZEBRA BOOKS are published by

Kensington Publishing Corp.
850 Third Avenue
New York, NY 10022

All Kensington titles, imprints and distributed lines are available at special quantity discounts for bulk purchases for sales promotion, premiums, fund-raising, educational or institutional use.

Special book excerpts or customized printings can also be created to fit specific needs. For details, write or phone the office of the Kensington Special Sales Manager: Kensington Publishing Corp., 850 Third Avenue, New York, NY 10022. Attn. Special Sales Department. Phone: 1-800-221-2647.

Zebra and the Z logo Reg. U.S. Pat. & TM Off.

First Printing: May 2004
10 9 8 7 6 5 4 3 2 1

Printed in the United States of America

*To my daughter, Sarah, with infinite love*

# One

*Bath, England, 1818*

"Is someone there?"

Sarah Kittling heard her voice echo about Queen Square, but there was no answering response. She was sitting in the park across from her family's modest town house, reviewing again a novel she wished she had not written, when she thought she heard someone call to her.

"Ghosts," she murmured, smiling to herself and returning to the task at hand. She had composed a sequel to her first novel and found she was regretting profoundly that she had once more put "quill to parchment." What terrible demon had possessed her to do so, she would never fully comprehend, except of course for the very pressing need for an income. Yes, there was that, but surely, if she had tried very hard she could have achieved a better manner of providing for her family than trading in the comings and goings of a complete stranger. Surely!

Faint whispers reached her ears again. This time she stood up, clutching the calf-bound book tightly, holding her place with her finger, and whirling about. "Who is there?" she called again.

The square was unusually silent. A cool, early morning breeze billowed the skirts of her pelisse. Perhaps it was her conscience that was calling to her, reminding her that what she had done was unforgivable. How apt that would be, ghosts and her conscience joining together to torment her.

Her gaze searched the nearby streets, but she saw no one. A strange sentiment coursed through her suddenly, of a profound longing, a desire for her life to take a hard turn and go in another direction entirely, even perhaps for her heart to be awakened. How odd that a little incomprehensible whispering, undoubtedly the mere fancies of her mind, would cause her to think such thoughts.

In truth, there was little chance for love to bloom in her life. She understood her society exceedingly well. She was an impoverished miss, without a proper dowry, and therefore quite an ineligible match for any gentleman, unless of course he were very wealthy. Gentlemen of some substance were not, however, all that plentiful, especially not in Bath, which had, over the years, become a rather stodgy old city, hardly the place where such men desired to congregate.

Here she laughed, and the ghosts about the square disappeared. She rarely succumbed to such gloomy reflections. Hers was not such a nature, not by half. Not for Sarah Kittling to be commanded by a long string of "if only her life was thus and so." No, far better to keep her chin pointed in the proper direction, her eye fixed on the real objective—to keep her family from sinking yet further into real poverty.

She drew in a deep breath and ordered her nerves to be still. She sat down, opened the book, and continued the task of reading her latest novel. Her gaze settled upon the paragraph at the top of the right page. "Lord Daventry caught his enemy hard by the throat. He had been waiting for this moment since he first settled his gaze on the Duke of Widenhall so many years ago."

She closed the book with a snap and in her mind abbreviated the remainder of the plot. *The duke would die by his hand, a fitting end for the man who had seduced Lord Daventry's betrothed in the first novel, having subsequently led her into a life of the worst sort of degradation and folly.* This was the vision she had concocted for the final climax to Daventry's ill-fated existence—he would vanquish his enemy.

She closed her eyes. She wished the deed undone, but it was too late. In a matter of weeks, every bookseller in Bath would have her second novel ready for sale, for reading, for madcap gossiping that would go on for months, and she would once more have to pretend to be curious, astonished, even shocked, and everything else that was required to keep her identity as the authoress of both books a secret.

If only she hadn't used Daventry as the hero's appellation, a name that rhymed so pointedly with Lord Gaventry. What an ill-judged decision that had been and yet, because Lord Gaventry was famous for his roguish escapades, it was the rhyming of his name which had created so many sales and in turn royalties that had allowed her family to remain in Bath, in Queen Square, in the same town house she and her sisters had inhabited for some seven years.

Still, she should never, never, never have taken what had been years of gossip about the very real Lord Gaventry and turned it into a novel. She could only imagine what he thought of her for having written the book, nothing charitable undoubtedly. She pressed her hand to her forehead and squeezed her eyes shut. She tried very hard to dispel a strong sense of foreboding which had been dogging her heels since dawn. Why, oh, why had she written *A Rogue's Tale*, but worse, why had she agreed to write the sequel in which Daventry takes his revenge?

"Do but look at her, Brixham. I tell you she's the one. She will do very well for my purposes." Lord Gaventry peered around the corner, his gaze fixed on a young woman seated in Queen Square Park. She seemed distressed or perhaps had the headache for her hand was pressed to her forehead. "She has the look of a typical, prudish Bath maiden."

"How can you tell? She is nearly a hundred yards away."

"The way she sits as though she is wrestling with her conscience, only I ask you, what the deuce could any of these prosy ladies have done to warrant such contrition?"

"Kissed the footman, no doubt," Brixham whispered, chuckling.

Only with the strongest effort did Gaventry keep from barking his laughter. "Well, wish me good fortune," he said.

"I wish you to the devil."

"That deed, I fear, has already been accomplished," he countered crisply.

He was about to begin his quest, but his good friend stayed him with a hand on his arm. "Gaven," Brixham said, a sudden frown furrowing his brow, "are you certain this is what you want? So much has changed since *A Rogue's Tale* was first introduced. Perhaps you will be made as welcome in Bath as you were beginning to be in London."

The question startled Gaventry, though he was not certain precisely why. He snorted disbelieving laughter. "And what of next year and the tides turn yet again? What then? No, Brix, I shan't rely on society again. I shall cut my own path as I have been doing for the past seven years."

Brixham's smile was sympathetic. "Very well then. Have your bit of fun."

"I shall," he responded brightly, popping his hat a little more firmly on his head as a new breeze flipped the tails of his coat.

Without further conversation, he entered the square and began crossing quickly to the central garden, where the lady sat.

He had come to Bath with one purpose in mind—to find the authoress of *A Rogue's Tale*, to beguile her with a careful flirtation, then once her heart was his, to entice her into a scandalous situation from which he would subsequently abandon her. The harpies of Bath would have a fine feast in the devouring of her. Yes, that would satisfy the rage he felt at having been exposed publicly through the lady's book.

Only one thing disturbed him—the authoress had written more closely to the actual events of his life than she could possibly know. Only a handful of people had ever truly been versed in precisely what had happened so many years ago, so how was it that Miss Aurelia Kittling, whom the publisher of *A Rogue's Tale* had informed him was the novelist in question, had stumbled on even a portion of the truth?

These were questions he meant to have answered before he quit Bath, not least of which was Brixham's most recent query, *was this what he wanted?* He had been plowing through the waters of his social exile for so many years now that he realized he had never before given the matter a great deal of thought. What was it he had wanted before the disaster of his flirtation with Miss Fulbourne had intruded so fiercely on his existence? He simply could not remember. He had been young then, scarcely six-and-twenty, and rather naive as events proved. Now, with a great deal more experience on his shoulders, he felt capable of achieving anything he set his mind to, including the storming of Miss Kittling's snug little life in Bath.

But all that would play itself out in time. For the present, he intended to announce his arrival in the quiet, dull little town, by taking that which he should not, from a lady who was completely unknown to him and who was presently tapping her finger on her forehead. With a smile, he began to walk more quickly.

The closer he drew, the more he smiled. He was never so happy as when he was creating a little havoc in the lives of priggish maidens and even more so, very pretty priggish maidens, as the lady now appeared to be.

Sarah heard the footsteps and turned sharply. A man, a gentleman by all appearances, was fairly marching in her direction. Was this, then, her ghost?

She felt there was a measure of determination in his gait as well as in his countenance and was made certain of it when he caught her eye, lifted what appeared to be a rather devastating brow, and smiled. *She*, it would seem, was his object. But why?

Her heart began to race. She glanced quickly around the square. She was alone and unprotected. Was there no one to emerge from a doorway to disrupt the man's strong, deliberate march? Why was he approaching her in the first place? Did he think he knew her, for she was certain he was completely unknown to her?

She met his gaze again, and her heart skipped at least two beats. He was a very handsome gentleman, perhaps just thirty or a little more. His hair, beneath his glossy beaver hat, was very blond and his eyes, even at a distance of twenty yards, were a very fine blue. She felt suddenly dizzy and looked away from him. She opened her book hastily and began to read.

"That will not do," he stated decisively, calling to her.

"I beg your pardon?" she queried, her pulse jumping about madly as her gaze shot to his face again. "Were you addressing me?"

"Of course."

He was but ten yards away now. Oh dear. She should rise from her seat and hurry away. Surely she should. Surely this man, with his hat sitting at a rakish angle on his head, meant nothing good by his approach.

"Whatever did you mean by your words, sir?" she asked instead.

Suddenly, he was before her. He caught her wrist, lifted her abruptly to her feet, and the wretched novel fell to the path below. "What are you doing?" she asked in a tight whisper.

He tugged hard on the ribbons of her bonnet, and the bow, traitor that it was, gave way easily. He pushed her bonnet off her brown locks and as it rolled down her back and plunked onto the bench behind her, he slid a firm arm about her waist. He caught her chin with his fingers. "I chose a pretty one," he stated, a wicked smile suffusing his face.

She meant to ask him what he meant by having chosen anyone, but he made his purpose clear by placing his lips against hers. She struggled at first and drew back, but his arm held her like a vise. "Do stop at once!" she cried, but still she was whispering.

He laughed, very low. "You do not really seem to mind else you would raise your voice to the rooftops instead of whispering."

This she could not allow and opened her mouth to set up a caterwaul, but he prevented a single sound from reaching the air by kissing her in a manner she had never been kissed before—fully, ravenously, and with all the experience in the world.

The fight died so quickly in her it was as though a bucket of winter water, still chilled from a layer of ice, had been thrown over her protests. In its place was a feeling of rapture so profound, so unexpected, so exhilarating, that she found herself leaning into the quite wicked rogue and allowing, even engaging in, his hearty exploration of her lips and mouth. Somehow her arms made their way about his neck, and somehow she began giving kiss for kiss as though not to do so would surely be the end of her life.

There was within her a whisper of warning that she was behaving scandalously, but for reasons she could not explain, she did not care one whit. She had a powerful conscience that kept her almost hourly in a state of nervous despair lest she break one of society's careful rules, so it was an extraordinary circumstance that she was partaking of a completely improper kiss, with something she could only describe as utter recklessness. In truth, she wished the stranger would go on kissing her forever.

He drew back suddenly, a deep furrow between his brows, but she hungered for the forbidden kiss and sank against him once more. This time, a strange awareness arose between them. He kissed her once, then looked at her, searching her eyes. She kissed him again then also looked at him, taking in the shape of his brow, the strong cheekbones, the stern line of his lips, which of course needed more kissing. He received her kisses with tense restraint.

"Who are you?" he asked at last, his arms still holding her firmly against him.

"Miss Kittling, Sarah Kittling," she breathed against his lips. She heard his breath catch. She asked, "Do you know of me?"

He shook his head. "No," he responded. "But it would seem providential to be meeting you this morning."

"In what way?" she asked, wishing he would not speak so much.

"In this way," and he kissed her again, full on the lips.

Sarah felt all her cares dissipate like strong sunlight in a heavy fog. She felt free and happy as she had never felt in her entire life. How could a kiss achieve so much and that with a gentleman completely unknown to her? A sense of mystery and wonder enveloped her. She was no longer earthbound but was flying among the heavens. She could hear Vulcan's forge and the clang of steel on the anvil. She heard the whispers of Diana and Venus, playful Psyche and Eros. She tasted ambrosia on the stranger's lips, and she knew, *she knew*, she would never again be the same.

The clatter of a carriage on the paved street could be heard, a sound which divided her from him as though a sword had severed the strange connection.

"When you speak of this, as undoubtedly you will, Miss Sarah Kittling, you may tell your friends that Gaventry was the gentleman who so ruthlessly abused your wonderfully sweet lips."

She gasped and took two steps away from him.

A hard, mocking light entered his eye. "Just so," he responded. He glanced down and saw the book. Fortunately, the cover which held the title was face down on the pavement. He picked the book up and without examining it further, handed it to her.

She thanked him, but quickly hid the book behind her. A clarity grew in her mind, a sharp awareness that she had behaved in a terrible manner with a man she had already betrayed, even though she was just now meeting him for the first time. At the same moment, she thought, *So, this is Lord Gaventry of whom I have heard so much. Why did no one tell me that he was perhaps the handsomest man in the kingdom?*

He bowed very low to her, then turned and began his march briskly in the direction from whence he had come.

Sarah's knees failed her, and she sank down on the bench, barely missing her bonnet. She brought the novel forward to stare at it. The title condemned her completely—*A Rogue's Revenge, the Continuing Adventures of Viscount Daventry.* Her thoughts became a jumble of fears, recriminations, wonder, and sweet recollection. She did not know what to think first, whether to dread the knowledge that Gaventry had actually come to Bath or whether to delight in the wondrous encounter which had just occurred between them? Yet why had he chosen to kiss a complete stranger, and was it possible that fate had brought him to her in such a stupefying manner? Above all, she had the worst sensation that she had just met her ideal. But that was absurd, for Gaventry was one of England's most notorious rakehells. How could he ever be any woman's ideal?

Fear now worked in her, fear that he was here, fear that he knew who she was as an author and that he meant to do her some manner of harm, fear that he would destroy her family if he could because of the ill turn she had served him.

These reflections, of course, were ridiculous since he could not know who she was. No one knew. She had sworn her publisher to secrecy, and even then she had used her elder sister's name instead of her own. With this thought, therefore, she began to be more at ease. She glanced at his retreating back, now a mere sliver in her eyesight as he rounded the bend. She released a profound sigh. Whatever the future might hold, she did not think she could ever truly regret this most extraordinary kiss.

Of course she should have. It was wholly scandalous, but maybe that was the very reason why she had given herself to

Gaventry's embrace in the first place. With a dawning awareness, she realized she was sick to death of always being
responsible for her family, for being wise and good, and never
having even the smallest of adventures. This morning, however,
adventure had come to her, if in a very small way, in the guise
of Viscount Lord Gaventry, the subject of her two novels.

No. So long as she lived, whether or not scandal and being
ostracized resulted from Gaventry's sudden arrival in Bath,
she would never regret the kiss she had shared with him. With
that, she clutched the novel in her hand, picked up her bonnet, dangling it from the ribbons, and made a slow progress
back to her house.

"What the devil was that?" Brixham asked, clearly stunned.

Gaventry laughed. "I have not the faintest notion."

"Ripe for the plucking," he stated.

At that, Gaventry's temper flared and he raised a caution-
ary finger to his good friend's face. "Do not even think such
a thought," he cried, though surprised by his need to defend
Miss Sarah Kittling. "She is a complete innocent."

"I see I have wounded your sensibilities," he returned face-
tiously. "But now you have amazed me or did I not quite
understand what I saw just now?"

Gaventry shrugged not knowing what to say.

"What happened then?"

"I cannot explain it," he responded, shaking his head. He
gestured for them to begin walking in the direction of the
Royal Crescent, and when they had begun their ascent up
the gentle rise to the gravel walks, he added, "I felt as though
I had known the lady for years and had even kissed her
before, but that could not in any manner be possible."

"Perhaps you met her once at a masquerade," he suggested.

Gaventry pondered this possibility. "She would never have
attended that sort of masquerade and the only lady I ever
kissed at a proper ball was Miss Fulbourne."

At the mention of her name, his friend shuddered. "Do not speak of her. I cannot but hear her name without the most ignoble thoughts of murder rampaging suddenly through my head."

"Such thoughts tend to plague me as well," he added. "None of this would have happened were it not for her. There would have been no reputation to survive, no gossip to hear bandied about again and again and in so many different forms that it makes my head swim to think of it, and certainly no novel to put the final cap on the entire escapade, which leads me to say that the lady I kissed was the authoress's sister, Sarah Kittling."

"Good God!"

Gaventry laughed. "I sense the gods at work and I am begun to be terrified."

"Do you mean to pursue the chit?"

"Good God, no!" he exclaimed. "What a ridiculous notion. You know perfectly well what my intentions are and a kiss or two will not change that."

"Rather looked like a dozen—"

"Did you watch the entire time?"

"Couldn't help it. Wanted to see the chit give you a severe dressing down. Never thought she would wrap her arms around your neck. But that is always the way with you. You have but to smile a little and the ladies swoon in your arms."

"It is no such thing as you very well know and I beg you will not talk in this ridiculous manner. You make me sound like a coxcomb."

Brixham merely laughed.

Gaventry wondered as well why Miss Sarah had failed to protest his amorous assault and more critically, why she had engaged herself so fully in the rather sumptuous exchange of kisses.

However, from the moment he had kissed her in earnest something profoundly mysterious had occurred. All vile thoughts had fled him, and the only one to remain was an odd notion that never had a lady fit so perfectly against him. He had become so enraptured with kissing her that everything was forgotten; his original purpose in very soon seeking out her elder sister, his intention of creating a bit of gossip before he had even been presented to the master of ceremonies of the Assembly Rooms, his desire to avenge himself on any female. Instead, an entirely new sensation had coursed through him of a deep regret that his life had been so derailed that although he could love kissing so sweet and so obviously an innocent young lady, nothing good could come of it. He had felt young again and full of ideals, as he had once felt when he was intent only on making his mark in the world and on finding a woman he could love and take to wife.

That she had proved to be Sarah Kittling, described to him as one of two sisters that Aurelia Kittling possessed, was in some manner portentous, only what did it mean?

"I only hope that she tells everyone of this evil I have forced on her."

His friend merely stared at him and shook his head in some disapprobation.

"What the deuce is the matter now?" Gaventry cried.

"I begin to think you have become the biggest sapskull of my acquaintance."

Gaventry laughed. "I have always been that," he returned, not in the least offended.


From the window of a nearby town house, Lady Haslingfield let a gauzy muslin drape fall back into place. She was still shocked by the sight she had just witnessed, but had acted swiftly enough so that she had sent her hostess, Mrs. Catesby, into another room before the truly extraordinary scene had played itself out before her eyes. She was a woman of some perception and knew instinctively that whatever motives her godson had had in kissing Sarah Kittling, the tender assault had not gone precisely as he had planned. Miss Kittling had done the impossible; she had confused Gaventry.

It was all so intriguing, so exciting, so rife with possibility! She was a shrewd woman and cognizant of the power she wielded in Bath society as its most prestigious hostess. She lived in the Circus, a distinguished address, her societal favors sought after by everyone, and had an uncanny instinct for the truth hidden within each individual.

She had known Gaventry since he was in the cradle and had never believed half of what he was reputed to have done, both in the past seven years and in that horrid scandal involving Miss Fulbourne, now the Countess of Stewkely. She had never had a very great opinion of Miss Fulbourne, even when her conduct had been above reproach and Gaventry had introduced the lady to her with his eyes full of stars. How it was possible he could have ever loved so unworthy a female, she would never know nor did she think she would ever learn all that had happened seven years ago. These ruminations, however, were entirely irrelevant. She had never approved of how Gaventry had conducted himself once the London hostesses, most of whom she had always believed were beneath contempt, had cut him from their guest lists. She had more than once let him know that she thought his conduct as absurd as it was shocking, to which he had always returned a bitter laugh.

Sarah Kittling, on the other hand, was something of an enigma to her. There were unsuspected depths to the young woman who had somehow survived her uncle's deplorable misuse of her annuity. She had her own suspicions as to just how the Kittlings had remained this past year in Queen Square when as a lot they should have been consigned to the poorhouse. Although her suspicions were entirely outrageous in nature, she thought, she believed, that the middle Kittling child was the authoress of *A Rogue's Tale*. At the same time, it seemed impossible, for there were facts in the novel that Miss Kittling could not have been privy to, not in even the smallest sense of probability. If, indeed, she was the author of the novel, how then had she been able to guess at the truth?

Mrs. Catesby returned to serve her a very nice cup of tea and prattled on, as was her way, about the latest gossip, which afforded Lady Haslingfield the opportunity to sip and to ponder as the hour wore on.

The kiss—that was the important factor, she mused. Sarah Kittling had kissed her godson as though she had known him forever. A spate of gooseflesh traveled in lightning speed down her neck and both her arms. There was something mysterious and fateful about that kiss, one that had set all her instincts to whirring and buzzing like a swarm of bees in her head. Gaventry and Sarah Kittling, now why did that seem the most delightful prospect of all?

Her only present concern was whether or not the scandalous embrace had been observed by anyone else this morning. If so, she would need to quash such gossip before it had a chance to run riot in the Pump Room. Once it reached Beau Nash's statue, there would be nothing she could do to still any of the resulting rumors.

"Emily!" she exclaimed, rising to her feet. "We must away. I am feeling the need to take the waters this morning, on the instant!"

"Now, Lucretia?" her friend queried, obviously shocked.

"Now!"

Her sudden command was far too much for the nervous Mrs. Catesby. She was a confirmed peagoose who rose too hastily in her intention to obey Lady Haslingfield's decree. She made a complete circle, tripped on her own slippers, and promptly fell flat on her face. "At once, m'lady!" she cried, peeping up at her from beneath a lace cap that had fallen forward over her eyebrows.

# TWO

"Have you yet seen the man who kissed you?" Meg whispered in Sarah's ear, at the same time nipping her beneath her elbow and causing her to twitch.

Sarah turned to scowl at her sister. She was standing at the far end of the octagonal entrance hall of the Upper Assembly Rooms, having just heard a rumor that suggested that Lord Gaventry was due to arrive at any moment. Even now, there was a current of excitement in the air that was almost palpable.

When her sister had stolen upon her so suddenly, she had nearly jumped a foot in the air. "I beg you will not do that, Meg," she returned quietly, all the while fanning herself. "You may not credit it, but I do not fancy being pinched in the least."

Meg tensed and rocked her shoulders. "It is just that I have never been so excited in my entire existence!" Once more she lowered her voice. "To think that you were so thoroughly kissed, in full view of all the occupants about Queen Square, and that so wickedly. Only you must tell me, have you yet seen the gentleman who kissed you?"

"No, I have not," she returned calmly. How shocked Meg would be were she to know the gentleman's identity, that he was the very one for whom all the ladies in the crowded entrance hall were waiting with rather breathless anticipation.

She had not informed Meg of Gaventry's identity. She had wanted to, particularly when Meg had told her she had seen a dashing, tall, and quite handsome gentleman kissing her, but she had been unable to coax the words from her tongue. Instead, she had sworn Meg not to tell a soul that she had permitted a perfect stranger to take such liberties with her. The last thing she wished for was that either her cousin, Charlotte, or her eldest sister, Aurelia, would know of her shocking conduct. Even now, she felt as though she had only dreamed the kiss, that it had never truly happened.

Meg warmed to her theme, all the while whispering close to Sarah's ear. "Only tell me how it was that you not only allowed the man, who must be a confirmed rogue, to kiss you but that you slung your arms about his neck as well?"

"Do but hush," she returned in an undertone. She wished her sister would not mention the kiss quite so frequently, for every time she did, Sarah could not help but remember just how she had felt in Gaventry's arms, as though she had been waiting for him to come into her life since she first dreamed of love and romance. These thoughts, however, would not do in the least, for she was reminded as well of Gaventry's truly wretched reputation, and all fanciful images would dissipate as quickly as they had come. The very nature of a rogue did not allow for the usual sequence of events. Surely he no more thought that a kiss might lead to love and marriage than a snail might think of flying. No, it was imperative that she forget all about Gaventry's devastating kisses and instead concentrate on how she might advance either of her sisters into more promising social opportunities. Therein lay the sole hope of the Kittling sisters, that one or the other of them might contract a respectable marriage and to some extent secure a future for them all. Lord Gaventry was nearly the last man on earth who could possibly be interested in fulfilling these more practical, essential requirements.

So it was she addressed Meg anew. "I wish you would cease prattling on about an event that I not only wish to forget, but wish undone, and one which I certainly do not mean to continue discussing here at the Assembly Rooms!"

Meg fanned herself quickly. "I beg you will not be prig-gish, Sally, for I am glad you allowed the kiss! I thought it wonderful and most *encouraging!*"

Sarah turned to regard Meg closely and gave her a hard look. She could hardly wish that her own misconduct would prompt her younger, and quite volatile, sister to begin entic-ing young men to take such terrible advantage of her. Margaret's disposition was such that she always took a mile when only an inch had been granted!

Meg was her younger sister by two years and had the most incorrigible tendency to speak her mind on any subject. She had unluckily seen her indiscretion in the park and, given her romantical nature, thought that nothing short of love had magically enveloped both her and the roguish stranger and that once "the mysterious gentleman" found her, whether this evening at the Assembly Rooms, or anywhere else, he was certain to declare himself.

Sarah, of course, thought nothing of the sort. In fact, given her more practical turn of mind, she thought that rather than of-fering for her out of a sense of infatuation or even honor, Lord Gaventry was far more likely to attempt to kiss her again or ig-nore her altogether. He was the sort of man, if even a small percentage of the gossip about him was true, who would crimp the edges of propriety whenever he had but the smallest oppor-tunity. Indeed his final comment to her, that she should tell everyone that it was he who had kissed her, indicated that that was precisely his intent in having done so in the first place.

She smiled to herself suddenly. Yes, instinctively she knew it to be true and now had the profound satisfaction of know-ing that save for Meg, the beau monde of Bath was entirely ignorant of his devilish conduct, for she had told no one of her, of their, indiscretion. Poor fellow. She believed he would be quite disappointed that he had not succeeded in becoming scandalous even before he had been properly met by the mas-ter of ceremonies and permitted to put his name in the Assembly Room subscription books.

Aurelia, who had been conversing across the entrance hall, approached her sisters at that moment, having squeezed herself through several score of personages all awaiting his lordship's arrival. Aurrie, the acknowledged beauty of the family, was dressed charmingly in a prettily embroidered muslin gown, her blond hair caught up into a cascade of ringlets. She looked, as she often did, quite like an angel.

She rolled her large blue eyes. "I cannot believe how crowded the rooms are this evening. One would think the Regent himself were due to arrive instead of Lord Gaventry."

Sarah could not help but chuckle. "A great fuss over nothing," she said. "I suggest we adjourn to the ballroom. I daresay Gaventry's arrival is only a hum anyway. Why would such a purportedly outrageous creature have the smallest interest in our little assembly? Come, we should at least be dancing."

Meg negated this with a swift cutting motion of her hand. "On no account!" she cried. "You may be prosaic if you wish but I for one cannot wait to see the man who has figured so prominently in so much gossip these many years and more. I believe this moment shall be one of the most enjoyable and satisfying of my life."

At the tail end of this speech, Charlotte Mears joined their family group, her smile rather knowing and cynical all at once. "Of what are we speaking?" she inquired. "Although I do believe I can guess." She was their cousin, a widow of some nine years, and for those years had served as chaperone in Bath to the Kittling sisters. She was as much a part of Sarah's family, however, as an elder sister or even a mother would have been and had made secure their rather quiet place in Bath society by her presence in Queen Square.

"Gaventry, of course," Aurrie stated.

"A great botheration," she proclaimed, in obvious agreement with Sarah's general opinions, "and over what? All for a gentleman who has been maligned for reasons we will probably never fully comprehend."

"Charlotte," Meg complained on a deep sigh, "do you mean to have as little sensibility as Sally tonight?"

"If not desiring to see Gaventry above all else means that I am lacking in an appropriate amount of sensibility, then I confess it is true. However, I believe I could easily exhibit the qualities you desire in me were you to show me a properly set stitch, for example, or a lovely autumn day, or even the seven hills of Bath shrouded in mist. Men of reputation, however, who have been castigated by an ignorant society, will never become objects of my interest, delicacy of perception, or artistic enjoyment."

Sarah laughed. "Have you the headache, Charlotte, for I vow you seem out-of-reason cross to be speaking so vehemently on the subject of a rogue?"

Charlotte shook her head, but a smile formed on her lips. "No, of course not. But I will admit I have little patience for this." She flung a hand outward, the gesture encompassing an entire host of muslin, silk, and satin gowns, and indeed, not one black or blue tail coat among the lot. It was the ladies, it would seem, who were all agog to meet the man who had been the subject of their gossip for the past several years.

"Then let us retire to the ballroom," Sarah said. "I would much rather watch the dancing anyway. Come, Meg, Aurrie?"

Her sisters, however, would have none of it and remained fixed where they were, to the side of the domed entrance hall, their gazes settled in the direction of the doors. Charlotte, however, hooked arms with her, and together they squeezed their way in the direction of the ballroom.

Sarah was glad to be going. For one thing, the longer she had awaited Gaventry's supposed arrival, the more strained her nerves had become, and for another, the crowd in the hall had made the chamber unbearably warm. Upon arriving on the threshold of the ballroom, she was at once solicited for a country dance and soon found herself forgetting her present cares as she went down the dance.

Another set, another partner, and the evening hours began

to while away. The ballroom grew more and more crowded as the ladies, one by one, relinquished their posts in the entrance hall, for it would seem Lord Gaventry had decided not to attend the assembly after all. She wondered if he would ever know the commotion he had excited merely by the presence of a rumor indicating he had meant to attend. She also wondered if he understood that the assemblies ended precisely at eleven o'clock. Whatever the case, it was nearly a quarter past ten now and the chance for an evening's entertainment for him nearly over.

She had just finished dancing the quadrille and was conversing with Charlotte when Lady Haslingfield approached her. Sarah greeted her warmly, for the countess had always shown her a great deal of kindness over the years. She had been a friend to her mother, and though Sarah had always sensed that her ladyship wished she had been able to do something to forward the interests of the Kittling girls, Sarah understood that this was all but impossible, given their relative degree of poverty.

Regardless, Lady Haslingfield always acknowledged her at the Pump Room, the Assembly Rooms, and in chance encounters about town. It was no surprise, therefore, that her ladyship requested that Sarah take a turn about the rooms with her.

They had not gone far when the countess led her to the tearoom and found an unoccupied corner. This did surprise Sarah, for it had all the hallmarks of a desire for a little private conversation. She was a formidable woman in both appearance and demeanor, for she was tall and large-bosomed, and carried herself as though she wore nothing short of a crown on her head. What the subject could possibly be, however, Sarah could not guess and was more than a little startled when Gaventry's name crossed the lady's lips.

"He is my godson. I can see by your expression that you are surprised. Did you not know as much? Of course, very few people do. But did you also know that because of *A*

*Rogue's Tale* he is beginning to be received again in London? I see I have shocked you anew. But so it is. The authoress of that novel has aided my godson, albeit unwittingly, more than she will perhaps ever know for I sent word to my friends who reside in Mayfair, when the novel first took my attention, informing them that I knew the particulars to be very close to the truth!"

Sarah gasped. "Is this indeed so, ma'am?" she cried.

Lady Haslingfield nodded.

Sarah, however, could not help but wonder if Lady Haslingfield had told a whisker or two in such missives merely to change her godson's fortunes, for how likely was it that her novel could have actually hit upon the truth? However, she did not feel it at all appropriate to confess to any such skepticism. Instead, she responded, "Then it is no wonder that his arrival in Bath has attracted such notice and not of an unkindly nature. You must be pleased he is finally come to our fair city."

"Very much so. Naturally, I have not seen a great deal of Gaventry in the past several years. He had long since attained his majority with interests of his own when this dreadful business began some seven years past with that wretched Arabella Fulbourne. Well, I daresay he had no wish to hear my opinions on that score. She is the culprit of all this mischief, as much as Lucinda Hardcastle is in *A Rogue's Tale*."

Sarah's skepticism now received a jolt. She had never before heard of Arabella Fulbourne, and if she was anything like Lucinda Hardcastle, the villainess of her novel, then she had indeed served Gaventry an evil turn. Lucinda Hardcastle entrapped Lord Daventry in a brothel, an establishment which had figured prominently in all the gossip about Gaventry, for the purpose of staging an event in which the Duke of Widenhall must rescue her. Afterward, for completely heroic reasons, Lord Daventry refused to tell what really happened since, given his chivalrous nature, he refused to darken the lady's name. It was no wonder Lord Gaventry had begun to be received. But to think that there really was a Lucinda Hardcastle!

"I do not know of a Miss Fulbourne," she said at last, her heart hammering suddenly in her chest, for she hoped to hear a great deal more of the lady.

"What I tell you now is not generally known but I believe I can rely on you to be discreet."

"I hope that I am worthy of such confidence."

"You have never given me cause to think differently and so I shall tell you a few facts of which I am certain you are unaware. Seven years ago, my godson fell violently in love with Arabella Fulbourne. I had several opportunities to converse with her over what was her first Season in 1811. During my initial encounter with her, I found her to be a beautiful young lady with manners as polished as they were delightful. However, after a few weeks I noted that there was frequently a certain wildness in her eye that I could not like, the look of a fox, so much so that to my way of thinking she was every much a vixen as Lucinda was in *A Rogue's Tale*, and we both know what a dastardly character she turned out to be!

"Regardless, Gaventry tumbled head over ears in love with the chit and she, of course, encouraged his suit, for I came to believe that she longed for a handle to her name more than life itself. But there was another gentleman besides my godson who had formed part of her court that Season, someone whom I have grown to believe was well suited to her in the depth of her vile temperament and shocking lack of morals."

Sarah felt dizzy. A new character had been introduced in Lady Haslingfield's story which so closely paralleled her own novel that she found herself dumbstruck. "And his name?"

"The Earl of Stewkely."

Sarah had heard of Lord Stewkely, and by reputation he was equally as notorious as Gaventry, if not more so. "Of course I know what is said of him, but do you think him a very bad man?"

"Fiendish. You can have no notion and are still of such a

tender age that I would not sully your ears with the stories I have heard of him or of his wife—formerly, Arabella Fulbourne."

Sarah's mouth fell agape. "So she married Lord Stewkely?"

Lady Haslingfield nodded. "Indeed, she did, not a month after she ruined my godson's reputation. Some of the gossip we have all heard is true; for instance, he was discovered having been in a brothel for days. What is not generally known, however, was that while there he sustained some serious injury."

"Indeed?" she cried, astonished. "Do you believe he was wounded as though in some manner of altercation?"

Lady Haslingfield nodded. "I have little doubt of it. One of my friends in London wrote a letter mentioning that a fortnight later she chanced upon Gaventry in New Bond Street and was surprised to see a cut above his eye, though healing, as well as a faded bruise on his jaw. He also walked with a limp."

"And you have no idea what happened to him?" Sarah was greatly shocked.

"None. The only information to reach my ears was that he had enjoyed a drunken revelry, lasting for days, in a notorious brothel, but this you must have heard yourself. However, my godson will not discuss even the smallest detail of what transpired during that time, but I tell you now, that was not all or perhaps not even in part what truly occurred. And if I do not miss my mark, Miss Fulbourne was in the very center of the maelstrom."

"Do you believe she was actually there?" she inquired on a whisper.

"I do, but not as an innocent."

Sarah gasped, for this did, indeed, follow the plot of her story. "Just as in *A Rogue's Tale*!" she cried.

Lady Haslingfield nodded. "It is my belief that she had devised a scheme by which to bring Stewkely up to scratch, one which somehow involved luring Gaventry to this particular brothel, but for this I have no proof."

"And Lord Stewkely?" she asked. "Where does he figure into this mystery?"

"I can only hazard a guess that she was somehow in league with him, but in what way or to what purpose where he was concerned, I simply do not know. I have often wondered if Gaventry ever understood what happened, but as I said before, he will not discuss the matter with me in even the smallest detail, so I can only be content with conjecture as the true facts have come to me in bits and pieces as they are wont to do. 'The truth will out,' so said Shakespeare, and so it will one day, mark my words!"

Sarah could see that Lady Haslingfield was passionate about this subject. For herself, she was fascinated and intrigued by what she was hearing. She was also a little astonished to learn that the events of her novel paralleled these so closely. "I must confess I am quite stunned by this information, my lady, for having read *A Rogue's Tale*, I can only think that the authoress—whoever she might be—must have been in some manner privy to all that you have just told me."

A strange smile suddenly twisted Lady Haslingfield's lips. "I, too, had always wondered not just who the authoress of *A Rogue's Tale* was but how she had learned so many details of the horrid affair that fairly ruined Gaventry's life. Although I suppose if a young lady were to use her imagination she could concoct something near to the truth without knowing the incidentals."

"I would have to agree with you," she said, utterly astounded. She began to understand a little how it had come about that Gaventry was being more accepted in society, whether in London or Bath. If Lady Haslingfield had lent credence to the details of *A Rogue's Tale*, then that would have set into motion a general softening in the *haute ton's* attitude toward Gaventry. "I must confess that I find myself amazed. It is quite odd to think that something to be found in a novel has actually transpired."

"Quite odd. You may imagine my shock when I first read *A Rogue's Tale*. Have you never wondered if perchance the authoress resides in Bath?"

Sarah kept her countenance as best she could and responded with an answer she had rehearsed many times. "I should think it far more likely that such a person would be a resident of London. How else could she know so much of your godson and his activities?"

She watched as Lady Haslingfield's eyes narrowed perceptively. "A very reasonable answer."

For the first time since they began conversing on this subject, Sarah began to wonder if it were possible that her ladyship knew the truth. For effect, Sarah added, "I never thought very highly of someone who would write such a book and make no effort to conceal the identity of the main character." She spoke only the truth since she had always felt the worst manner of guilt in having written the novel in the first place.

"I must confess that I thought so at one time but then I began to speculate that it was entirely possible that a lady who would do so might be above reproach in all respects but suddenly find herself in desperate circumstances. Do you not think this would exonerate our authoress a trifle?"

Sarah met the countess's gaze fully. She tried to still the sudden pounding of her heart. "So you think the novel was written out of necessity?"

"I do," she responded firmly.

"But surely you must agree there must be a dozen other means by which a real lady might earn an income? The authoress for instance, who clearly has some command of language, could have easily served as a governess or a companion."

At that, Lady Haslingfield grinned. "I would imagine that a lady who enjoyed composing imaginative tales would find such labors as the instruction of young ladies in the use of watercolors, the pianoforte, the globe and perhaps a foreign language, dull work, indeed. No, no, pray do not protest. Ah, but you fence delightfully. However, I should like to revert to our former subject, namely, Gaventry. I had always regretted that he was unable to escape to the Continent for a time, to absent himself from all polite society in order to regain his bearings. That, I suppose, is one more crime of Bonaparte's, to have deprived our young gentlemen of the Grand Tour. Had Gaventry been able to separate himself from the situation, I think he should have recovered far better than he did."

Sarah watched the countess carefully, unable to comprehend either her purpose in telling her this story, or what the point to the story might be. Out of respect, she smiled politely and waited, her hands clasped about her fan in front of her.

Lady Haslingfield smiled, even chuckled. "Yes, yes, I suppose I am rambling. Now you are surprised that I have guessed your thoughts, but you have a very penetrating expression of feature that gives a general and sometimes readable animation to your face." She sighed. Leaning close, she whispered, "You should not go about kissing young men in Queen Square. I do not need to tell you it is not at all the thing."

Sarah gasped and immediately lifted her fan to her face and began wafting the lace confection over her suddenly hot cheeks. "Oh dear," she murmured.

"Just so, but never fear. I have made certain that no one will know of it and it is quite apparent to me that you were wholly fortunate in that no one but myself seemed to have witnessed the event. I made certain of it by attending the Pump Room shortly afterward and intercepting anyone who I thought might have seen you. You are safe, my dear, but I must warn you against any such future indiscretions. There are limits to my powers."

"Yes, my lady."

"I have but one question, which the circumstance of seeing you locked in my godson's arms can be answered only by you. Namely, were you per chance acquainted with him before he, er, kissed you?"

Her expression was not in the least condemning, which surprised Sarah. "No," she responded.

"You had never met him before?" Lady Haslingfield's eyes grew very large.

Worse and worse, Sarah thought. It was one thing to have been indiscreet in such a scandalous manner with a gentleman one knew, but quite another to have kissed a perfect stranger. She swallowed hard. "No."

Lady Haslingfield frowned. "But he made himself known to you," she stated.

Sarah strove to keep her blushes from overtaking her completely as she responded, "Afterwards, yes."

"Good God," Lady Haslingfield remarked.

Sarah watched as a half-dozen more questions flitted through Lady Haslingfield's eyes, and when none of them arrived upon her lips, she found herself not only intensely grateful but willing to offer an explanation of what had happened.

"He approached me, I now believe, with the sole intention of stealing a kiss from a stranger for the purpose of arousing a great deal of gossip in Bath. Perhaps he feels his reputation demands such a thing. However, something odd happened when he kissed me. I had meant to cry out, but found I could not, that I did not want to."

"But you have been kissed before?"

Sarah cringed at the nature of the question. "Once or twice but nothing to signify," she responded earnestly.

"Were you any other lady, I should not believe you, for I know what I saw. But in all these years, it is your honesty I think that has caused me to acknowledge you on every occasion. I believe I can trust what you are telling me now, only it is most incredible. Pray, continue, if it is not too distressing."

"The only distress I have, my lady, is that I do not in the least comprehend how I could have so recklessly kissed your godson in return, without knowing a single thing about him! Yet I did and though I fear I will give you palpitations by saying so, I enjoyed every moment of it. Indeed, it is only with the strongest effort that I keep the experience from overwhelming one thought out of two since it happened."

"It is love," stated Lady Haslingfield. "There can be no two opinions on that score."

"No, no. I am persuaded it is not. An odd, though quite powerful, momentary infatuation, nothing more. I do enjoy a good novel on occasion but I am not so romantical in nature that I would ascribe anything virtuous and worthy in my encounter with Gaventry this morning."

At that, Lady Haslingfield laughed, and not a polite ballroom laugh, but something very near to cackling. She did not let her amusement continue for long and then apologized for making such a spectacle of herself. "Oh, but you are too adorable. It is no wonder my godson kissed you so thoroughly. No, no, do not protest or try to convince me of something I will never believe. Instead, let me address the seriousness of this matter. I was able to forestall gossip of the most damaging kind on this occasion, my dear, but most certainly I cannot caution you enough about taking the greatest care in the future, particularly since I believe Gaventry means to remain in Bath for several months."

"Several months?" Sarah queried in a voice that sounded very small even to her own ears.

A slow smile overcame Lady Haslingfield's face once more. She nodded. "So, you believe yourself to be in some danger, eh? Well, well, all I shall say at this juncture is that I expect to be invited to the wedding breakfast!" With that, she inclined her head and moved away.

Sarah watched her go, her heart feeling as though it were being plucked, at a rapid pace, by a highly experienced musician. Lady Haslingfield's words brought numerous questions rushing to her mind, and she found she could hardly breathe. Married to Gaventry? Married to the man who had kissed her so wondrously? Married to the man whose life she had so cruelly put into print? Married to a man who was a confirmed rogue? What terror! What bliss! What a complete impossibility!

She blinked several times and began walking slowly, if blindly, in the direction of the octagonal entrance hall. She commanded her heart to grow quiet. Unfortunately, the moment she reached the doorway, she heard a terrible pronouncement by a lady not ten feet from her. "It is confirmed—Gaventry is arrived!"

Sarah turned around on her heel and made a quick but very long circuit back to the ballroom, where she knew most of the assemblage to still be gathered. She took up a chair in the least conspicuous part of the room and once more strove to quiet her heart. Would he know her? Would he recognize her? Would he even desire to speak with her? Oh, and what could he actually be thinking of her now?

She was sitting in a chair at the perimeter of the ballroom when Meg hurried toward her, a rather shocked, even concerned expression on her face. She plopped down and immediately leaned in the direction of Sarah's ear. "I have just learned something dreadful," she whispered.

A noise from the vestibule drew her attention slightly away from Meg, but Meg pulled her back. "You must listen! I have seen Gaventry!"

Sarah turned toward her sharply. "I know that he has arrived. I heard as much already."

"Oh, Sarah, it is truly dreadful!" Meg cried. "For there is something you must know." Her gaze was suddenly drawn away to what was now a loud rustling at the door to the ballroom. "Too late. Only do but look at Gaventry and tell me if you recognize him. However, if you feel faint I have brought my vinaigrette."

Sarah glanced at what was now a throng at the doorway and saw Gaventry, dressed quite to perfection in white breeches, a black coat, and an immaculately tied white neckcloth.

"There, you see!" Meg cried, still whispering. "Gaventry is

the man who kissed you! Are you not shocked? Oh, Sally, what was it like to kiss such a rogue?"

Sarah thought with some amusement that he did not look like a rogue at all. Somehow, in her mind, and certainly within the context of *A Rogue's Tale*, Daventry had always been dressed in quite exotic clothing, whether sporting a turban while attending Drury Lane and shocking all the tabbies, or wearing very long box coats of brocade with a sword fixed to his side like a pirate merely for the purpose of riding in Hyde Park! Here was the real man, however, appearing quite magnificent in clothing clearly designed *à la Brummell*, and not even an enormous nosegay in his buttonhole to bring a scowl to the faces of the numerous social dragons gathered nearby and assessing him with daggerlike expressions.

Though her heart had previously been leaping about nervously, a very strange thing occurred at the sight of him; the organ relinquished its erratic conduct and settled into a strong, measured rhythm. How very odd and completely inexplicable! She would have thought the poor thing would explode from so much anticipation. Instead, it was as though her heart knew something she did not.

Whatever the case, she could not help but admire the viscount as surely as a hundred other young ladies were doing at this moment. Even in profile he was quite handsome. He wore his blond locks in long waves, curling over the edge of his neckcloth, which lent him a poet's countenance, his only apparent salute to his profession as a rakehell. His blue eyes were narrowed in the fashion of the hunter. She wondered just what he was looking for since he was ignoring several fans fluttering all about him, trying to attract his attention. He had lifted his quizzing glass to one eye, and was presently surveying the left side of the chamber. He seemed perfectly serene in the face of the obvious stir he had caused by his late arrival, an interesting quality to be sure.

He was nudged suddenly by the man next to him, a gentleman, Sarah noted, with reddish brown curly hair, freckles, and dark blue eyes. She found that this gentleman was looking directly at her, his smile crooked and almost sympathetic. For that instant, when her gaze met his, she had a strong impression she would like him very much indeed were she ever to come to know him. Gaventry glanced down at him and in the next moment his friend directed his attention to her. Goodness, was it possible that the viscount had come in search of her?

When he immediately settled his gaze on her and smiled, she realized her supposition was correct—Gaventry had come to the Assembly Rooms purposely to see her, though why was a complete mystery to her. Other than a shared, albeit extraordinary, kiss, he knew nothing of her save her name.

On the other hand, seeking her out was precisely what a confirmed rake might do. She had little doubt that he, too, had enjoyed the kiss, so perhaps he meant to steal another. But here? At the exalted Bath Assembly Rooms! Even Gaventry would not be so audacious as that! Surely!

Yet even as he met her gaze, he began to smile in that manner peculiar to him, as though he knew all her secrets, and she understood his intentions entirely. She sincerely doubted he would be so brazen as to attempt a kiss, but that would not prevent him from attempting something else of a wicked nature, such as approaching her without a proper introduction! It was one thing to assault her in an empty square and kiss her, but quite another to address her in public when they were veritable strangers to each other. How did he suppose they were to explain their acquaintance to the curious multitude?

Meg whispered into her ear. "What do you think now that you know? I must say you do not seem to be overset in the least . . . unless . . . you knew!"

Sarah nodded. "But only afterward."

"Yet you said nothing to me." Meg appeared crushed by this fact.

"Pray do not be distressed, Meggy. I could not bring myself to tell you or anyone. It was all so strange and his reputation so vile."

"There is not a lady in Bath who believes all that gossip anymore. *A Rogue's Tale* made the truth known."

Sarah glanced at her sister, startled to hear such an opinion from her. "Is this truly what you believe?"

"Of course. For heaven's sake, Sally, it is as though you live in another world entirely. Do you not pay even the smallest heed to what is being said?"

"To gossip? No."

Meg grunted as if disgusted with her sister, and the conversation was dropped. For this Sarah was grateful since Gaventry was heading quite determinedly in her direction. So, he meant to do this wicked thing! There was nothing for it but to summon every reserve of strength and dignity and afterward to attempt somehow to explain to her friends, her acquaintances, and the high sticklers of Bath just how it was that she was known to the infamous Lord Gaventry but had never once let on.

He stood before her and bowed. "Well met, Miss Kittling. May I have the honor of the next dance?" He extended his hand to her.

She glanced left and right and saw numerous mouths hanging decidedly agape, a score of shocked countenances, and more glares, especially from several young ladies who had awaited Gaventry's arrival with more dedication and patience than she had ever seen or endured in her entire existence. All appeared to be angry at having been outdone by a mere Sarah Kittling.

At this last thought, at the knowledge that because her family was known to be in rather straitened circumstances and therefore not included in the first circles, something punishing rose within her, of defiance and pride. She lifted her chin. "With pleasure, my lord, and may I say how delightful it is to see you again." She had spoken with such clarity that anyone who was not already staring at her and at Gaventry now did so.

Though he seemed a little surprised by her speech, his smile became a grin, and he nodded approvingly.

She rose and settled her hand on his arm as he guided her onto the floor. The last dance of the evening was a country dance. She wondered how well he would know the steps. Do men of a rakish propensity enjoy dancing? Do they excel at the art? She would soon know.

Other couples followed suit, and very soon the floor was alive with dancers going down the country dance.

"I only wish to know one thing," she whispered, when the steps of the dance drew them closely together.

The dance parted them and when once more together, he queried, "And what would that be?" His lips twitched and she could not keep from giggling. How very much like a rogue to enjoy the predicament in which he most certainly was aware he had placed her.

"You know very well what," she returned with an arch of her brow. He opened his mouth to speak, but they were parted again.

Once more together, he laughed. "Very well," he whispered. "I shall put it about we are old acquaintances."

At that, her laughter was loud enough to draw more stares. She immediately composed herself. "That is impossible."

"No it is not."

They were separated again.

Finally, she spoke quickly. "Because I would never be able to explain, in the face of so much gossip, why I never once admitted the acquaintance."

He moved away then back again. "That will be easy." Away once more.

Back again. "In what possible manner could that be easy?"

He smiled as he drifted away to offer a turn to the lady nearest him. Turning Sarah again, he said, "You only have to claim intense mortification and your diffidence will not only be perfectly comprehended but applauded as well."

The dance took them in opposite directions once more. Together again, she said, "It speaks wretchedly of my character, however. I hope I would never disavow a friend."

"I did not say we were friends . . . acquaintances, merely."

She giggled again, for he was being utterly ridiculous. When they were brought together anew, she said, "But, my lord, you cannot be serious. A gentleman does not approach a mere *acquaintance* as you did me just a moment ago."

He appeared to contemplate this seriously as he moved away. Once returned to her, he said, "I see you mean to be difficult."

"I?" she cried. She saw at once, however, that he was merely trying to get a rise out of her. "Oh, very well. We are old acquaintances. I suppose the tabbies will sort it out for themselves." She slipped away from him.

Once again together, her hand in his as the dance turned them, he said, "Now you have a good understanding of how best to proceed. Ignore them all!"

She might have been offended, but there was such a look of laughter in his blue eyes that she could only give her head a shake and continue the rest of the dance in more silence than the first part. When at last the dance ended, he returned her to Meg. "May I call upon you tomorrow?" he asked.

"Yes, for I believe we have much to discuss."

"So it would seem."

The master of ceremonies was hovering nearby, and the moment Gaventry bowed himself away, he was accosted by that good man, who in turn began a series of introductions to the most influential ladies of Bath.

Sarah watched him go, feeling rather dazed by his sudden arrival, the rather amusing dance, and now his intention of calling upon her. Really, if she did not comprehend his reputation as well as she did, her head would be completely turned by the attentions he had just paid her. She could only wonder, however, just how she was to explain both her supposed acquaintance with him as well as his purposefulness in seeking her out at this, the last moment of the assemblies.

She did not have very long to ponder these thoughts, for she was suddenly besieged by a score of friends all demanding to know, and some of them none too politely, just how it was she had been singled out by Lord Gaventry. She responded just as had been agreed upon, that though she had known his lordship for many years, she had been too distressed by all the gossip to acknowledge her acquaintance with him. She tried to keep the references to a first meeting between them as vague as possible and was relieved suddenly when the hour was announced and everyone began departing the premises.

Later, upon reaching Queen Square, Sarah found that instead of being permitted to retire to her bedchamber, she must take up a seat in the drawing room and explain to her sisters and cousin just how she knew Lord Gaventry.

Meg, however, turned the object of the discussion slightly by complaining anew that Sarah had withheld such vital information from her as the astonishing fact that the man who had kissed her earlier that morning was none other than Gaventry.

This outburst, however, prompted both Charlotte and Aurrie to cry out in unison, "Lord Gaventry kissed you this morning?"

Sarah stared at the gaping, shocked expressions of her cousin and her elder sister, which she thought was in amusing contrast to Meg's disgruntled scowl. "Pray sit down and I will tell you all."

Her family quickly pulled chairs close as she took up a seat on the sofa. She began at the beginning, how she had been reading her book—oh dear, now she must fabricate a title for she could hardly tell them she had been reading *A Rogue's Revenge*! She told a whisker and said it was one of Maria Edgeworth's elevating tales, but for some reason she could not at present recall the name of the story to mind.

"Oh, what does it matter!" Meg cried. "Tell them of the kiss!"

Sarah felt a blush climb her cheeks. There was nothing for it now but to acknowledge the truth and even to tell them a little of her conversation with Lady Haslingfield, who had also witnessed the quite scandalous indiscretion. At last, the recounting of her adventures came to a close. "And so, in truth, I cannot say why he singled me out at the assemblies. It is to me the greatest mystery."

Aurrie sat back in her chair. "That is because," she began in her simple way, "you always were far too modest about how pretty you are and how lively you dance and converse. It is no wonder to me he sought you out. Why, when the pair of you were dancing, I believe he was wholly enraptured by you."

"Nonsense," Sarah returned, but there was a very secret place in her heart that suddenly wished it were true.

Meg turned to Charlotte and Aurelia. "And he asked to call tomorrow. What do you think of that?"

Once more, the ladies appeared quite astonished.

Having stunned the ladies to silence a second time, Meg finally seemed satisfied, as though she had been given her proper due. Not long afterward, Charlotte announced that she felt the time had come for all the ladies to retire, especially since they would have such an exalted visitor on the morrow.


With the hour closing on midnight, Gaventry sat with Brixham in his study, swirling brandy in his glass. His gaze was fixed upon the flame of a candle situated on the mantel. His thoughts, however, were on the assembly and on a certain beautiful young lady. Sarah Kittling exceeded his memory of her from that morning. She had been gowned in a simple pale pink silk ball dress, the light color not only befitting her maidenly status but setting her dark looks to advantage. He had already determined to dance with her, to make her his object so that he might have a reason to invade the Kittling household, but he had not expected to have enjoyed himself so much as he did during the all-too brief dance with her. She had held her own against his onslaught of teasing rejoinders and a smile now reached his lips.

"You seem excessively well pleased with yourself," Mr.

Brixham observed. He was reclining on the floor, his glass balanced precariously on his chest, a cushion beneath his head.

Gaventry's smile broadened. "I suppose I am, a little."

"Well, you ought to be. You appeared to have charmed Miss Sarah Kittling quite thoroughly. I have never seen a young lady laugh more as she went down a country dance. Quite amazing, really, since she did not miss her steps, not even once."

"She is an excellent dancer."

Brixham chuckled, which of course caused his chest to rise and fall erratically, but he caught the rocking wineglass before it toppled over. "Yes, she is that."

"Your meaning?"

"I think her deucedly pretty and very much in your style if I do not much mistake the matter, dark hair, lovely brown eyes."

"She is not, however, the equal of her sister."

Here, Mr. Brixham sighed heavily. "No, she is not. What lady could be? Aurelia Kittling is clearly a diamond of the first stare."

Gaventry frowned. "She ought to have gone to London and made a brilliant match instead of writing that wretched novel."

"From what I heard this evening, the Kittlings live on the fringes of Bath society, being not in the least plump in the pocket. Lady Haslingfield—you know, that old dragon who apparently rules Bath—acknowledges them but they are not invited to the first houses."

"Then I will have to change that," he stated emphatically. "I suppose I shall have to do the pretty and call upon my godmother."

At that, Brixham leaned up on his elbow, catching his glass with his hand. "You have a godmother?"

"Indeed, I do."

"Which lady is she? Did I meet her last night?" He took a sip of his brandy.

"Why yes you did, as it happens. Lady Haslingfield."

At that, Mr. Brixham promptly spewed brandy over his coat, which he quickly dabbed at with a hastily drawn kerchief. "What the devil? Good God, she eyed me as though I had snakes for hair and she meant to bite the heads off each."

Gaventry lifted his glass to his friend. "You have described my godmother to perfection."

Brixham leaned back down on the pillow and once more took to balancing his glass on his chest. "And now you must abase yourself at her feet."

"I may have to do just that. I have not spoken with her in some time. I would suppose of course that she has heard all the gossip. I only wonder if she will offer me even the smallest assistance."

Brixham chuckled again, catching his glass once more just before it toppled over. "I suppose she won't if you tell her why you've come to Bath."

Gaventry rolled his eyes. "You have had far too much brandy, my good friend, and if you continue holding it unprotected on your chest, you will spill it."

Brixham sighed again. "I only wish the younger sister, Sarah, were the authoress."

"Why?"

"Because I had a chance to converse with the eldest Miss Kittling and I think her a deuced fine girl, very sweet and unspoiled. For reasons I cannot explain, I do not wish to see her hurt."

At that, Gaventry snorted. "Unspoiled? Sweet? You would describe the authoress of *A Rogue's Tale* in such a fashion? My dear fellow, I begin to think your wits have gone a-begging."

Brixham looked at him apace. "Gaven, we should leave Bath," he said urgently. "Tonight. No good can come of this scheme of yours. So she wrote a story featuring events of your life; it was only a novel, nothing of consequence, nothing that will be of any interest in a year or two. What do you really care if Miss Kittling earned a few pounds because of your reputation?"

"A few!" he cried. "I understand it was several hundred."

"Hardly a fortune and if all that I heard of them is true just barely enough for the family to continue living in Bath, nothing more. Regardless, I say we return to London, the sooner the better."

"Why are you taking up their cause?"

"I liked them, both of them, and I hear there is a third, a Miss Margaret Kittling."

"Brixham, you amaze me. How can you say you like either Miss Kittling or Miss Sarah when you have not met either one of them?"

"Drink more of your brandy, Gaven. You are becoming sadly out of temper. As for Miss Sarah, there was something in her smile I liked very much and while she was dancing and conversing with you there was something so completely artless in her manner and her laughter. I like her, I tell you! Very much, indeed!"

Gaventry ground his teeth. He, too, had liked Miss Sarah, a great deal more than he wanted to. He could not remember having enjoyed a dance more. She was an elegant, accomplished dancer, and the fact that she could entertain the flirtatious discourse he thrust on her while not once glancing at her feet was quite remarkable. It was almost as though she were not in the least in awe of him.

To Brixham, he said, "I suggest you do not take to liking any of the Kittling girls overly much and no, we are not returning to London. If you wish to leave, you may do so. I have come here for a purpose and will not quit this ridiculous place until I have succeeded in my object."

Brixham sighed. "No, I shan't leave. Wouldn't be at all chivalrous."

Gaventry had not the faintest notion what his friend meant by this, but because the glass of brandy, still sitting on his chest, suddenly toppled over without the smallest provocation, and Brixham sat up cursing, the subject was soon forgotten.

# Three

On the following morning, Gaventry stared at his footman as though he had gone mad. "You are telling me that Lady Haslingfield is come to call."

"It would appear so, m'lord," the servant responded, swallowing very hard. "She . . . she does not seem to be in spirits."

"I see." Gaventry had no doubt whatsoever that his godmother had used an intimidating manner when she arrived at his lodgings, although he suspected that her reputation alone would have been enough to overset his manservant.

A friend had lent him the use of his very fine town house in the prestigious Royal Crescent, an accommodation that included his staff. The staff, in turn, were themselves residents of Bath, and each knew to perfection the full reaches of the local *haute ton* society. Lady Haslingfield served as its primary dictator. To have her call, therefore, was not an insignificant occasion. But why had she come? This visit was so completely out of character for her that he grew suspicious, though he could not conjecture in the least as to what her motives might be. Regardless, he was a little relieved that rather than having to abase himself by seeking her out and begging for her assistance, she had instead come to him.

He turned to Brixham, who had been busily employed for the past two hours preparing his own peculiar blend of snuffs, and found his friend staring at him, his mouth agape.

"What do you make of this turn of events?" Gaventry queried.

Only then did he realize that Brixham's exquisitely tied neckcloth seemed suddenly too tight. His face was red, his eyes bulging slightly, and a panic had taken hold of every feature.

Gaventry chuckled. "Easy, man! I promise, I will not let her eat you."

"I believe she puts me far too much in mind of my own mother to make me in the least comfortable. I suppose you must receive her but I only have one shoe on. Lost the other. Kept thinking it would show up."

Gaventry glanced at his friend's feet and laughed again. "Tuck your foot beneath the table and when you stand to offer your bow, move behind me a little." After these sage words of advice, he turned round and addressed his servant. "Please show her ladyship in and afterwards would you please search the rooms until you find, er, which is it, Brixham, the right or left?"

"Right, with a small silver buckle."

Gaventry nodded to the servant.

"Very good, m'lord."

Gaventry rose to his feet and moved to obscure Brixham a trifle from view. There was no sense in waiting until Lady Haslingfield marched into the room to attempt to arrange matters.

He heard her commanding voice. "I should think he would wish to receive his godmother," she said, clearly addressing the poor servant. A moment more and she swept into the chamber, followed by her husband and Miss Whittle, the latter of whom having been introduced to him last night as her companion.

Lady Haslingfield did not meet his gaze at first but rather cast her own about the receiving room, an imperious brow lifted in a long, encompassing and quite critical sweep. The furnishings in a soft gold and brown were quite unexceptional, a circumstance her ladyship apparently noted with a soft harrumph as she finally settled her gaze upon him.

He made his best bow, his guests responded with bows of their own, and he offered, "Won't you sit down?"

Lady Haslingfield took up a chair adjacent to him while her spouse crossed the chamber, procuring a seat at a great distance from his beloved. Miss Whittle, a rather thin, meek woman of indeterminate age, fussed in quick jerks and starts all about her mistress, placing a footstool beneath her feet, plumping up a pillow for her back, and generally giving the impression she would have groomed her feathers as well had Lady Haslingfield presented any for that purpose. She continued in this fashion until the countess dismissed her with a swift snap of her wrist.

Miss Whittle then took up a chair behind and to the right of her mistress, folded her hands on her lap, and quickly gave the impression of suddenly having turned to stone.

Gaventry watched his godmother carefully, all the while wondering if she would reveal her reason for coming. He smiled, if coolly, and said, "I have been trying without the smallest degree of success to determine to what honor I owe this visit. I should have thought you would be at the Pump Room at this hour."

Her ladyship smiled thinly. "You clearly know very little of the matter for we have already been to the Pump Room. Haslingfield is often afflicted with the gout, though he imbibes but the smallest portions of wine, and must take the prescribed three glasses of water a day before breaking his fast."

Gaventry glanced at Lord Haslingfield, who seemed quite absent. He was not certain if he was an imbecile or if his mind was continually set in other pastures to avoid present truths and realities. He appeared not to have heard a word of his wife's explanation.

Lady Haslingfield continued. "As for the purpose of this call, I shall explain momentarily. First, however, I feel it my duty to set at least one thing to rights." Shifting toward Brixham, she addressed him abruptly. "Where is your other shoe? I have never seen such an example of ill-breeding. How do you explain this lapse?"

Brixham cleared his throat. "Simple matter, really. I couldn't find it this morning. Beg pardon. Wasn't expecting company."

"Well, it is most improper," she said in a much-aggrieved tone. "Do go locate your shoe at once, if you please. The sight of your stocking, which has a tear in it, is aggravating in the extreme."

Brixham rose hastily from his chair and in doing so disturbed a quantity of snuff that spilled on his blue pantaloons and rose in a soft billow toward his nose. He began to sneeze.

"Snuff, is it?" she called out. "A nasty habit. I do not permit Hasley the use of it and more than once he has thanked me for it. Is this not so, my love?"

Gaventry glanced at Haslingfield apace, who blinked several times before stating, "Very true, my pet, very true, indeed."

As Brixham hobbled from the chamber, Gaventry watched him go with a mounting temper. He would have immediately remonstrated with the dragon before him, but she merely laughed and said rather hastily, "Now, now I can see that you are become out of temper, but I mean no unkindness. Having it in my power to keep at least the observances of society in check, I do not hesitate to wield such power. You, on the other hand, are dressed in just the manner a young man ought to be—following Brummell's lead, who I must say, has done more to relieve us of a thousand foolish lads thinking it very fine to be dressed in shirt points up to their eyebrows and lapels as wide as their shoulders, than even the finest tailors. Yes, you are to be commended, which leads me to say, Gaventry, that I have come to give you this." She held up a missive, a motion which served to launch Miss Whittle from her seat.

Gaventry rose at the same time to retrieve the note, but Miss Whittle was before him, and as he fairly fell back to his seat, she had delivered what proved, upon quick examination, an invitation to a ball not three days hence. He glanced at Lady Haslingfield. This was an attention entirely unlooked for.

A smile curved her ladyship's lips and almost, for the barest moment, her expression was somewhat pleasant. "I see I have given you a shock. I must say, nothing pleases me more."

"But, my lady, surely you risk offending half the matrons in Bath by inviting me."

She swelled her bosom and narrowed her eyes. "Others follow my lead and those who don't, I ignore. I invite whom I choose and that is the end of the matter. Although, I must say, I believe the authoress of *A Rogue's Tale* has contrived to change things for you. Even my few London acquaintances have told me that because of the novel's success and the general belief that some of the information presented within must be true, that you are being invited to many homes heretofore closed to you. Is this so?"

"It is, although as you may imagine, I do not accept such late-coming invitations."

"I hope you do not intend to be so mulish during your stay in Bath," she cried.

Gaventry found himself torn. He wished nothing more than to state that he intended to refuse all invitations, for then he would have the supreme pleasure of annoying his overbearing godmother. On the other hand, doing so would certainly defeat his purpose entirely, and he knew Lady Haslingfield's own stubbornness well enough to suppose that she would turn her back on him even now should he prove abrasive and obstinate.

A dart of amusement flickered in her brown eyes causing Gaventry to wonder about her. Perhaps at heart she was not all dragon. She added, "I can see that you wish nothing more than to do so, but I beg you will not be a fool."

Gaventry remained silent but did not permit his gaze to waver from hers.

Lady Haslingfield did the same.

A tension rose in the chamber which caused Miss Whittle to begin a series of brisk, dry coughs and Lord Haslingfield to cross and uncross his legs several times.

A thumping on the stairs soon brought Brixham back into

the room, a most propitious circumstance, particularly with the sight of him wearing not the companion shoe on his right foot but rather a top boot. At least he was no longer hobbling. Lady Haslingfield's attention was diverted instantly.

"Did you do this purposely to aggravate me, Mr. Brixham?" her ladyship exclaimed

"Good God, no!" he cried, horror writ in every feature. "Lost the silver-buckled shoe. Only have these boots."

"Why did you not put on the other boot as well, then?" she cried, clearly dumbfounded.

Brixham bowed, begged pardon, but he could not find his other boot. He remembered taking it off but not where he put it. " 'Tis a mystery, I fear, where it has gone."

Since these words left her ladyship with her mouth agape and her eyes wide with wonder, Gaventry could only shake his head as he addressed her. "I have sent a servant to search for his shoe, so I beg you will forget my friend for the moment. We were not expecting visitors this morning, else we would have been properly prepared to receive you. Let us say for the present that I shall accept all invitations you deem of sufficient worth during my stay in Bath, only tell me this, what has prompted *you* to overlook all the gossip, even going so far as to call on me this morning?"

She narrowed her eyes thoughtfully. "I suppose it is simple, really. Your mother was a good friend of mine whose correspondence was a constant source of joy to me and which did not cease until her unfortunate passing. It would be singularly remiss of me not to honor our friendship by recognizing her son."

Gaventry could not make her ladyship out. She was at once both ridiculously imperious in demeanor and conversation and yet held to matters of friendship and honor in a way of which he very strongly approved. "Then I will be happy to attend your fete, provided that Mr. Brixham may attend as well."

"Of course. I shall send another invitation round this afternoon." She then rose, her business concluded to her apparent satisfaction. "Good day, Gaventry. Oh, but there is one more small matter I feel must be addressed."

Gaventry rose to his feet. "Indeed?" he queried in his most imperious manner, hoping to match her own.

Another glimmer of amusement raced through her eyes. But she quickly lifted her chin and returned a frosty, "Yes. If you hope to be received in more homes than just my own, then I trust you will take greater care where you do your kissing. Mrs. Catesby happens to reside in Queen Square."

A smile tugged at his lips. He bowed in acknowledgment of her advice and with that, and another harrumph, she took her leave.

He stood staring at the empty doorway for a considerable length of time.

"Does she know of your having kissed Miss Kittling then?" Brixham asked.

"Undoubtedly," Gaventry murmured, his suspicious nature trying to understand his godmother. "Only what I do not comprehend in the least is why she did not give me a dressing down."

"Perhaps she is addled," he said, tapping the booted foot.

Gaventry chuckled. "No, I think not. Only what is her game, I wonder?"

"I have heard she is very fond of whist. Oh, I see what you are at." He then laughed at his mistake.

Gaventry clapped his friend on the shoulder and said, "Now, let's go find your boot and your shoe."

Brixham smiled broadly. "You always were a right one, Gaven."

"And it means a great deal to me, old fellow, to hear you say so."

Later that morning, Sarah, her sisters, and her cousin returned from a walk to Sidney Gardens only to find several cards left at their house.

"But this is not possible!" Sarah cried, handing them one after the other to Aurrie, who passed them to Meg, who in turn read each name to Charlotte. She had of course been expecting Gaventry to call, but not until that afternoon and these cards each bore a lady's name, a *prominent* lady's name.

"Lady Haslingfield, Mrs. Catesby, Lady Riseley, Mrs. Tempsford, and Lady Everden."

When the last of these names was read, silence fell in the small entrance hall, a sound which put Sarah forcibly in mind of church services at Easter. To say there was something holy about this list of names was perhaps going beyond the pale. However, Sarah knew, as did her sisters and Charlotte, that there was something quite extraordinary about so many visits in one day, from exalted personages who had heretofore never darkened their Queen Square doorway.

The maid began gathering up bonnets, gloves, and pelisses and very soon disappeared up the stairs.

Sarah turned to lead the way into the drawing room, her thoughts quite scattered. What could possibly be the meaning of so much attention from Bath's leading hostesses, and more to the point, what precisely had changed to bring the ladies to their door? She could not comprehend it in the least.

Meg addressed her bemusement. "I know that Lady Haslingfield often makes a point of conversing with you, Sarah, for you always were one of her favorites, but why did she call today? Is it because of Gaventry?"

"I cannot imagine how that could be, or why. Really, I am completely baffled."

Meg still held the cards splayed in her fingers like a fan as she sat down in a chair near the doorway.

"One thing is for certain," Charlotte said, taking up her place opposite her tambour frame and unlacing the needle from the border of the fabric, "these calls must be returned tomorrow. To do anything less would be most uncivil."

All the ladies agreed to it and immediately began discussing in which order the visits ought to be repaid, when a carriage was heard in the street and stopped in front of their house.

Sarah glanced out the window and saw that Lord Gaventry and his friend had just arrived.

" 'Tis Gaventry," Meg called out.

"And his friend, the gentleman at the ball," Charlotte said.

"That must be Mr. Brixham," Aurelia said. "I heard Lady Haslingfield introduce him to Mrs. Catesby."

When the knocker sounded, Sarah felt her heart begin to race. *Gaventry, again.*

In a swift bustling of movement, the ladies rose in preparation of receiving their visitors. Sarah found that she could hardly breathe. Though she had tried very much to keep her mind occupied in general with anything other than images and recollections of Lord Gaventry, he had invaded her thoughts hour upon hour from her first leaving her bed this morning.

She knew nothing good could possibly come of forming an attachment to such a hopeless sort of gentleman, especially one who reminded her constantly of her perfidy as an authoress, but on the other hand she truly had enjoyed dancing with him last night as well as engaging in a very light flirtation with him. If there was also part of her that reveled, though mildly, in the sensation she, as a mere and impoverished Sarah Kittling had caused, she knew these particular sensations to be as transient as they were vain. However, it was very nice to have been such an object of attention, when generally she was confined to so small and to so proper a place in Bath society. For that, she found herself grateful to her guest.

The maid announced Gaventry as well as Mr. Brixham, and the ladies exchanged bows with their visitors. Once this formality was accomplished, Charlotte asked Sarah to make the introductions, "For we are not all known to Lord Gaventry or his friend."

Sarah would have done so immediately, but for the oddest

moment her tongue had been quelled, and all that she could think as she looked into Gaventry's striking blue eyes was that he was so very handsome. He must have for years set all the young, maidenly hearts a-flutter each Season in London, whether he had been deemed an outcast or not. His cheekbones were high and chiseled in appearance, his nose slightly aquiline, which gave a strong cast to his features, matched only by the angled line of his jaw. His eyes, however, were his most dominating feature for they were a brilliant blue and deep-set in a manner that made her think that he had looked harshly upon life for a very long time. She felt in that moment as though she understood something significant about him.

She gave herself a mental shake and through years of practice made the formal introduction of Gaventry, while he in turn introduced Mr. Brixham. When this task was performed, the ladies took up their seats, and at the same time she begged their guests to sit down, which the gentlemen did, each drawing a chair forward. The small receiving room decorated in soft hues of blue, though serviceable, was not lavishly furnished and a few scattered hardback chairs accommodated the rare occasion in which more seating was required. Sarah wondered suddenly if they would be in need, in forthcoming days, of adding to their furniture.

Gaventry addressed Aurelia. "Your home, Miss Kittling, is very well-situated for enjoying the pleasures of Bath."

Sarah felt her muscles tense as she watched her sister struggle to digest these words. Aurelia, for all her beauty, was not quick-witted. "I think it a very fine thing when a house faces north," she said at last.

She saw the slight start in Gaventry's manner and expression. "Yes, I suppose it is. The summers must be comfortable, indeed."

"I love the month of August," she returned.

"I do as well," Brixham announced suddenly.

Aurelia cast him a beaming smile. "I do not mind winter,

either, as most do. For when it rains and is very cold, I curl up by the fire like a cat."

Mr. Brixham chuckled. "I stretch out like a happy hound."

Sarah did not think she had seen Aurrie so content in a conversation before, and since it had proceeded so very well, she felt she could give their discourse a slight turn and draw the attention away from Aurelia, whose ability to sustain a dialogue was somewhat limited. She was a beautiful ninnyhammer, with more hair than wit, but as sweet and gentle a creature as ever was born. Sarah therefore queried, "Do you intend to remain long in Bath, Lord Gaventry?"

He turned his slightly frowning gaze from Aurrie and replied, "We have no fixed date for leaving. I suppose we will merely cast our days and hours upon fate."

She felt the answer was evasive. However, to have inquired further would have been uncivil. "And how do you like our fair city thus far?"

"I have not been here long enough to have fully tasted of what I understand the numerous delights of Bath to be, but thus far, particularly with Queen Square, I must admit I find myself greatly content." His words were too pointed to be ignored, and a decided twinkle shone in his eyes. She knew he was referring to events of the morning before.

She feared that a blush would quickly steal up her cheeks if the subject was not changed instantly, but for the life of her she could think of nothing more to say. Her mind had become snagged, for reasons she could not explain, on the memory of having been kissed by Gaventry, and that so thoroughly. How had it come about that she had not only allowed the kiss but had given herself so completely to the experience. An odd warmth flowed suddenly over the surface of her skin, and a spattering of gooseflesh raced over her neck, shoulders, and arms. For the most ridiculous moment she wished he would kiss her again.

"Have you been to Sally Lunn's?" Meg asked, the calling cards now settled in a small stack on the table in front of her as though she had taken possession of them.

Gaventry winked at Sarah before turning toward her sister. What a devil he was, and surely he had earned his reputation more by experience than anything else. Clearly, he knew how to invade a woman's heart!

He addressed Meg. "No, I have not, but Brixham insists we rise early tomorrow and break our fast there."

"If you had stayed at the White Hart, that would not have been far from Sally Lunn's," Aurrie commented. "But Cook tells me you are residing in the Royal Crescent."

Sarah felt herself blush for Aurelia. To refer to having listened to a servant's gossip was quite inappropriate. There was nothing for it, however, and even though a frown creased Gaventry's brow once more as he settled his gaze on Aurrie, he addressed her politely. "I suppose our comings and goings are spoken of everywhere."

"Indeed, they are and have been for these many years and more. I am very happy that you have come at last to Bath for now we may know you a little. You were very kind to have danced with my sister last night." Here Aurelia smiled in her most angelic manner. "Indeed, you have lifted us up so high in the eyes of our friends and neighbors that even today we were acknowledged as never before." She rose, and picked up the cards before Meg, then carried them to him. In her simple way, she handed them to him. "Do but look who has come to call. You did this for us and we will always be grateful." She sat down in a chair beside him

Gaventry took the cards and found himself utterly confused by Aurelia Kittling in so many ways that he hardly knew where to begin in sorting out his thoughts. For one thing, had he not known that she had written *A Rogue's Tale*, he would have believed her incapable of composing a letter, much less an entire novel. For another thing, how could someone behave so sweetly and so ingenuously who had used him so ill? He was dumbfounded, unless of course she was playacting, which, given her imagination, was quite probable.

Glancing down at the cards, he saw his godmother's name

and recognized two of the ladies as having been friends of his mother's as well and understood Miss Kittling's pleasure. Certainly, these five cards represented the cream of Bath society.

He looked at her once more, trying to make her out. She had the countenance of a goddess, that much he and Brixham had long since decided, and in this moment he would have found the warmth of her expression to be utterly endearing had he not known the truth of her character.

Regardless, he had but one true object in coming to Queen Square, which was simply to worm his way into her good graces, which it would seem he had done merely by dancing with her sister last night. He felt very satisfied that the beginning of his campaign to win her heart had appeared to commence with such ease. For that reason, he smiled. "I sincerely question that my presence here has had such a profound effect on your social enjoyments. However, if such is the case I can only say that I am happy to be of service."

She held his gaze for a long moment, not in what he would describe as a flirtatious manner, but as though she were assessing him. Her pronouncement was forthcoming. "I like your eyes, my lord. Some reported them last night to be cynical, even cruel, but I see only kindness."

He was completely taken aback. Kindness in *his* eyes? She must, indeed, be a simpleton if she saw kindness in his eyes.

Charlotte, again seated before her tambour frame, interjected. "You must not mind our dear Aurrie, Lord Gaventry. She does not mean to be impertinent. It is merely that she is blessed with the ability to see into the souls of her friends and acquaintance. The compliment she has paid you is of great merit."

Gaventry again regarded Miss Kittling. "And thus you take everyone's measure?"

She nodded.

"Are you never wrong?" he inquired. He was certain she was in this case.

She shook her head. "No, never, though sometimes I wish

I were. In your case, whatever the past injustices of your life, I can see that you have a very kind, if wounded, heart, even the heart of a poet, and I hope you will treat our home as your own."

This seemed to make sense to him. He had often thought that the authors of imaginative tales must have unsuspected abilities, and so it was with Miss Kittling. He still, however, did not believe his heart was kind. It might have been deemed such in his youth but not, he feared, anytime during the past seven years. And what the devil did she mean, "the heart of a poet"? No matter. As the ancient phrase "lamb to the slaughter" came to mind, he was not in the least unhappy that she held such ridiculous beliefs of him. He relaxed happily in his chair and smiled. "With so sweetly proffered an invitation, I believe I shall."

Sarah watched Lord Gaventry settle his blue eyes upon her elder sister and a smile she could only describe as devastating appeared on his lips. She was not certain what precisely had just transpired before her, but in anyone other than Aurelia, she would have known a very serious flirtation to have just transpired. Certainly Gaventry seemed to have cast out a lure to her with the broadest of smiles and open manner, but the obvious truth of it caused a whole series of most inelegant thoughts to race through her head. The uppermost of these involved a terrible scenario in which she took her elder sister by her hair and pulled every fine blond ringlet from its careful mooring.

She mentally castigated herself for such ungenerous notions. After all, it was not as though she could ever have any serious interest in a rogue, nor would Aurelia, who, though her intelligence was of an uneven nature, did not lack for common sense. At least, she hoped she would not be so silly as to tumble in love with Gaventry.

She settled her gaze carefully on Aurelia to see just how his attempt at dalliance would be received by her. Aurrie smiled in her gentle manner and responded, "Then it is settled. You and Mr. Brixham"—here she nodded to his friend—"are to think of Queen Square as your home."

"I hope you will enjoy having more visitors," he said, "though if these cards are an indication I predict the charming Kittling sisters and their most charming cousin will soon be besieged by callers."

Aurelia overlaid his arm in a confiding manner. "That was very kindly said, but you must know that it will not at all be likely, or if so, then certainly of a very short duration."

"And why would that be?"

"Because we have no dowries, I fear, and as such we are ignored by all the matchmaking mamas, who Sarah says are in great fear of putting any of us in the path of their sons lest love blossom. Is that not so, Sally?"

Sarah wanted to sink into the sofa and disappear. She could not imagine what had possessed Aurrie to begin offering such confidences to a man she hardly knew, and one whose consequence was so far above the Kittlings. However, there was nothing for it now but to face the music. She swallowed hard and with a lift of her chin turned her gaze to Gaventry. He, on the other hand, appeared to be taking great delight in her discomfiture. It was clear to Sarah that he had gained a swift understanding of Aurelia and, good heavens, was managing her to perfection.

"Very true," was all the satisfaction she intended to give him. Gaventry chuckled.

"It is true!" Brixham suddenly cried, moving closer to the circle by rising from his seat and taking up the chair to the left of Aurelia. "Never noticed it before, but now that I've heard you say it, I can recall a dozen times when I would see a pretty young lady at a ball, look for her at a dozen more and never find her again. When I think of them now, all those pretty young ladies had the same quality—small dowries!"

Aurelia smiled in his direction, clearly happy to be understood.

Sarah could only smile herself in that instant as she met

Gaventry's gaze. His amusement was vast, she realized, and after a moment she found herself giggling and unable to stop, for suddenly everything about this odd social call seemed ridiculous in the extreme. For one thing, the very man who had figured so prominently in her first novel was actually sitting in her drawing room, and for another, Aurelia, who rarely showed to advantage, was being supported by the calculated flirtations of one man and the admiration of another.

Meg, who had been oddly silent, suddenly interjected, "Why are you laughing, Sally? I see nothing amusing in having our shortcomings bandied about as though they had no significance. Whenever I think of the mold of our society, I become infuriated, not at all amused, I assure you."

She was as mad as fire, which only made Sarah laugh more heartily still. Meg was a firecracker, always speaking her mind and more often than not setting up the back of some tabby or other by venturing a bold opinion when she would have been wiser to have kept her thoughts to herself. And if she was not mistaken, Gaventry now understood to perfection that there was more than one reason why the Kittling sisters did not receive more invitations. In other circumstances, she might have been inclined to give Meg a hint that she ought to curb her present impulse to speak her mind, but she decided she might as well allow the gentlemen to comprehend at the outset the full scope of her family's shortcomings. Even Charlotte cleared her throat by way of encouraging her to draw in the reins on Meg.

She met Charlotte's gaze and gave a small shake of her head. Meg, for her part, continued in her oblivion. "Lord Gaventry," she began, also leaving her seat and closing the circle more tightly by moving to sit next to Sarah on the sofa, "do you not think it a grave injustice that every lady's worth is measured on the basis of her dowry and every gentleman his land and fortune? I think a great deal of our gentlemen take to drinking far too much rum punch than they ought merely to avoid these unhappy truths. Is that why you sank into some of the seedier aspects of society? Did you become sickened by so much hypocrisy, for I know you to be a man of substance?"

Even Sarah was a trifle surprised by these exceedingly personal questions. She bit her lip and looked carefully at Gaventry, wondering just how he would take these unsolicited opinions and queries. Dear, dear Meg. She had so many notions and on so many subjects that surely these queries would put her beyond the pale in his eyes. Surely he would be offended.

Gaventry, however, looked at her thoughtfully for a long moment. "In all these years, I've never had anyone ask me these particular questions."

"You need not answer," Charlotte intervened, apparently unable to bear more. "Meg, I fear, has crossed the bounds of propriety. Indeed, Margaret, you ought to offer an apology. Your questions, even the proffering of your opinions, were highly impertinent."

Meg's color grew heightened. "Oh, yes, of course you are right!" she exclaimed. "My lord, I am very sorry. I tend to speak without thinking and I fear I allowed my improper curiosity to better my manners. Pray forgive me."

Sarah could see that Gaventry's expression had become more guarded. "There is nothing to forgive. You are right in one respect. I am grown cynical, more so than any reasonable man ought to be."

Sarah could see by Meg's expression that she meant to press her point, and she reached out hastily, taking hold of her arm. She shook her head, negating the thoughts, even the questions, clearly poised on her sister's tongue.

"No, let her speak," Gaventry cried. "I wish to know what she was so anxious to ask this time."

Meg waited for Sarah's approval. Sarah could find no reason to forbid her now that Gaventry had given his permission. "Very well," she said, addressing the viscount. "If it does not distress you."

"Not in the least."

Sarah was not convinced and wished that Meg would choose discretion, but she did not.

"I wish to know, for I have been more curious than you may imagine, whether or not *A Rogue's Tale*, mirrors more truthfully than any of the gossip we have heard, the events of your life?"

Sarah had already learned from Lady Haslingfield that this was so, but she wondered just what Gaventry would say. The room grew very silent. Even Brixham looked a little worried as he watched his friend. All eyes were upon his lordship.

He seemed to fall into something of a brown study, his gaze more than once shifting to Aurelia in a speculative manner. Aurrie, apparently thinking he was asking for encouragement, said, "I believe you would do well to answer. These matters have weighed on your heart far too long. To speak of them might be very relieving."

Sarah was stunned by her sister's observation and exchanged a startled glance with Charlotte, whose needle was poised in midair. She was about to jump from her seat and suggest that a brisk walk around Queen Square would be just the thing to make the most of the fine weather they were enjoying when Gaventry began. Instead of addressing Meg, however, he directed his answer to Aurelia, perhaps because she was the oldest or perhaps because she was the one who had prompted him. "I must confess, I was stunned when I read the novel. I was even a little resentful. Mostly, however, I was dumbfounded by the relative accuracy of the information presented within. From the moment I finished the last page I have been wondering just how the authoress knew so much of the truth of what happened seven years ago, for it is not generally known."

Meg cried out, "I knew it was true."

Charlotte whispered, "Good God!"

Sarah, however, stared very hard at Gaventry. She could not believe he was speaking of these events to her family. From her conversation of last night with Lady Haslingfield she had learned that, indeed, a Miss Fulbourne had been the source of his social ruin, though in what manner she did not as yet know.

A memory returned to her suddenly, something she had completely forgotten, a conversation she had had with Lady Haslingfield perhaps some three years past in the Pump Room. Gossip had once more been rife about Gaventry. He was even reputed to be a Napoleonic spy and a smuggler of brandies and silks. She had laughed at the time as Lady Haslingfield had done as well. Then the countess had let something drop, the smallest detail. "There was a young lady once," she had said, "who was the cause of his downfall. I have never forgiven her for that."

Sarah had wanted to ask her more about it, but Lady Haslingfield had become flustered. She had begged her to forget she had said any such thing to her and had quickly made her excuses and moved away. Neither she, nor the countess, had mentioned the matter again. At the time, Sarah had not given the matter much thought, and she had forgotten all about the odd conversation. Now, however, she came to believe that that was how she had conjured up the story in the first place, only she had never put the facts together before. The information Gaventry's godmother had imparted unwittingly that day had become the bedrock of her story—a young lady had been the cause of Gaventry's social ruin. Miss Fulbourne had become Lucinda Hardcastle.

After Gaventry confessed that there was a correlation between *A Rogue's Tale* and the scandal that had severed him to a large degree from London's polite society, the chamber once more fell silent for a long moment. It was not surprising that it was Meg who was the first to speak, but this time her voice was gentler, less forceful. "How kind of you to entrust this knowledge to us. I, for one, promise to repeat nothing of what has been said today."

Sarah agreed, as did Aurrie and Charlotte.

"I shall hold you to it," Gaventry returned, but he was smiling.

Mr. Brixham, however, was regarding him in some wonder. "Do you know, I have never heard you speak of this to anyone. I think it very odd in you."

"This, from a friend!" he countered playfully.

Brixham shrugged. "Glad you said it. I believe it's time the truth came out about all the rubbish that happened so long ago."

"That will do, Brix. I did not offer to amplify what has been said."

"So you did not. Well, this is a good beginning then and all because Miss Kittling persuaded you to do so." He turned to Aurelia. "I vow I shall forever be in your debt. As Gaven's friend these many years and more, it has always made me as mad as fire that the young lady was to blame but Gaven's sense of honor would not allow the truth to be known generally."

"That will do!" Gaventry snapped. "I have answered Miss Margaret's question, but that is all that will be said of the event." He then turned to Aurelia and gave the subject a hard turn by asking after her interests. Aurelia responded in kind and began speaking of the pianoforte, her love of music, and of dancing, and of how many partners she had had at the assembly last night.

Sarah was glad that he had ended so prickly a discussion and that he was giving his attention so fully to Aurrie, for she had much to ponder. She stared at him, aware that for some reason her heart had been jolted severely by Brixham's further revelation, which not only cast the viscount in the right, but even in the role of a chivalrous knight, perhaps having gone so far as to protect an unworthy Miss Fulbourne's reputation. A piercing curiosity swamped her every sensibility. She needed to know what had happened, what had really happened. Her novel was one thing, but the truth quite another.

A deep stillness within her heart caught her attention, and she listened very hard to understand the musings of her soul. She looked at Gaventry a little more and she listened more intently to the whisperings of her heart. She remembered kissing him on the day before, throwing her arms about his neck and kissing him as though her happiness had depended upon it.

All at once, comprehension dawned—she understood now that she needed to know more than anything else in the world whether she had kissed a rogue yesterday or a knight. Only how was she ever to discover the truth?

# Four

"Why are you smiling?" Brixham asked.

"Am I?" Gaventry returned, picking up the reins of his matched pair of grays.

"Yes, and I do not like it, not one whit, for that is not a kindly look in your eyes. More like the way you looked just before you popped a hit over Jackson's guard."

Gaventry chuckled. Perhaps that was the way he felt after all, he thought, setting his curricle in motion. He would not, however, own the truth to anyone, not even to Brixham, whom he accounted the best friend a fellow could ever have. "I would hardly equate a boxing ring to a drawing room."

"Nor would I, " Brixham said. "So why do I think you just have?"

Gaventry shrugged and gave the horses another slap of the reins. In truth, he could not have been more pleased with the progress he had made in this the first of his assaults on Miss Kittling's heart. She had warmed to him quite strongly, at least from the moment she encouraged him to speak of his past. She had even touched his arm, which in his experience was a quite telling gesture. If matters continued on this course, he could expect to have achieved his object within no less than three weeks, at which time he would be utterly grateful to quit so tedious a place as Bath.

For the present, however, he fixed his mind on what he must do next. Ignoring Brixham's question, he asked one of his own. "How would you feel about doing the pretty at the Pump Room?"

"Good God!" Brixham exclaimed. "I begin to think you have gone mad!"

"I take that as an affirmative?" He turned his curricle down Gay Street in a general southerly direction toward the Pump Room. Bath was a small city and the genteel quarters even smaller, so that the journey from Queen Square to the bathing pools, Pump Room, and Abbey were not far distant.

"Yes. No. Oh, I suppose I don't give a fig what we do, besides we always do what you want anyway."

Gaventry glanced sharply at his friend. "I beg your pardon? That is not so. Tell me you do not truly believe what you have just said."

"Of course I believe it. Not that I am complaining, mind. Easier not to have to make too many decisions."

"Brix, you have but to say the word. We shall do whatever you wish."

His friend laughed suddenly. "What I wish is to return to Queen Square where I might be at liberty to stare at Miss Kittling for the next year or so."

"Besotted?" he queried uneasily.

"No, hardly that," he said on something of a sigh. "She's devilishly pretty. All the ladies were of course, but the eldest . . . ! I vow I never saw anything so lovely before, not even in London. A perfect angel in appearance, manner, and speech."

"I cannot allow you to call her thus or have you forgotten already that your *angelic* Miss Kittling is the author of *A Rogue's Tale*? No angel would have written that book."

"I suppose that much is true. However, Gaven, I must confess that I have never quite understood why that novel made you as mad as hops particularly when you were cast in such an heroic role, one that I know very well was in fact precisely what happened."

"The story could have been accurate in every essential, which it most certainly was not, and I would still be exceedingly vexed that my life, my actions, my deeds were put into a small calf-bound volume and read by half the ladies of the kingdom."

At that, Brixham laughed heartily.

"I see nothing amusing in what I have said."

"Gaven, do but think! Half the ladies of the kingdom cannot even read."

In spite of himself, Gaventry smiled. "Do stubble it, will you?"

Conversation came to a complete halt when Brixham quickly raised his quizzing glass and ogled several damsels also walking in a southerly direction. He sighed anew. "You may think Bath a dead bore but I vow I have not seen so many pretty ladies. I wonder if it is because they all drink the waters?"

At that, Gaventry laughed. "I have never known the waters to serve as a cure of being platter-faced. For the gout, for rheumatic and lung complaints, for diseases of the skin, but never for a stubby nose, a pronounced forehead, or the lack of a chin."

"She winked at me," was Brixham's response. "The middle one with the sweetest freckles across her nose. I hope I shall meet her at the Pump Room."

A few more turns, a few minutes more, and Gaventry drew up his horses. Brixham immediately jumped to the ground. "Brix, be a good chap and fetch that intelligent-looking lad to mind the horses, will you?"

When the horses were properly attended to, Gaventry led the way to the Pump Room and spent the next half hour greeting the few faces he recognized and permitting himself to be introduced to anyone he felt might be of use to him in the coming weeks. If several of the young ladies and not a few of the matrons who offered their bows to him also tended to dazzle him with their smiles and expressions of hope that he might enjoy his sojourn in Bath, he found himself cursing Miss Kittling beneath his breath once again. This had been the primary result of her horrid novel, that now he was no longer seen so much as a villain but as a misunderstood knight of old. He truly did not know which displeased him more, being an outcast, or this new brand of social absurdity in which he was now treated as something of a dashing Byronic creature.

Having promised at least two young ladies to go down a dance with them at Lady Haslingfield's fete on Friday—should she allow dancing in her expansive drawing room that evening—he at last took his leave.

Upon taking up the reins once more, he realized Brixham had grown oddly silent. Tossing a shilling to the lad who had watched his horses, he turned to his friend and saw that Brixham's complexion was white and his lips were turned down in a truly marvelous grimace.

"What the devil is the matter with you?"

Brixham swallowed hard. "Tasted the waters!" he croaked. "Swallowed a full glass until I realized how vile they were. Why did no one warn me!"

At that, Gaventry laughed heartily and did not stop until his friend's complexion had returned to normal, and that was not until he finally made his turn into the Royal Crescent.

Later that afternoon, Sarah sat on the small chaise-longue, situated by the front window overlooking Queen Square, and marveled at how beautiful the trees were now that they had begun leafing out. A wind was sweeping through the seven hills that surrounded the city, causing the leaves to dance about and shimmer in the waning light of the May evening. A peculiar excitement had taken hold of her since Gaventry's visit, though he was certainly only part of the reason her heart had been in a state as near to exhilaration as she had ever before experienced. The rest was due primarily to the fact that what had begun as a disaster, in the loss of their annuity at their uncle's hand, appeared to be transforming into something of a miracle. She had but to finger yet again the calling cards which she had been holding for the past hour to be reminded of their changing good fortune.

A footman, in livery she did not recognize, entered the square and crossed in her direction to the southerly row of houses. Her heart began to beat strongly in her breast the closer he drew, and just when she thought he meant to pass by her house, he approached her door, at the same time withdrawing a missive from the pocket of his coat. The knocker sounded, the maid responded, and in a moment more she brought her the missive.

"A response is requested, ma'am."

Sarah glanced at the maid and saw that her complexion was aglow. She offered her an inquiring glance, and the maid whispered, "Lady Haslingfield's man."

"Oh, I see." She broke the seal quickly and read the note, which proved to be an invitation to her fete three days hence.

Her heart leapt anew and tears burned her eyes. She was not mistaken. For reasons that were not in the least apparent to her, Lady Haslingfield had invited the three Kittling sisters as well as Cousin Charlotte to her party. "Bring me my writing things at once, Betsy."

"Yes, miss. Indeed! At once!"

A few minutes later, while cradling the portable table on her lap, Sarah strove to keep her nerves quiet, but even so, as she penned the necessary letter, her fingers showed an abominable tendency to shake. Betsy stood nearby, dancing from one foot to the next, the significance of this remarkable turn of events not lost on her.

When at last she had sanded and sealed her missive, she handed it to Betsy who received it as one taking possession of a holy relic. She walked proudly in the direction of the entrance hall and disappeared, but only for a moment.

From the window, Sarah watched the footman begin his return journey heading in the direction of the Circus. Betsy reappeared in the doorway. "Begging yer pardon, miss, but should I perhaps summon yer sisters and Mrs. Mears?"

"Yes!" Sarah cried. "By all means, yes! Do so at once!"

While she waited for her sisters, Sarah became so excited that she could no longer remain sitting sedately on the chaise. Setting aside the portable table, she fairly jumped to her feet and began pacing the room. She could scarcely contain the thrill she felt at just what Lady Haslingfield's invitation could mean for her family. Why, even Charlotte might find a match now that they were to be invited into the first circles of Bath!

Only how was this to be managed? How were they to make five calls tomorrow or could some of them wait and what about . . . oh, yes, what about *new gowns* for them all! If they were to call in the Royal Crescent and the Circus on a regular basis, they must have more modish apparel. Nothing of course that would indicate they were trying to be anything they were not, nothing above their station, but at least a muslin each that did not show so much wear as their current wardrobe and perhaps silk gloves all around.

When the ladies had descended the stairs, each appearing a trifle bemused at her summons, she blurted out, "Milsom Street! We are to go to Milsom Street on the instant!"

Meg, Aurrie, and Charlotte frowned at one another. "But it is nearly four o'clock. The shops will be closing soon," Meg stated reasonably. "Sally, why are your cheeks so red and your eyes glittering?"

Sarah's spirits plummeted. "Yes, yes, of course. Well, there is nothing to be done. We must wait until morning. But then it is imperative that we visit the dressmakers."

"In Milsom Street?" Aurrie queried. "But are they not a trifle dear?"

"Yes, but it must be done," Sarah responded.

"Why?" Charlotte asked, taking a step forward. "Whatever has happened to put you in such a state for it is not at all like you to recommend a shopping expedition when there is scarcely a tuppence to spare for extra sugar or even beef."

Sarah had thought of that. Of course she had thought of that. She had thought of little else for years; how to squeeze every tuppence possible out of a wholly inadequate quarterly allowance and later royalties, which were only but a trifle better in order to keep her family safely ensconced in Queen Square. In truth, she was sick to death of having to be so careful, of having to make decisions that were in her own view dishonorable, like writing novels about the lives of complete strangers. She calmed her mounting frustrations and addressed the matter at hand. "In ordinary circumstances, I would agree with you. However, circumstances have changed and . . . and I have been saving a portion of our annuity for an emergency."

"What emergency?" Aurrie cried, appearing anxious. "Indeed, Sally, you begin to frighten me! Whatever is the matter? Are you become ill? Now that I look at you I think you must have the headache."

She shook her head. "Not by half, dearest. Something wonderful has happened, something which might alter our fortunes completely!" With that, she lifted the invitation for all to see, but she could not speak. She could not remember the last time she had been so completely overcome.

Charlotte took the invitation and read it aloud. Afterward, with all the color draining from her face, she staggered backward and was caught by both Aurrie and Meg before she toppled over in her dazed state. Though she appeared as though she might faint, she did not. All three ladies stared at Sarah.

Aurrie shook her head in utter bewilderment. "We . . . we have been invited to Lady Haslingfield's fete on Friday evening?

Meg cried, "A fete, a real fete!"

Charlotte, finally gaining her balance, proffered, "But how . . . why . . . when did this happen? How is it possible and she even included me?"

"Well, of course she included you," Sarah said. "She knows very well that you are part of our family."

Meg took the invitation from Charlotte and read it for

herself. "Oh, but how wonderful! The Circus! We have never been into even one of those elegant homes before. So that is why you wish us to go shopping!"

Sarah took up a seat and gestured for her sisters and Charlotte to do the same. A serious discussion of what next must be done was certainly in order. "Precisely so. I only wish it were not so late in the day."

Charlotte took up a chair nearest her, fairly collapsing into it. "But how did this happen? And why, after so many years living in relative poverty, have we now been given the entree?"

"Yes, why?" Meg intoned, also taking up a seat.

"It is a mystery," Sarah said. "I vow I truly cannot account for it."

Only Aurrie remained standing. She sighed heavily, which brought Sarah's gaze to her face. She discovered there a beatific expression and was not surprised when Aurrie whispered, "I should like a gown of pink satin overlaid with the softest sheerest tulle which floats behind in a demi-train over two rows of small satin ruffles. I could wear Mama's pearls and in my hair a scattering of pink artificial flowers and a few white ones, too." She once more released a deep sigh and moved to sit down. But because she was not paying attention she sat on Charlotte's lap, a circumstance which set all the ladies to giggling.

Sarah, feeling happier and more hopeful than she had in years, felt tears fill her eyes once more. "And so you shall, dearest! The precise gown you have just described."

The next two days were the most unusual for the Kittling household in a very long time. Once they had made the requisite morning calls, there were numerous shopping trips and excursions to dressmakers. Charlotte was not willing to be deterred on one particular point—she had insisted from the outset, and much to their joint advantage, that the very best price for fabric was to be sought and that the sewing would be done by a group of widows in the Westgate Buildings, who would welcome their business and who would perform the required service for the ladies at a much lower cost than that which the Milsom shops would charge.

Sarah did not demur for very long, particularly since the need for economy had long since trained her out of every extravagance many years ago. So it was that with a judicious purchase of fabric and other notions, the ladies saw numerous enhancements to their wardrobes, even the addition of several pelisses, shawls, and hair ornaments which could be shared among the sisters and of course with Charlotte.

At long last, when the night of the fete came to pass, and sedan chairs had been ordered for each of the ladies, Sarah soon found herself ensconced in what was for her a luxury which proved invaluable since, as the carriers began the gentle ascent to the Circus, it began to rain. She treasured every moment of the ride, not caring about the occasional jostle when a curb was mounted or one of the carriers stumbled slightly. She felt in that moment like a lady, a real lady, a very odd sensation to be sure, but one which reminded her suddenly that for so many years of her life she had served more as a housekeeper, watching over every groat that the household spent with the meticulous eye of a clockmaker, so that she was never without some occupation to perform or some trying decision to be made, like whether to replace a worn-out umbrella or two or to purchase a new linen tablecloth because Betsy said the present one had become ragged beyond repair.

Tonight, therefore, regardless of what had happened in the past or what might happen tomorrow, she meant to savor every moment of the occasion.

Two hours later, however, she found herself standing beside a palm at the entrance to Lady Haslingfield's drawing room, quite alone but watching her sisters in some stupefaction and not a little fear.

At one end of the elegant rose and green drawing room, Aurelia was seated in a winged chair with her small feet settled daintily on a footstool. She was surrounded by several beaux, each wearing a quite besotted expression, and why wouldn't they be besotted for she was quite the prettiest lady present. There was one gentleman fairly reclining at her feet and reading poetry to her, another making frequent inquiries about her comfort—was she too hot, too cold, was she in need of refreshment—while a third and a fourth gentleman had drawn chairs forward to flank her, clearly intent on listening to every word that fell from her lips. Sarah did not wish it so, but she lived in constant dread that the gentlemen surrounding Aurrie would realize suddenly that she was something of a ninnyhammer and desert her without the smallest regard for her feelings.

At the opposite end of the room, Meg stood by the fireplace with no less than three young gentlemen dancing attendance upon her. From this quite lively group could be heard frequent bursts of laughter, usually as a direct result of something Meg would say. Sarah fanned herself nervously. Would Meg offend her listeners with some suddenly expressed and quite volatile opinion or would she burst out laughing, as she often did, and so loudly that all three men would feel a disgust of her?

She sighed a brief, anxious sigh and fanned herself a little more. Her gaze flitted back and forth. After a moment, she drew close to Aurrie's group and heard her sister say, "Why, Mr. Catesby, I think you are very much like a sailing ship. I see adventure in you or at least the desire of it."

Sarah gulped. Aurelia was using her Gypsy ways in telling her audience their strongest guiding force, a powerful intuitive gift she possessed which often misled people into thinking she could converse equally on other subjects. She could listen to no more and moved as surreptitiously as possible toward Meg. She arrived in time to hear her youngest sister say, "I could walk up and down the seven hills of Bath before sunset if given the challenge. What of you, Sir George? You appear to be a gentleman of some strength. Could you do as much?"

Since the young baronet ran his finger about the inside of his neckcloth and his face darkened, it was no surprise to Sarah, when he cried, "Good God, no!"

All the gentlemen laughed once more. Thank goodness the subject was harmless enough, yet she feared the next would not be. When one of her admirers spoke of driving, and Meg immediately announced that had she had the opportunity to learn she would have been proficient before the cat could lick her ear, Sarah's heart quailed and she moved away. Why was it that her sisters must be so extreme? Why could they not be more like Charlotte, which led her to wonder where her cousin was, precisely. She moved from chamber to chamber and found her in the card room.

Once there, however, she blinked, for Charlotte was no less surrounded, though the set was much older. Charlotte and Mrs. Catesby were partners playing against Lady Haslingfield and Mrs. Tempsford in what appeared to be a very serious round of whist. Once more, Sarah groaned inwardly, for though Charlotte was quite docile in many respects she was not when she played at cards, which was her favorite pastime. On these occasions she became an absolute tiger.

Once more, Sarah trembled inwardly. When she heard Charlotte proclaim her victory in a loud voice and Lady Haslingfield's complexion turned the shade of a plum in her displeasure, she could bear no more. She turned abruptly on her heel and would have quit the doorway, except that she now collided with Lord Gaventry.

"Oh, I do beg your pardon!" she cried. He must have just arrived, for she had not seen him earlier.

"My fault entirely," he said, a crooked smile on his lips. He had grabbed her shoulders in order to keep her from falling backward and for a long moment did not let her go. "I fear in standing so closely and failing to inform you of my proximity, I created the mishap. On the other hand, I certainly did not expect you to whirl around so abruptly. Is something amiss?"

"No," she responded, trying to smile. At the skeptical lifting of one brow, she hastened to add in a low voice, "Yes, that is, not yet. Oh, I do not know. I think I worry far too much than is at all necessary, certainly for my own peace of mind."

"Indeed?" he inquired, his expression curious.

"Yes, it is my greatest failing," she added confidingly. "If it is raining I worry that the clouds will suddenly break, the day grow hot, and I will be suffering in my woolen pelisse—"

"And if it is hot, you fear it will rain."

"Precisely," she responded, a sense of some relief striking her at being so easily understood. "Do you suffer from a similar defect?"

He shook his head. "No, I fear mine is the opposite, I rarely give a thought to the weather at all!"

"You know very well that is not what I meant," she retorted, laughing. Only then did she realize that all conversation in the card room had ceased. Glancing in the direction of the whist table, she saw that Lady Haslingfield was staring at them in some curiosity, a little bow of a smile on her lips, and that the entire group had followed suit.

She felt a blush begin to climb her cheeks, particularly since she knew of her ladyship's opinions where her relationship with Lord Gaventry was concerned, and would have undoubtedly turned the precise shade of a ripe tomato had not the viscount suddenly offered his arm and asked, "Would you care for some refreshment, Miss Sarah?"

She did not hesitate but wrapped her arm quickly around his. "Yes, very much, thank you."

A moment more and they had quit the doorway.

Gaventry whispered, "Our hostess may be my godmother, but sometimes I think her conduct completely beyond the pale. I hope you will not be overly disturbed by her stares and smiles."

"I would have been, had the moment continued even a fraction of a second longer. Thank you for suggesting a little refreshment. I have been attempting to pass myself off creditably this evening but had my blushes overtaken me just now, I should have failed miserably."

At that, he chuckled. "You do worry far too much, indeed," he responded. "I believe the curiosity was directed more toward me than you, though now I fear I sound like a braggart."

She glanced up at him. "Perhaps a little, but since you have done so in order to give relief to my feelings, I should be ungenerous not to overlook it. Would you not agree?"

"Completely."

He guided her into the dining room, which had been arranged to provide refreshments throughout the evening. Several footmen stood nearby awaiting their pleasure. "Champagne?" he asked of her. When she nodded, he procured two glasses and returned to her.

"Thank you," she said, relieving him of the proffered drink.

Once more he offered his arm and began guiding her out of the dining room and into the library, which was less crowded. Another turn and they were settled in a quiet corner in wing chairs set at a close angle to each other. Sarah seated herself and realized she welcomed it. "What an excellent notion. I have either been dancing or moving about the receiving rooms since my arrival and that was at least two hours past." She took a sip of the champagne. "And the wine is lovely."

He joined her. "So it is."

She regarded him over the rim of her glass and felt a dizziness assail her that had nothing to do with the delicate, bubbly wine. She had felt this way on Monday, when he had first accosted her in Queen Square as though something about his mere presence overthrew everything she knew to be true about herself and about what she believed would make her happy. In a thousand years, she would never have thought that kissing a rogue as she had would have made her happy, yet in those few minutes, when she had been locked in his embrace, she had known happiness. But why?

Therein lay the mystery. She could not explain what had happened to her that morning, not in all the ponderings and wonderings she had engaged in since that time. He had kissed her, she had loved every moment of it, and that should have been that. Instead, every time she saw him again her heart was pierced anew with longings she did not truly comprehend.

Knowing that her musings had caused a silence to begin stretching between them, she felt obliged to break it and that as swiftly as possible. She introduced a subject therefore that had become something of a conundrum to her. "Do you know, that in all the gossip I ever heard of you, which has been quite formidable over the years, I cannot recall any lady ever having spoken of how handsome you are." He was clearly taken aback. "Oh dear! Ever since our arrival, I have been fretting that my sisters would say or do something outrageous and disgrace us all, but here I have done so instead."

He grinned. "You have not committed a capital offense. I was merely surprised by your frank compliment." He leaned forward slightly. "So you think me handsome?"

"Only a simpleton would think otherwise."

He appeared to assess her. "Do you mean to flirt with me, Miss Sarah?"

"Of course not," she responded quickly. "I was merely making an observation. I cannot account for why you were never described to me before."

"I believe I have your answer—because the meat of the gossip was so much more scintillating than the beauty of my person."

She smiled. "Perhaps. But I begin to think there might be a simpler answer."

"Indeed?"

"Yes. I begin to think that no one had ever seen you before. This is, after all, your first visit to Bath."

"Very true."

"On the other hand, you are known exceedingly well to Lady Haslingfield. She must have always known precisely what you looked like."

"Yes, but I have not seen her in years. Perhaps time has improved me."

Sarah could only laugh.

She watched as a speculative light entered his eye. "So you think me handsome, but am I as handsome as Lord Daventry in your opinion?"

His sudden and quite surprising reference to the hero of her dreadful novel caused her heart to constrict. She shrugged. "That ridiculous story. Mere fabrications. You, on the other hand, are real. The hero of that story is not. Therefore, there can be no comparison."

He stared at her very hard. Questions rose in his eyes and passed over his features, yet he remained silent. She wondered precisely what he was thinking, or more specifically, what it was he was not asking.

Gaventry stared at Miss Sarah in some bemusement. *She speaks so easily of the novel. Was her response rehearsed or is it possible she does not even know that her sister is the author of* A Rogue's Tale? That seemed an utter impossibility particularly since even from his short acquaintance with her, he knew her to be a woman of some sense as well as intelligence? How could she reside in Queen Square and not know that Aurelia Kittling was the author of that deuced novel? For the barest moment he wondered if the publisher of *A Rogue's Tale* had misinformed him. At the very least, thus far there was simply no indication that any of the ladies had a connection with the novel.

"So you think the story absurd?" he queried. Perhaps he might glean an inadvertent confession from her about her sister.

"Of course. How could it be otherwise, for surely no friend, no true friend who would be privy to the particulars of your comings and goings would actually publish such a story. From the beginning, I assumed the essentials presented in the novel to be erroneous."

"Are you so naive as to think that a friend cannot betray?"

He was not certain from whence the question, so clearly laced with bitterness, had arisen. He watched a frown crease her quite pretty brow.

"Are you saying then that you were in some manner betrayed by a friend?"

He regarded her carefully, a thousand doubts rampaging through his mind. Did she actually know nothing of the truth? "I was not discussing the story," he said at last, "merely the concept of a friend being capable of betrayal."

"Never a true friend, surely," she said.

He shrugged suddenly and could not help but laugh. "We are grown so serious and I risk the quite wretched solecism of either boring you to distraction or giving you a fit of the blue-devils."

"Nonsense," she responded promptly. "I enjoy an occasional debate on such subjects." She sipped her champagne.

"Debate? Is that what we were doing?" He glanced about the chamber, which had thinned of occupants. There were but three others remaining.

"Very nearly. Do you dislike the notion?"

"Not in the least," he responded, settling his gaze on her. "But I must say that I find you a rather unusual female, Miss Sarah Kittling."

"And you have surprised me as well. Given your reputation, I would not have thought it would be so easy to converse with you."

"Did you imagine that a gentleman who drinks wine from skulls would have no ability for discourse?"

She laughed outright. "Is it true then?"

"I fear I shall disappoint you exceedingly," he responded, thinking yet again that he liked her a great deal more than he ought, "when I tell you that I have never done so. That sort of thing belongs to Byron and his set." He finished his champagne and settled the glass on the table at his elbow.

She had grown quiet again and was regarding him in that open manner that ought to have made him uncomfortable yet for some reason did not. Finally, she grinned, yes it was a grin. "I thought it was all a hum!" she cried. "I suspected it from the first."

He found himself laughing, his spirit lighter than it had been in years. She had done this in just a few short minutes of conversation. "Why from the first?" From the corner of his eye he watched as the last of the guests quit the library. They were essentially alone.

"I cannot say precisely. Perhaps it was because of the sheer magnitude of the gossip. Early on, I had become convinced that what was said of you, at least in Bath, was done so primarily because Bath is a rather dull place. You may not consider it a service, but your sad reputation has brightened many a drizzly day in the Pump Room."

"For you?"

"No," she returned quickly, laughing and grimacing at the same time. "I always thought the stories ludicrous. Even from a practical viewpoint, how could you possibly have been in both Scotland and Greece, committing every manner of impropriety, on the exact same day of the same year?" She sipped her champagne again.

"Was I in both places?" he asked, his smile broadening again.

"Yes, you were in Scotland ravishing innocents and in Greece drinking wine from skulls. That was a twelve-month past, May, of 1817. Do you have a twin perhaps? That might account for such a disparity."

"No twin," he murmured. His gaze drifted over her brown curls and across what he believed was the prettiest cheek he had ever before witnessed. Miss Sarah's complexion was quite lovely, her skin bronzed if but a trifle, perhaps from walking about the hills quite often, and accompanied by an apple blossom bloom sweeping along a pronounced and very beautiful cheekbone. All the gentlemen of his acquaintance would probably account Miss Aurelia Kittling as the beauty of the family, but he did indeed by far prefer the softer, understated beauty of the lady before him.

He was reminded suddenly that but a few days past he had held her in his arms and kissed her quite thoroughly. A powerful desire to repeat the experience suddenly shot through him. If she was so brazen as to speak of his reputation without the smallest blush, why not let her feel the force of it again? After all, it would serve his interests of the moment far better to offend her since *her* heart was not his object, but rather her elder sister's. Besides, he had no serious interest in her.

As though fate were somehow taking a hand in this little adventure he was contemplating, the door began to slowly swing shut. They were now alone.

"I wonder who did that?" she queried, rising to her feet. He saw the panic in her eyes, which further prompted his wicked scheme.

He rose as well, but as she reached for the latch, he was before her and overlaid her hand with his own. "Not yet," he whispered against her ear. "We are not finished with our discussion, particularly of all the gossip surrounding me. Would you like to know how much of it is true?"

He felt her grow very still, a circumstance that delighted him. He would kiss her again, and there was no doubt in his mind that she would not refuse him. He took her glass of champagne from her hand and settled it next to his own.

Once the glasses were safe, and without a moment's hesitation, he hooked her elbow, turned her into him, and gathered her up in his arms. He kissed her fiercely, knowing that if the door was not opened in a minute or less, their seclusion would become a scandal as quickly as dry tinder catching fire. Oh, but she was a delight to hold in his arms.

Sarah, for her part, did not understand even the smallest mite why she was permitting him to kiss her again. Regardless, she received the gentle assault as one caught in a dream from which she neither could nor wanted to escape. He kissed her with such ferocious abandon that she felt all but devoured and in the devouring sank into an exquisite oblivion of pleasure and joy. Time ceased to exist, every earthly care disappeared like vapor beneath a burning sun. She was reborn in a place of such sweet delight that there was no returning now.

She understood that this was not love, at least not yet, not in this present fiery form, but if not love then what precisely, because it was as sweet and wondrous as a baby's first steps, as a schoolgirl's perfect copperplate, as a sonnet by Shakespeare's hand.

Her own hand still touched the latch as if in doing so she could remain tied to the present and to the obligations to family and society. Yet all the while her free hand touched the curls at the nape of his neck, which just barely clung to the edge of his neckcloth. His arms held her tightly about her waist. He had pulled her shockingly against him, so it was that she felt the power of his thighs and something within her gave way. She could no longer breathe.

After a long moment, she drew back ever so slightly, and while he kissed her lips tenderly now, she could just see the line of his cheek, the firm arch of his brow, the way he tilted his head to reach her lips more fully. She let her arm fall away from his neck, yet she still held the door latch by the smallest of fingerholds. He drew back and she was left supporting herself against the door. There was a savagery about him. She remembered that he was a rogue and had lived in such a fashion for a very long time, seven years to be exact, for that was when the gossip about a duel in a brothel had begun.

"Did you kill him?" she whispered, needing to know suddenly all that he truly was.

He lifted a brow and a crooked smile twisted his lips. "What a very strange question to be sure. To whom are you referring?"

"The man in the brothel."

She expected him to become angry, instead he leaned over

her, an arm pressed into the door beside her head. He traced her lips with his finger. "I should have."

"Then it is true. You were not alone."

"I was not alone."

"And he was there."

He nodded.

"Who was he?" She wanted to hear him speak of Lord Stewkely.

He shook his head. "I shall never tell, not even a woman who kisses like heaven. You do, you know."

She smiled faintly looking at him. " 'Tis not my skill, my lord," she murmured, laughing.

"Then what is it, for kissing you is like holding moonlight in my arms."

"A poet?" she whispered, smiling again. "A poet's words?"

"My words, but no poet."

"A poet's soul. That is what Aurrie said of you, did she not?"

"Yes, but it was ridiculous."

"Not ridiculous." She reached up and touched his cheek. He caught her hand and held it couched in the safety of his own strong grasp.

"Who the devil are you?" he asked on a sudden, intense whisper.

"Sarah Kittling," she whispered.

He almost leaned down to kiss her again, but from beyond the doorway another voice called out, "Sarah, where are you?"

"That would be Aurelia," she said to him. In a strong voice, she called out, "I am here, Aurrie, with Lord Gaventry." At the same time, she stepped away from him and opened the door wide.

Aurelia swept into the chamber, her blue eyes wide. "My lord, 'tis you I seek. Lady Haslingfield has asked that you go down the next set with me, for she said she has a desire to see us dance together, that is, of course, if it would be pleasing to you."

"Nothing would please me more," he responded, offering his arm to her.

"That is very kind of you. I thought you might not like to."

"Why would you think that?"

"Because you arrived so late at the Upper Assembly Rooms."

"But that was not my fault at all. Poor Brixham had lost his dancing slippers and we had the deuce of a time finding them."

"Poor Mr. Brixham! I wish I had known for I could have offered him my sympathies."

"Do you often lose things?" he asked.

Aurelia smiled up at him as she moved into the hallway. "No, but sometimes I misplace things."

Sarah watched a briefly startled expression pass over his features. A moment more and she was left alone in the doorway, Aurrie's innocent prattling a balm to her overtaxed nerves. Had she just permitted Gaventry to kiss her again? Good God, she must have gone mad! Or had it truly happened? Was it possible she had merely imagined his lips pressed to hers, his arms wrapped so tightly about her, the way his kisses teased and tormented her lips?

The remainder of the evening became a strange blur to Sarah. She never again found herself alone with Gaventry, nor did he seek her out either to converse or to dance with her. He did, however, make a point of joining the court that had so quickly formed around Aurelia, something for which she found herself grateful on several score. For one thing, there was little chance she would again be left alone in his company, which she found rather dangerous in a terribly exciting way, and for another, the more Aurelia was viewed by other men to be of some interest, the greater the chance the right gentleman would take note and hopefully tumble in love with her. Her chief object must be to see either or both of her sisters settled happily.

# Five

Meg leaned over Sarah's shoulder and whispered into her ear. "Gaventry is just arrived! How handsome he is in a blue coat. I vow every lady in the Pump Room has turned to stare at him. Did you notice how broad his shoulders are?"

Because Meg described Lord Gaventry in so thorough a manner, Sarah found it not in the least necessary to even glance his direction. For this she was grateful. Ever since the kiss of last night, not to mention a ridiculously jumbled sleep in which she became tangled in her bedcovers, she had been fretting about just what she ought to do when next she met Lord Gaventry. Unlike the kiss in Queen Square, last night's assault on her lips had been kept entirely secret so that no one, not even her sisters, was aware of what had transpired in Lady Haslingfield's library. She still could not credit that the rather disastrous event had occurred at all, but the state of her nerves all morning reminded her that Gaventry, indeed, had somehow succeeded in taking another kiss from her.

In many ways she was still astonished that he had done so, but then she had never before been so closely acquainted with a man of roguish propensities, and she could only suppose that what he did last night was something he accomplished quite frequently. With how many ladies, she wondered, a new blush climbing her cheeks at the mere thought of what his reputation alone suggested.

One thing was certain, regardless of how many hearts he had vanquished with his dashing looks and cunning ways, she was too sensible to lose her own over a kiss or two, or three or four or however many he had actually taken from her between Queen Square and the Circus. Goodness! He had kissed her over and over on each occasion. How had that happened and she so lacking in experience? Really, her very short acquaintance with Gaventry, scarcely six days old, had dumbfounded her completely.

With her gaze still averted from the entrance to the Pump Room, where it would seem everyone else had fixed their attention, she felt at some liberty to do what she had been doing all morning, to steel herself against Gaventry. Though he had not conversed or danced with her the remainder of the evening at Lady Haslingfield's, she felt it was critical at this juncture to make certain he understood that she was neither going to kiss him again nor was she interested in furthering a flirtation with him. Only how to go about this, she was not at all certain. How does one repulse a rogue?

At least because of this resolution, she could be at ease on one score—she need never concern herself with the possibility that he might discover her secret concerning *A Rogue's Tale*. The very thought of it caused her to breathe a new sigh of relief. If she maintained a somewhat disinterested acquaintance with him, then she would be assured of never having the subject brought forward in such a way that he might come to know the truth.

"He is now but ten feet away and conversing with Miss Catesby," Meg whispered. "Do but look before he comes much closer, Sally! Tell me he is not the absolute image of Adonis!"

At that, Sarah found she could not help herself. She turned slightly and glanced at him over her shoulder. He was smiling at Mrs. Radwell now, Lady Haslingfield's eldest daughter. Sarah's breath caught. In all her careful plans about hinting Gaventry away and establishing a platonic relationship with him, she had forgotten one thing—how the mere looking at him caused her to feel as though she were floating.

"Oh dear," she murmured.

Meg pinched her very lightly on her arm. Sarah glanced at her and saw that her sister was grinning broadly. "You are greatly struck with him!" Meg cried, her voice still a whisper.

"I believe every lady in the room is," Sarah returned, unwilling to admit her sentiments could be more than mere admiration.

Meg surprised her by hooking her elbow and drawing her away from the crowd slightly. "But you are not *every lady*," she said quietly. "Sally, all these years, you have kept your heart so tightly bound, even from two quite eligible *partis* either of whom would have made an excellent husband for you, and yet here you are, besotted with Gaventry."

At that, Sarah recoiled. "I am no such thing," she cried, but her heart was racing and unexpected tears darted to her eyes.

"Yes you are. I noted it from the first and how could you not be when he kissed you so well on Monday. I wonder, is it possible that you are afraid of love?"

Sarah shook her head. "But, Meggie, do but think. You are suggesting that I am losing my heart to a rogue, a man in possession of so dreadful a reputation that I would be the greatest fool in Christendom were I to do so."

At that, a frown creased Meg's brow. "I had not thought of it in that manner. Are you saying then that you do not believe the essentials of *A Rogue's Tale*, even though he has confessed they are true?"

"I wish you would forget about that novel that some lady, or perhaps even a gentleman, wrote perhaps because he or she was bored of a Sunday afternoon. And even though Gaventry admitted some of it was true, not all of it was."

"Enough, however, that our stodgy Bath tabbies have accepted him into their dull circles without the smallest hesitation."

Sarah frowned. "Even if he is accepted into a hundred drawing rooms of merit, does it excuse all of his conduct over seven years' time?"

Meg lifted her chin. "Had he not been so misused by the

lady he loved, I am persuaded he would not have behaved so very badly."

"He has only admitted that there was a lady like Lucinda Hardcastle, nothing more. We still do not know the particulars and I greatly fear that you are affording him far too much grace, of that I am convinced."

"And you are not affording him enough!" With that, Meg moved away.

Sarah was left to stand near the stage, upon which a small group of musicians played a delicate Mozart sonata. To the right of her, there was a great deal of noise near the pumper, where a large family had gathered. The gentleman who appeared to be the grandfather of the brood, and quite gouty, was seated in a Bath chair, his left foot elevated and bandaged as he took the waters. On his lap he held the smallest of the children.

"How do you go on, Miss Sarah Kittling?"

A little startled, Sarah turned to find herself addressed by Lady Haslingfield. "Very well, I thank you," she responded. "I was just regarding that dear old man and noticing how kindly he holds his granddaughter."

"Quite a noisy lot."

"Yes," she said, smiling. "With seven children, all younger than ten, I should think it would be."

"Did you enjoy the fete last night?" she inquired.

Sarah looked into brown eyes that held more than a question. "Prodigiously," she remarked.

A faint grunt was heard in her ladyship's throat. "And did you have much opportunity to become better acquainted with Gaventry?"

"Yes, as it happens I did. We sat for some time in the library, sipping your quite excellent champagne and conversing."

A slow smile overspread the lady's features. "I am glad to hear it since I went to such extremes to make certain you enjoyed a few minutes of privacy."

At that, Sarah opened her eyes very wide. "Did you close the door?" she whispered.

Lady Haslingfield chuckled. "Do not look so surprised. I was young once, though I fear that was a long time ago. I see that Mrs. Catesby is waving to me. Good day, Miss Kittling."

Sarah bowed politely, her head reeling, as the countess moved away. She did not think she had been more shocked in her entire existence. It would seem that Lady Haslingfield meant to encourage what she perceived to be their interest in one another. This knowledge caused her, if but for the barest moment, to doubt her own resolve to hint Gaventry away. Was it possible that Lady Haslingfield, an older woman wiser in the ways of the world than herself, saw something that she did not?

Sarah gave herself a strong mental shake. She wished her ladyship had not quit her side so quickly, for then she could have begged her not to make any particular effort where she and Gaventry were concerned. In fact, she ought to speak to her before she left the Pump Room. Yes, that is what she would do, even now!

"I am not surprised you appear to have been blasted with cannon shot. Lady Haslingfield can be something of a cross-patch. I have known her since I was a boy."

Sarah turned to find Gaventry at her elbow. She started, then held a hand to her bosom. "You have given me a shock, which is not at all useful since her ladyship, this very minute, has just done the very same thing."

"Did she lecture you on the proprieties, perhaps," he queried, smiling, "or did she criticize the cut of your gown?"

"Neither," she responded, though she could hardly tell him the nature of their discussion and quickly gave the subject a turn. "So you have known her since childhood?"

"Yes, she was a very great friend of my mother's."

That would explain in part, then, Sarah thought, the count-ess's interest in Gaventry. A promise, perhaps, made to a dying woman to find him a proper wife? It was all so surprising and so strange.

"I believe she may think of you as her son," Sarah observed.

At that, the viscount uttered a crack of laughter. "I do not think so. Our conversations, even from the time I was in leading strings, were that of a commanding officer speaking to an inferior. There certainly was not the smallest display of affection."

Sarah regarded him thoughtfully for a long moment. "Perhaps not, for that is not her way. Not in the least. But your interests, even your future, that would be a different matter entirely."

"And what leads you to that conclusion?" he inquired.

"How else do you account for your general reception in Bath? Surely, your acceptance here could not be solely the work of that dreadful novel? That would be expecting far too much from even the broadest minded person."

"Which Lady Haslingfield is not."

"I did not say as much," she countered, glancing around quickly to see if anyone had overheard such a careless remark. Lowering her voice, she added, "And would you please take care not to say such wretched things."

Lord Gaventry realized he was caught. He had not meant to approach her this morning, quite the reverse in fact, but he had become curious as to what his godmother was saying to her that would have caused her to blush. Besides, she looked so devilishly pretty in her blue and pink calico walking dress and a straw bonnet trimmed with white silk flowers.

He drew close to her. "I like saying them if for no other reason than to see you blush anew."

She gasped as she stepped away from him. "You are a ridiculous man," she cried. Lowering her voice once more, she added, "And I beg you will not do that again!"

"Do what?" he countered provokingly.

She narrowed her eyes, but at the same time, a smile curled her lips, a very enticing smile. "Move near me in that wholly inappropriate manner, of course. Do you intend to set all the tongues a-wagging this morning?"

Yes, he was caught, indeed! He had not had the smallest intention of singling Miss Sarah out, and yet here he was, ready to continue this most promising flirtation with her once more. He could not believe that with but a brief exchange of words, a few smiles, a gasp or two, she had completely captivated him. Worse yet, he knew she had not done so to a purpose. His rank had given him years of experience in that regard— he knew quite well when a lady had set her cap for him. Miss Sarah Kittling, far from appearing in the smallest degree determined to pursue him, had kept her distance from the moment he entered the Pump Room. Any other lady intent on capturing his fancy would have fairly raced up to him when he appeared in the doorway.

But this would not do, he lamented. He had his own purposes in coming to the Pump Room, which had nothing to do with either taking the waters or flirting with the lady before him. No, his quarry was at present near the statue of Beau Nash, surrounded by several hopefuls, one of whom was Brixham. Aurelia Kittling ought to have been his prime object. Instead, the moment he had caught sight of Miss Sarah across the room, he seemed to have had no other object in mind but to flirt with her . . . again.

So, here he was teasing her and tormenting her, whispering in her ear when he should not, taking steps toward her so that she had to back away if she meant to keep a maidenly distance between them. In other words, he was engaging her in a quite serious and quite provocative flirtation. Worse, still, she seemed to be responding, or so the curling smile on her lips would indicate and the glittering of her lovely brown eyes.

He drew in a long, slow breath as he let his gaze take in every feature. She was lovely, there could be no two opinions on that score. Her complexion held a luminescent quality, enhanced perhaps by the grand volume of light that streamed in through the tall windows of the Pump Room. Her brown eyes, so wide, open, and thoughtful, were quite magnificent. And there was so much humor in her expression that he knew a strong desire to stay beside her the remainder of the day. There was something earthy and quiet about her, even serene in the elegant line of her nose, her pronounced cheekbones, and the soft oval of her face. Add to this the tendency of her words to be bold and almost vixenish, and it was no wonder he remained fixed by her side, gaping at her like a country rustic, instead of tending to the far more critical matter at hand.

Sarah Kittling, he concluded, was something very near to his ideal, and for that reason he found a powerful sensation growing in his heart that was as strong as it was unwelcome. After all, the last time he had felt this way, some seven years past, he had been cast into a dark scandal that had changed his life in a myriad of hapless ways.

Remembering the beautiful Miss Arabella Fulbourne caused much of his present excitement to abate. Yes, he had felt this way once before, and the lady had been as dark in beauty as Miss Sarah, and a degree more beautiful. He had given his heart to her completely, but how could he have known that she was not to be trusted? Indeed, what was there now, in the lady before him, that gave him cause to believe she was worthy of trust? If anything, because of her sister, he should be inclined to distrust Miss Sarah all the more.

"You cannot possibly be offended!" she cried suddenly, disrupting his reverie.

He gave himself a shake and realized that something of his feelings regarding the heinous Miss Fulbourne had clearly betrayed his expression. "I beg your pardon, Miss Sarah, of course I am not offended."

"Then why did you suddenly appear as mad as hops?"

"It is a long story," he said, honestly. But the spell had been broken. He made his bow. "If you will excuse me, I promised Brixham we would not stay long this morning."

"As you wish."

Sarah watched him go, thinking he was the most quixotic gentleman she had ever known. In one moment he was flirting outrageously with her, and in the next, he, well, she was certain had she been a fly, he would have taken a swat at her.

Meg ran up to her. "Why did Gaventry take a pet?" she cried.

Sarah shook her head. "I have not the faintest notion but come, let us not concern ourselves with him. Aurelia means to go with Miss Catesby to Sydney Gardens but I was hoping you might accompany me to Sally Lunn's."

"Indeed, I will. Should we inquire if the gentlemen wish to join us? I daresay Gaventry would not be so peevish were he to have a toasted bun, a little Devonshire cream, strawberry jam, and a nice cup of tea. I shall be happy to extend the invitation if you wish for it."

Sarah shook her head. "I do not understand in the least why you would even suggest such a thing."

"Because you are in love with him, goose! Even a sapskull could see as much merely by the way you looked at him just now."

Sarah rolled her eyes but refused to rise to the fly. "What a baggage you are become!" she cried. She then hooked Meg's arm and drew her away from the crowd and toward the door. A moment more and they were marching on the flags in the direction of Sally Lunn's restaurant.

At noon, when the ladies had all returned from their various activities to Queen Square, Aurelia informed them that a drive through the countryside had been planned. Mr. Brixham would be tooling his gig and Lord Gaventry his curricle and pair. When Sarah learned that it was Gaventry who had suggested the notion, she immediately refused, saying she had rather remain at home reading her newly acquired book of poetry.

"But Charlotte already accepted for us," Aurrie said, "and besides we are all invited. Lord Gaventry was most particular on this point. He wanted, I am certain, to observe the social niceties."

Sarah placed a marker in her book and frowned at Meg and

Charlotte, who were presently exchanging glances. "What is it?" she asked.

Charlotte, who returned her gaze to her tambour frame, in which a bouquet of pink roses was coming to life with each intricate stitch, said, "It is simple, really. The gentlemen intend to drive out in a Stanhope gig and a curricle. You know my fear of horses and I have little interest in being squeezed into a seat meant only for two." Here she smiled. "The invitation may have been extended to myself and to Meg, but I believe the spirit of the outing was meant only for you and Aurrie."

"But this is nonsense," Sarah said, turning her attention to Meg, "as you very well know. I am perfectly content to read and, like Charlotte, I do not care to be squeezed into a curricle or gig meant only for two."

Meg wore the most aggravating smile on her pretty bow lips. "I daresay 'tis not I with whom Gaventry wishes to drive out."

"That much is true, Sally," Aurelia offered quickly, "for he most pointedly said that I was to sit beside him all the way to the top of the hill."

At that, both Charlotte and Meg exchanged another glance, which began to annoy Sarah quite fiercely. "What intrigue are the pair of you concocting? This will not do, not by half!"

Meg rolled her eyes. "There is no intrigue. Merely, that I am disinclined to drive out as well."

"Indeed, there is not," Charlotte stated. She did, however, cast an expressive glance in Aurrie's direction. Aurelia in turn was staring at her sleeve and plucking at the small row of ruffles at the wrist.

Sarah understood. Charlotte wished for a little private speech. "Will you excuse me for a moment, Aurrie? I believe I must speak with Cook."

She rose as she spoke and had not taken three steps when Aurelia said, "Yes, you should see if she can prepare cold meats, bread, and perhaps some fruit for the picnic."

"Picnic!" All three ladies cried at once.

"Well, yes, did I not say as much? We are to picnic at the top of Lansdown Hill. I told the gentlemen we would pack a very nice basket. Mr. Brixham, which I thought was excessively kind in him, said that he would bring a bottle of wine although I do hope he means to include glasses, but if he does not, perhaps we should." She looked hopefully at Sarah, who was now standing in the very middle of the room.

"Now it is a picnic?" she queried.

"Yes, I have said so. Was I not clear when I spoke of cold meats and bread?"

"Yes, of course. Perfectly," Sarah responded. "But I must have a word with Cook." She quit the drawing room and made her way to the servants' stairs, where she waited for Charlotte to join her. Scarcely a minute had passed when Charlotte arrived.

"I am sorry, Sally," Charlotte said. "And I do beg your pardon but Meg has been telling me all that has been going forward where you and Gaventry are concerned."

"What has she told you?"

"Only that you seem to be smitten with him. Is this true?"

Sarah could have easily contrived a simple, acceptable answer to such a question that would have satisfied Aurelia, but Charlotte was a different matter entirely. She was a woman of experience and had been married, quite happily, many years before. Just how she was to explain her sentiments to Charlotte, therefore, became a matter of some delicacy. "Meg has chosen to interpret my admiration for him as something more."

"But you do admire him?"

"Yes, of course. What lady of our acquaintance does not?"

Charlotte nodded, a faint frown between her brows. "But he kissed you. I have wondered if his having done so has somehow turned your head."

"Quite the opposite, I assure you, for his actions merely served to remind me that there is a clear basis for all the gossip about him, even if he is perhaps not guilty of the whole of it."

Charlotte nodded again, but still the frown remained. "It would not be unusual for you to form such an attachment, even if you were being careful of his reputation."

"Are you giving me a hint?"

At last her visage relaxed, and she smiled. "You, of all ladies, my dear cousin, have always known how to manage your affairs. I would only say to you that sometimes love arrives when we least expect it. No, no, it is not necessary to argue the point further. I understand quite thoroughly how Meg's fancies tend to overrun themselves and I do not intend to coax you one way or the other." With that, she turned on her heel and began walking on her brisk step in the direction of the drawing room.

Sarah blinked rapidly several times as she began to descend the stairs in order to speak with Cook. Had Charlotte actually *encouraged* her to open her heart to Lord Gaventry? It was one thing for Meg to do so, for she was already convinced that she had tumbled in love with him and in her belief would refuse stubbornly to either join the outing or to take up her place instead. However, Charlotte's words had completely overset her peace. What had she meant that *sometimes love arrives when we least expect it*?

She dared not ponder such a notion. She already knew she was painfully susceptible to Gaventry—the second kiss in Lady Haslingfield's library had convinced her of that! Nor did Charlotte know that there had been a second violation. Perhaps had she known as much she would not have suggested that she open her heart. No, she was convinced that had Charlotte known of the second kiss, coupled with the terrible fact that she was the authoress of *A Rogue's Tale*, she would not have given her even the smallest of encouragements.

There was nothing for it, however, but to attend Aurrie on the drive. Charlotte had spoken truly when she had said she was afraid of horses, and for that reason alone she would not impose on her cousin. Meg, of course, would dig her heels in and refuse to take part in the outing no matter what her arguments, so there was nothing to do now but to have Cook make up a basket for the picnic. At least she could be easy on one score; she would be driving with Mr. Brixham.

Gaventry slapped the reins, calling to his team to make the somewhat steep climb up Lansdown Hill. The lady beside him, Miss Aurelia Kittling, the authoress of *A Rogue's Tale*, had been oblivious to his flirtations thus far, or at least, he believed she was. In truth, he could not be certain. Since he knew her to be the authoress, he understood she was in some possession of intelligence, a very fine intelligence as her writing suggested. Having met her, however, and conversed with her, he simply could not make her out, since more often than not she at times appeared almost dull-witted. Miss Sarah had even confirmed this opinion while at the same time speaking highly of her other more intuitive qualities. He could only think, therefore, that her defects, particularly in social interactions, were a result of having developed the use of her pen to the exclusion of her tongue. He knew quite well that before his advent into Bath, her social invitations had been rather limited. He thought it quite possible that, given time, her ability to converse in general, and to comprehend things spoken to her in particular, would undoubtedly improve.

" 'Tis a very fine day," he observed.

"Oh, yes," she responded happily. "We have been enjoying a lovely May. I have not seen so many days of sunshine together in several months which was why, when you asked me if my family would enjoy such an outing, I responded most enthusiastically."

There, her answer was quite sensible. She merely needed more practice.

With his horses trotting along at a steady pace, he leaned

close to her. "Your bonnet is quite pretty but I hope to soon have it off you."

Her expression was completely mystified. "Whyever would you want to do that?" she asked, her blue eyes all innocence.

Oh dear. Had she truly not comprehended this hint? Had she no sense of subtlety? Whatever the case, he pressed his intentions. "Because I am hoping, Miss Kittling, to steal a kiss from you this afternoon."

Her eyes grew wide and considering. He glanced at the road, made a slight adjustment to the reins, and glanced back at her. She was smiling. "And you cannot do that while I am wearing my bonnet?"

He chuckled. "Of course I could, but hats in general tend to inhibit full expression."

She blinked several times as though attempting to comprehend the meaning of his words. At last, she said, "Oh, but I must say I do not agree with you at all. I think hats and bonnets express many things, a sense of style and color, even one's innermost thoughts and ideas."

He glanced at her apace. "I believe you may have mistaken me."

"Oh, I do not think so," she responded gently, a soft hand placed on his sleeve. "If you will remember, you said you thought bonnets inhibited expression and I disagreed with you. I suppose you are not used to being disagreed with which leads me to say that I do not think you should be speaking of kissing me when you have already kissed Sally."

His mind was snagged on the need to correct her misapprehension about what he had meant by *full expression*, but the path of their conversation had become far too muddied for that. Instead, he addressed the latter part of her speech. "So you know of our kiss, then?"

He could not help but wonder what she thought of it and whether her words were cloaking a desire for him to kiss her as well. He had flirted with so many ladies in a like manner and knew that often they said the very opposite of what they truly wanted. How many times, for instance, had he held a lady in his arms, she protesting loudly, but all the while holding him fiercely. On the other hand, Miss Kittling was not quite in the style of most of the ladies he had engaged in a flirtation.

Miss Kittling responded, "Yes, but I did not see it. Only Meg saw you kissing our sister and I must say, Lord Gaventry, that I think it very odd in you."

At that, he laughed. "Why? Surely you know of my reputation? Surely you have read *A Rogue's Tale*."

He watched her closely, for one telltale flinching or blinking of her eyelids, but there was nothing, only a prosaic nodding of her bonneted head. "Of course. All the ladies of my acquaintance have read that particular novel."

He could not believe her sangfroid. "And what did you think of the story?"

Keeping his horses moving up the winding hill, checking them now and then with a tug or slap of the reins, he waited for her response. Again he watched her carefully for even the smallest acknowledgment of her perfidy. Still, she did not blink or in any manner betray herself. He could only suppose that she was as fine an actress as she was a writer of novels.

She did, however, shrug slightly. "I thought it interesting in its way, but a little silly."

"In what way silly?" he inquired. How unusual for an authoress to regard her work as *silly*, or was this perhaps a very complicated ruse she was concocting, telling a string of whiskers and pretending to be simple when in truth she was leading him a merry little dance.

She answered his question. "Well for one thing, I do not understand in the least why Daventry would attach himself to such a worthless female. He must have been addled to have done so. Since the entire story is based on his *tendre* for Lucinda Hardcastle, I thought it silly."

Gaventry clenched his jaw. When he thought of how much

he had believed himself in love with Arabella Fulbourne, and how that love had sunk him so low in both spirit and social acceptability, he found he had to agree with Miss Kittling's assessment—a story, a life, based on the conduct of a worthless female, was silly, indeed. He realized that never had a truer word been spoken, but did the lady beside him understand just how true? "Do you think as much of me, then? That I was perhaps addled?"

She smiled, pretty dimples brightening her face. "Having become acquainted with you I may safely answer that you are not in the least addled."

"But I did allow a young lady to ruin my life."

"You said as much the other day, but I am not persuaded that it is entirely the truth."

"Indeed?" he queried. He felt aggravated, proving her earlier axiom that he did not like to be challenged. In this case, since Arabella Fulbourne had quite tidily ruined his London career, the lady next to him was grossly mistaken. However, he needed to understand precisely what she meant. "What do you believe the truth to be?"

"Only that you are like Sarah in that you wish for things that most people do not, something of magic and adventure, even for true love. You have said the lady ruined your life, but I think you wished it so."

He was shocked and did not know precisely how to respond to this observation. First, however, he wondered if she had spoken something of the truth to him. Then, as he glanced behind the curricle and saw Miss Sarah laughing at something Brixham was saying to her, he could not help but wonder if what was said of her was true as well. However, he could not help but address the question most pertinent to his present cause with her. "You cannot convince me that you do not wish for love."

She wrinkled her nose. "In all honesty, my lord, I cannot say that I do. What I desire most, should I ever have the good fortune to marry, is to be able to converse easily with my husband and to enjoy his company. I do not believe that I care for the notion at all of tumbling in love as some ladies do. Why, do you know that Miss Catesby has been violently in love no less than four times and each time she grows so wretchedly ill that she swoons and has spasms and has even been known to cast up her accounts? I promise you, there is nothing about her sufferings that has ever led me to desire to be in love."

"Yet, *Sally* does?"

"Oh, yes. Not perhaps in the way of Miss Catesby, but she once said that she would not marry a man unless she knew that her husband would be more important to her than the sun rising or setting. Those were her words."

Again, he glanced back at Miss Sarah, who was talking in an animated fashion with Brixham. He frowned slightly. "Was there never a gentleman to tempt her?"

"Oh, there were two very serious suitors, each with excellent prospects so that she would never again have to worry about housekeeping matters. But she refused them both."

Gaventry wondered what she meant about "housekeeping matters," but since this would have meant another digression, he queried, "And you, Miss Kittling? How many offers of marriage have you refused? A score, a hundred?"

She trilled her laughter, a beautiful sound that reverberated like a bird's song about the hills. He ought to have been even a little enamored of her, yet strangely he was not. "Oh, no," she cried. "Not so many as that. Only nine."

"Nine!" he exclaimed. "You must also be as fastidious as your sister."

For some reason, her spirits sank; he could see it in the suddenly crestfallen set of her shoulders.

"Now you must tell me what I have said to have made you suddenly blue-deviled."

"You will not credit it, my lord, but generally I do not converse so easily with most gentlemen. And . . . and I knew that the offers I received, which were each quite hasty in nature, would not have had happy outcomes."

He found himself touched by this confession, something, given his purposes, he should not have been. He strove to remind himself that the lady beside him had used him terribly ill, and that he should be satisfied by her unhappiness. Instead, he queried softly, "Was your heart never engaged?"

"Oh, no," she responded, brightening swiftly. "For I did not feel even the smallest spasm with any of my suitors."

At that, he could not help but chuckle. "Then all's well that ends well."

"Yes," she responded, tucking her arm about his. "Yes, I had never thought of it in that way before."

He glanced down at the small gloved hand wrapped about his arm and thought he should have felt a great deal more gratified by this gesture than he did. In any other lady, he would have known his success was not far distant, but with the complicated creature beside him he was not at all certain.

"Do you know, Lord Gaventry, you are like a brother to me, a brother I never had. I cannot tell you how happy you have made me today."

He groaned inwardly. She could have said nothing more dampening to him. However, he was not beaten yet. Guiding his horses round a bend, he leaned close to her once more. "Though I appreciate very much your having said so, I must confess, Miss Kittling, I do not in the least think of you as a sister."

Though he lifted a brow and hoped she would once again take up his hint, her expression fell. "Oh," she murmured sorrowfully. "Have I offended you then, in having said so? Would you not want me for a sister, even if we were just pretending?"

He laughed again in complete despair. Whatever gifts the lady possessed, they did not encompass subtlety. "You mistake me completely. I was not in the least offended and when I said that I confessed I did not think of you as a sister it was because I hoped to think of you as something else."

"A cousin?" she asked hopefully.

He laughed again. "A cousin will do," he responded, unwilling to try to explain himself yet again.

"Well, I suppose 'cousins' will do. Yes, we shall pretend we are cousins and if it would not be too tiresome, I should like very much to converse more with you. I believe it may be beneficial to me."

With this, he felt he had to be satisfied, and if nothing else he now had a tool by which he could command more of her attention. He would not hesitate in future to remind her of how "beneficial" it would be for her to take very long walks with him, for instance, and in that way he would work to win her heart.

Since she commented on the numerous buttercups lining the road, he ended his present and somewhat laborious attempts at flirtation and drew up his horses that she might collect an armful. He may not have been entirely successful in his conversation with her, but the joy she exhibited in holding the flowers in her arms served to give him hope that with a little patience he would find the key to her heart.

# Six

"Did you enjoy the drive with my sister?" Sarah asked, glancing up at Gaventry.

They walked along a wooded path, following in the wake of Brixham and Aurelia. Earlier, Aurrie had expressed a wish that she might see some lambs today, upon which Mr. Brixham promptly informed her that he had already noted several ewes and their progeny in a field a mere quarter of a mile distant. This pronouncement set Aurelia immediately in the direction of the appropriate pasture.

"Very much so," Gaventry responded. "She has what seems to be a very kind, even loving, disposition."

Sarah regarded his profile as she strolled beside him. He was frowning. Why, she wondered.

The drive from Queen Square to the top of Lansdown Hill had been pleasant, indeed, in Mr. Brixham's company, and the May afternoon a complete delight. Throughout the entire journey to the summit, however, Sarah had found herself curious as to just how well Lord Gaventry and dear, but slightly dimwitted, Aurrie had succeeded in sustaining a conversation. That they had engaged in considerable discourse nearly the entire journey up the hill had been much in evidence, in particular by how many times she heard Gaventry's laughter drift backward to Brixham's gig.

After Aurrie had gathered her buttercups and the carriages had at last reached their destination, Sarah had been able to determine, as much by Aurrie's relaxed expression as by her numerous smiles, that she had been properly entertained. With the prospect of sheep not too far distant, however, her sister had quickly taken up Mr. Brixham's arm and hurried in the direction of the faint bleatings of the nearby flock.

Now, as she watched Gaventry closely, she thought she detected something of a troubled expression in his eye. She felt certain she understood the cause of his disquiet. "The answer to your question is that Aurelia does lack something of understanding, she has from the time she was very young."

Turning to face her, he stopped her quite unexpectedly in her tracks, his brow pinched tightly together. "But how is that possible?" he asked, as one who had been attempting to solve a serious riddle.

Sarah was completely taken aback as much by his question as by his strident demeanor. "I do not take your meaning," she responded, moving away from him slightly.

She watched him weigh carefully the question he was clearly framing in his mind. He gestured once or twice with his hands, opening and closing them, then he rolled his eyes and shook his head as though completely bemused. "Your sister is a woman of accomplishment, is she not?" His blue eyes had taken on a rather piercing expression.

"Yes, she is. No one plays the pianoforte with greater brilliance than Aurrie and she is a very pretty dancer. I believe she surpasses all our friends in that particular art."

He again drew closer. "But what of pen and paper?" he asked, almost as though challenging her.

Sarah again took a small step away, even turning her shoulder to him. She wondered what he meant by such a question. Was he asking about *A Rogue's Tale*? However, that made no sense, since Aurrie was not the authoress. She answered his question. "Her correspondence is always quite legible, I assure you, if simple in composition."

"I see," he murmured, but there was something of a dark look in his eye.

"Lord Gaventry, I believe you are speaking in circles. Will

you not be frank with me? You seem to be suffering some frustration where Aurelia is concerned and beyond saying as politely as I can that she is lacking in understanding, I do not know what it is you wish for me to say."

His gaze remained fixed on her for a long time, his countenance still rather defiant, but to what purpose? When she said nothing, he finally relaxed. "I suppose I find her in possession of such extreme qualities that I cannot reconcile the whole."

"Why is it so necessary to do so?" she countered, beginning once more to walk along the shaded path. "My sister is a darling but she does not converse with ease. On the other hand, she plays and dances brilliantly and has an uncanny ability to assess one's basic character. Anything more, and you will look very hard before discovering either a flaw or a virtue. You may trust me in this."

"I suppose I shall have to."

She glanced at him apace, noting yet again a measure of bitterness in his tone. She smiled suddenly. "Did your flirtation not go as happily as you had planned? Is that why you are out of reason cross?"

At that, he caught her eye and smiled. "Am I so obvious, and in so many respects?"

"If you mean, are you easy to comprehend, yes. And if you are also referring to your intentions where Aurelia or any other beautiful young lady might be concerned, I will only remind you that you are an avowed rogue. Your conduct is implied."

At that, he laughed, and quite heartily.

Sarah found herself breathing an inward sigh of relief. She had felt instinctively that he had drawn near to the subject of writing and novels when he had mentioned "pen and paper" but she did not understand why. Was it possible he had somehow guessed at the truth and was now probing for a confession in speaking of Aurelia rather than herself?

She began to wonder anew just why he had come to Bath so unexpectedly, when he had never once shown an interest in their quiet "watering hole" before. Nor why he had so quickly connected himself to the Kittling interests . . . *unless* Mr. Bertram, her publisher, had been badgered into revealing secrets.

"You have grown very quiet," he observed.

Sarah glanced up at him, assessing him yet again. She decided to ask a few questions of her own. "Why have you come to Bath?"

"Not quiet anymore, I see."

She smiled, but her heart had begun beating anxiously in her breast. What if he did know something of the Kittling connection to *A Rogue's Tale*? Good heavens! What would she do then?

She pressed him. "Do you not wish to tell me? And pray do not offer even the smallest whisker about desiring to take the waters, for I shall not believe you, not one whit."

"Then I certainly shan't," he responded. Although he smiled, she could see he had grown wary. "Why have I come to Bath? For the pleasure of meeting someone like you, of course."

Again he smiled in a manner that she was certain had previously devastated more than one female heart. "After flirting with my sister," she cried, "you will now flirt with me?"

"No, no! Not flirting with either of you. Merely *trying* to flirt and thus far having no success at all."

She laughed. "You must be a little serious with me. I must have an answer. Why have you come to Bath when you have shown no interest in our fair city these many years and more?"

"Why must you have an answer?"

"That is not allowed."

"I beg your pardon?"

"It is not allowed to either answer a question with a question or to divert the subject by introducing another one. You have broken both of these rules just now."

"We are at rules?"

"Of course. Every conversation has its rules, spoken or not.

Although usually they are defined by propriety and civility. In this case, I am being completely self-indulgent; the rules are designed strictly for my pleasure."

"Then of course, as a gentleman, I would not for the world inhibit your pleasure."

"What gammon!" she cried. "You would do so in a heartbeat, did it serve your interests, and well you know it."

He gasped, perhaps a little theatrically, but still she could see she had shocked him.

"You have ascribed to me a terrible flaw," he said. "I do not like it in the least."

She laughed, slapping at soft, budding branchlets as she passed by the shrubbery. "But I have spoken the truth or will you now tell me that you are always considering the feelings, concerns, and sensibilities of others when in company?"

He sighed. "Perhaps I should, but I believe you have the right of it—I confess I am a very selfish creature."

"Which leads me back to the beginning of this circle—why have you come to Bath? What brought you here?"

He paused at least five steps worth of cogitation. "Fate," he responded at last, but he was grinning.

*Fate.*

Even though she knew he was teasing, a spate of gooseflesh traveled in lightning speed down her neck and back. She felt woodland spirits tugging on the hem of her walking dress and the whispers of the gods all around her. A strange excitement set her pulse to racing madly. Had fate brought Gaventry here? Was that what was prompting the rapid beatings of her heart and sending her thoughts fleeing in a hundred directions at once? She did not know.

There was a time when she had believed in fate, in magical things, in mystery, but that was a long time ago, when she was very young. Her present thoughts led her to recollections of her family's joyous country life in Hampshire, when both her parents had been living and the comings and goings of the Kittling household had been directed by her dear father. He had been a whimsical man, well-read, perhaps even a genius in his way. Sometimes Aurelia put her in mind of him. He kept his three daughters entertained and challenged. He oversaw their instruction generally and encouraged each of them to pursue interests suited to each. He hired a prominent music teacher for Aurrie and a riding instructor for Meg. For herself, he had supervised her reading, introducing her to the poets and playwrights and later to the novelists. She had written several plays for her family when not much older than thirteen or fourteen, and nothing was so pleasant during the long winter months than to prepare a play with her sisters, including scenery and costumes, which in turn would be presented to her parents and the servants at appointed times— usually when the snow had settled deep into the vales and a corresponding boredom into every bone.

"I realize I have not been often in your company, Miss Sarah, but I have never seen you either so quiet or with such a glow in your eyes before. Though I should wish it was because of my presence, I daresay I am utterly mistaken."

"Not entirely," she mused, glancing up at him. "What you said just now, setting your arrival here in Bath to the happenstance of fate, for some reason made me think of making plays for my family during the winter months in Hampshire."

"You are a playwright then?"

She laughed. "I was used to be, but that was a very long time ago."

"And when not in Bath, you reside in Hampshire?"

"No, not for eight years or more. My parents were living, then. We have been residents of Bath for what seems to be an eternity." He was not looking at her, but into the distance. Not far, the woodland could be seen to break and an expanse of blue sky dotted with clouds beckoned the traveler forward. Without giving it much thought, she said, "You would have liked my father, I think."

At that, his expression was full of surprise when he glanced at her. "Indeed?" he queried.

She laughed again, clasping her hands behind her as she strolled. She did not know why precisely she had said as much. The answer, however, came quickly, "Yes, because his thoughts were so unique, so independent of the prevailing modes. He despised London for one thing and thought the presentation at court should have disappeared centuries ago or at least with panniers. He never referred to the London Season except by calling it the Marriage Mart."

"The whole process of choosing a mate is quite barbaric," he stated, "even though it is cloaked in silks and diamonds."

"Then you were not unhappy to have been excluded?"

A faint smile appeared on his lips. "How could I have been unhappy when my separation from society allowed me to do as I pleased?"

She considered this, the woodland growing thin and the sky larger. "I must say, I am relieved to hear you say so. I was used to pity you. I shall not do so anymore."

"Pity," he cried. "Good God, I hope you are not serious. The day a man with a handle to his name and the command of a fortune should be the object of pity, is the day the world is turned upside down."

She touched his sleeve suddenly and caught his gaze. "You know very well there is a great deal more to happiness than such things."

"Ah, but *such things* can purchase a great deal of comfort and ease of mind."

"Very true. I will not deny you that. However"—and here she smiled—"you cannot kiss your pot of gold at night and feel warmth against your lips."

"It would seem I am in the presence of a philosopher."

She giggled. "Oh, indeed, yes!" she returned playfully. "A very great one!"

When at last the woody stretch gave way to pasture, Sarah saw in the distance her sister leaning over a drystone wall and petting a lamb. A wind blew across the grassy hill, setting the green slope into ripples of waves. The countryside was beautiful and particularly so in this moment beneath a lovely sunshine.

"If we walk to the rise," she said, "we will be able to see both Bath and Bristol at the same time or would you prefer to see the lambs as well?"

"Not by half. Bath and Bristol it is."

Within a few minutes, they had left Brixham and Aurrie behind as they made their ascent. Once arrived, Gaventry swept an arm. "Extraordinary view! I believe in this moment my entire sojourn in Bath has been redeemed. And that must be a great portion of the Bristol Channel and beyond, Wales."

"Yes, indeed, it is, but I must tell you that you have quite betrayed yourself."

He glanced at her sharply. "In what way?"

"Answer me this; why must your visit in Bath be *redeemed*?"

He laughed and chucked her chin. "I do not have to answer you in the least for you have just broken one of your own rules, answering a question with a question!"

"So I did!" she cried, grimacing.

The wind buffeted her bonnet, and she felt the need to secure it more fully beneath her chin. She untied the ribbons but chose a most unpropitious moment to do so for a particularly strong gust slid over the hill, plucked the bonnet off her head, and carried it away some distance. She gave a shriek and immediately followed after. She heard Gaventry laugh, but was soon outdistanced by him as he raced in pursuit of the whirling, tumbling hat.

"Oh, my bonnet!" she cried. She had but two in her wardrobe and after today's misadventure, one of them would be in serious need of repair. She was soon out of breath, but followed as well as she could in Gaventry's path. She watched him several times snatch at the errant hat, but the wind taunted him again and again.

Finally, the bonnet found a safe resting place against a stone wall, and as quickly as it had begun, the ridiculous adventure was over. He was dusting off the sad-looking hat, with lace hanging in places it should not, when she arrived. She would have taken it from him, but he kept it away from her. "What made you take it off in the first place?" he cried, but he was grinning.

"I meant to tie it more firmly about my chin. It was the most absurd thing!"

"Indeed, it was."

"You may give it to me now."

"First, you must thank me."

"Why? You did not fetch the bonnet, the wall stopped it." She did not know where such teasing, challenging words were coming from.

There was such a look in his blue eyes. "I suppose not," he responded. His gaze drifted to her lips. "However, if you want your bonnet back, I believe I shall require that you pay dearly for it."

"That sad, old thing!" she exclaimed. "I am not interested in the least." She crossed her arms over her chest.

"Then I shall toss it into the air and see how far the wind takes it this time." He threw up his arm, but she cried out and reached for it. "No, no! I was only teasing!" His arm being longer, however, prevented her from retrieving her hat while at the same time he caught her suddenly about the waist.

"A forfeit," he whispered against her ear. "Just one and you shall have your bonnet."

She ceased reaching for it and turned in his arm toward him but placed her hands quickly over his lips. "No," she whispered, giving her head a shake. "I cannot. I have made a very firm promise to myself."

"Promises are always meant to be broken," he returned, a devilish expression having taken hold of every feature.

"What a wretched thing to say."

He lowered his arm and now held her in the circle of both, the bonnet behind her. A smile played on his lips. "Perhaps, but very, very true."

He leaned toward her, but again she pressed her gloved fingers to his lips. "No, Gaventry. I forbid it."

"Now you are forbidding me? You should never say such things to a rogue, you know. They tend to incite rather than to calm."

"Were you always such a hopeless creature?" she asked.

"I believe I must have been for all my pretenses that a lady was at fault for my troubles. At least, that is what your sister would have me believe."

Sarah thought this might be a more hopeful direction for their present discourse, since the introduction of another subject, other than his wish to kiss her of the moment, would help to allay whatever passions he was presently experiencing. She therefore encouraged him. "What else did you discuss with my sister?" At the same time, she reached behind her, took his arms in hand, and attempted to dislodge them from about her waist, but he merely continued to smile in his maddening fashion, all the while holding her fast.

"I shan't let you go, at least not yet. And certainly shall tell you nothing more of what your sister and I discussed."

She looked into his eyes and saw something returned to her that frightened her more than anything she had before experienced with him. She thought she believed that he *understood* her. Though she had known him such a brief time, this above all else was true, but did he know how much? When his expression stilled, then softened, she thought it was possible he did.

"Please Gaventry," she begged quietly.

He released a resigned sigh. "Oh, very well," he grumbled.

She gave another gentle tug on his arms and they fell away. He lifted the bonnet to her head and gently settled it over her curls. He tied the ribbons firmly beneath her chin and worked to tuck at least two stray pieces of white lace back into place, then once again chucked her chin. "Shall we search for your sister and my friend?"

Impulsively, she gave him a hug, squeezing his arms tightly before releasing him. "Thank you," she murmured warmly.

When she stood back, he regarded her thoughtfully for a long moment. "You are a very odd female," he said at last.

"Yes, I suppose I am but I beg you will not let that keep you from allowing me to be your friend."

"My friend," he murmured. A smile once more touched his lips. "Well, I suppose friendship will have to do since that appears to be all you are offering today."

"Indeed, it is," she responded, but not without a smile.

"I must say, this is the most lowering experience I have ever had. Two ladies and one wishes to be as a cousin to me and the other a friend. My powers must be fading quickly."

"Did Aurelia say as much?"

"First she asked if I might be as a brother to her and when I responded I wished to be something else entirely, she became utterly downcast. She then asked if we might be at least cousins."

Sarah giggled. "Oh dear! Lowering in the extreme, for I suspect she did not comprehend your hints at all."

"Not in the least."

"Poor Gaventry," she offered.

"That is better," he said, extending his arm to her. "If you begin to pity me, perhaps you will relent and allow me a kiss after all."

She responded with another giggle but took the proffered limb and encircled it with her own. Walking beside him, she pretended to gaze at the verdant hills, made round by the persistent winds and lovely by the frequent rains, but her mind and heart were engaged elsewhere. For one thing, she found herself so deeply content as she moved beside him that she wished suddenly she might do so forever. She had taken the arms of many gentlemen in the past, but in this moment, knowing that in a very essential way Gaventry understood her, she felt happier than she had ever felt before.

* * *

Later, Gaventry leaned against the mantel, watching his friend preparing to take a pinch of snuff. Brixham opened his enameled snuffbox and carefully took the powdery substance between forefinger and thumb, lifting his preferred concoction to his nose. Inhaling sharply, he blinked rapidly several times and smiled. "What a ridiculous habit, eh?"

"Indeed," Gaventry replied. "One of many we have fallen into, I fear."

"At least it is not opium." He then laughed suddenly. "Remember that horrid stuff even Coleridge was said to have used? What was it called? Boom or something?"

Gaventry chuckled. "*Bang.* I believe it was called bang."

"Ah, yes. *Bang.* Smelled like the devil." Brixham took another pinch and frowned slightly. "You've been very quiet this evening. Not at all like yourself."

Gaventry knew this much was true. How could it not be when his mind had become fixed on two quite disparate circumstances. The first was that he could not seem to forget the moment when Miss Sarah, having begged him not to kiss her, had thrown herself against his chest and embraced him fully. The gesture had become fixed in his mind, but for what reason, he could not quite comprehend, except that the warm embrace had perhaps been the sweetest expression of gratitude and, he believed, affection, that he had ever before experienced. The feel of her pressed to his chest had lingered so that with but the smallest effort he could recall the entire experience to mind. This, however, he was unwilling to discuss with Brixham.

The second matter was much less personal so that he finally responded to Brixham's observations. "I suppose I have. I have been given much to ponder, as it happens. Do you know, Miss Kittling said something very odd to me while we were driving up Lansdown Hill."

"What did she say?"

"That I was very much like her sister, Miss Sarah, and that

not only were she and I alike, but that we wished for things that most people do not."

"Odd, indeed, and most surprising. Did she suggest what it was the pair of you wished for?"

"I believe her words were for magic and adventure; she may have even said for true love. Then she suggested that I had wanted Miss Fulbourne to ruin my life."

"Miss Kittling said all this?"

"Very nearly."

"Do you think she has described you accurately?"

He shook his head slowly. "I have not the faintest notion. I have never before considered it. I have always thought of what happened seven years ago in very simple terms. I loved Miss Fulbourne, she betrayed me in a manner that put a terrible blight unfairly upon my name, and I have lived with the consequences since."

"But have you enjoyed your exile? That may be the most pertinent question."

He stepped away from the mantel and took up a chair next to his friend. "The devil if I know. Perhaps in some ways I have."

"You would not have traveled so much if you had been married to Miss Fulbourne."

"No, that I would not and I have enjoyed my travels. I suppose it is possible Miss Kittling has hit upon an aspect of my character, my life, of which I have not been at all aware, which leads me to a puzzle I have been attempting to solve this entire evening, but with little success."

"Should be happy to have a go, if you wish for it."

Gaventry regarded his friend thoughtfully for a long moment. Brixham was very dear to him and had been these many years and more. However, delicacy of perception was not precisely his strong suit.

Brixham continued. "I see your thoughts and you are very right. I do not have your abilities. I daresay few men do. But sometimes a different view of things can help."

"Very well. I am thinking of our authoress."

"Of Miss Kittling still?"

"Yes."

"Ah. Miss Kittling. Our beautiful shepherdess."

"Miss Sarah tells me she is brilliant on the pianoforte."

Brixham nodded his head, but his eyes narrowed in some perplexion. "Where is the mystery in that?"

"Does she not strike you as a trifle, well, dull?"

Brixham closed his snuffbox with a snap, glanced at the lid, and laughed suddenly. "Forgot there was a lamb painted on my box." He chuckled a little more, then returned it to his pocket. He then fell into a study, from which Gaventry hesitated to draw him. Finally, Brixham said, "So you think Miss Kittling dull, perhaps even boring?"

"Not boring or dull. Dull-witted."

"A little like me."

"No. There can be no comparison."

"That much is true for I cannot play a single note on the pianoforte."

This comment caused Gaventry to regard his friend carefully. Miss Kittling had done very nearly the same thing on their ride to Lansdown, when she had mistaken him. Perhaps Brix was more like Miss Kittling than he had previously thought. However, watching him, he suddenly recognized the teasing light in his eye. "The devil take you!" he cried.

Brixham chuckled, then pursued the subject. "So you are trying to make out Miss Kittling, how she could be brilliant in some areas but not in others, such as in conversation."

"Precisely."

"Well, that is quite easy to explain. There are only a few who excel in everything. I know but a handful of men or women. You are such a one and it would not surprise me if Miss Sarah were another. However, the rest of us, well, we muddle through as best we can."

Gaventry was a little astonished and did not know in the least how to respond to these observations. He disagreed strenuously with the assessment of his own abilities, for there were numerous ways in which he knew he fell well short of the mark. However, since he wished to enlarge the discussion about Miss Kittling, he did not pursue this aspect of the subject. "Though I would argue your point, I really wish instead that you might explain to me how it is that Miss Kittling can have the appearance of a certain lack but still be able to write an entire novel?"

"Oh, I see what you mean. Now I understand your question." He shook his head and shrugged. "I have no explanation, really."

Gaventry sat down opposite his friend but leaned forward. "Then you will admit that there does seem to be an inconsistency?"

"Yes, I suppose so. Not a great one, really, but yes."

"Very well." He clasped his hands together, still holding Brixham's gaze. "How could she have written that novel when she cannot hold to a single thought?"

Brixham appeared to think for a long moment. Finally, he said, "Perhaps she did not write the deuced thing after all. Perhaps her publisher was gammoning you."

Gaventry sat back in his chair. Good God, what if it was true? "Where would that leave us?" he asked.

"Why do you not write to him and press him on this point?"

"Yes, I could. Perhaps I shall. Yes, it is an excellent notion. And just in case he has lied to me, I shall include a threat or two."

Gaventry composed his letter but rather than entrust the task to the mails, he sent a servant by way of the post. He received an answer in a very quick four days.

"My lord, I have given you accurate information. The name of the authoress about whom you inquire is Miss Aurelia Kittling, Queen Square, Bath. All remuneration is sent to her bank in Bath in her name. Yours, etc., H. Bertram."

* * *

Sarah took the letter from her maid, addressed to Aurelia, and recognized her publisher's handwriting. She immediately felt uneasy. Mr. Bertram never corresponded unless something of a critical nature was at hand. Her thoughts had immediately flown to the possibility, which had occurred to her many times since Gaventry's arrival in Bath, that he knew she was the authoress of *A Rogue's Tale*. However, several days had passed since the drive to Lansdown, and nothing in the daily, rather commonplace exchanges between herself and Gaventry which had occurred betwixt had given her the smallest indication that he was aware of her identity. If anything, his interests had become fixed upon Aurelia.

She broke the seal and quickly read the contents. She could not prevent a gasp of dismay from crossing her lips. The letter read, "Dear Miss Kittling, It is with the deepest of regrets that I must confess that after having been pressured quite seriously and in a legal as well as a personal manner by Lord Gaventry, I have revealed your identity to him. This terrible deed was accomplished three weeks ago but recently he demanded the information be verified. Having learned that he was presently residing in Bath, I felt it imperative to warn you of this circumstance. From my brief, and quite disturbing conversation with him in early May, I came to understand he was not in the least pleased with your novel. I can only caution you against his possible intentions. Knowing that he is residing in Bath when I begged him most fervently to leave in peace a gentlewoman who I believe brought him more good than harm in the publication of *A Rogue's Tale*, has caused me the worst apprehensions. I do not fear for your safety, for he is not the sort of man to do physical harm to any lady, but there are other means by which innocent young women can suffer injury. Having thus given you the warning I owe you under every bond of honor and chivalry, I can only offer my most sincere apologies for having broken those same bonds in revealing your identity to Lord Gaventry in the first place. Please know that only the harshest persuasions were applied to force this information from me. Yours, etc. H. Bertram."

So there it was, she thought rather numbly. Gaventry knew, or at least he thought he knew who the authoress of *A Rogue's Tale* was. Ironically, in order to sustain the pretenses that the Kittlings were continuing to receive the annuity from her father's estate, she had used not her own name, but Aurelia's, when the documents had been signed to cover allocation of royalties once the novel was published. Their uncle had always sent the annuity in her sister's name and for housekeeping purposes it seemed simplest to utilize her name with the publisher. Sarah had been unable to imagine what harm there might be in doing so since these matters were intended to be kept anonymous.

Now, however, it would seem there was to be harm after all, only what precisely would be the manner of trouble she could expect? If nothing else, it explained his increasing attentiveness to Aurelia. He might have begun his exploits in Bath by kissing her in Queen Square and at Lady Haslingfield's fete, but she could now see that her sister was his true object, only to what purpose?

For the next hour, she strolled about Queen Square and pondered the extraordinary circumstance of Gaventry having come to Bath. So he knew the truth, only what could he possibly mean to do to the Kittling family except to exact some sort of revenge for Aurelia's supposed, and her own in fact, perfidy? She was not without imagination and it seemed to her that Gaventry was indeed in possession of a plan. Though she had known him for less than a fortnight, she had been in his company a sufficient number of times to have noted the strain of bitterness often present in either his expression or his voice. A man who was bitter, who felt life had exacted an unfair toll upon him, who also had it in his power to woo and win the average female's heart, was a man in possession of the ability to inflict whatever damage he desired.

Mr. Bertram was correct on one score—there were many

ways to inflict damage other than actually doing physical harm.

There was, however, only one flaw in Gaventry's present plan—Aurelia was not an average sort of female. Indeed, there was scarcely anything normal about her. Her intelligence was not keen, but her perceptions were. She wasn't just pretty, she was beautiful, and instead of barely being able to perform on the pianoforte, she was a true proficient. The only attribute which seemed to fall straight in the middle was her unimpressive use of pen and paper, a circumstance which amused her vastly since because of Gaventry's belief that she was the authoress he was seeking, this skill should have been her greatest. No wonder he had previously expressed bemusement about her sister's expertise in composition. Only what precisely did his lordship mean to do?

Instead of feeling lowered by this knowledge, however, Sarah felt very odd, indeed, almost dazzled by the possibilities. So, Gaventry had come to Bath to hurt the authoress of *A Rogue's Tale*. Unfortunately, he had been misinformed as to her identity, through no fault of her publisher's, for even her publisher did not know the truth. Something about this so appealed to some truly wretched but latent part of her soul that she could not keep but smiling. She read the letter again and smiled a little more, and so it was that Gaventry happened upon her.

"Why do you smile?" he called to her from at least twenty yards across the square.

He seemed like another person to her entirely as she watched him close the distance. He was of course as handsome as ever, wearing his glossy beaver hat at a rakish angle atop his blond locks, and yes, her heart as usual did seem to skip several beats as he drew closer and closer, but now everything had changed. She realized she no longer had to fear him or his affect upon her. She understood that his intentions in coming to Bath were wholly ignoble, and that undoubtedly as soon as he accomplished his true objective, which involved hurting her sister, he would as quickly depart her lovely, happy city. Only how to avert disaster?

She pocketed her letter, securing it very deeply within her gown.

"You have not answered my question," he said, walking up to her, so confident in manner and demeanor.

She met his gaze squarely. "I am smiling and indeed, laughing, because I have just learned something so peculiar, and so unexpected, but very secret, that I find myself delighted in a way I cannot even express, nor even comprehend, actually."

He grinned. "Will you not tell me the nature of this unusual news? I promise I am quite excellent at keeping secrets."

"As am I and since this secret must be kept, I fear I cannot tell you."

"Will you at least give me a hint?"

She shook her head, then abruptly took his arm, something she had been resisting doing in recent days, but all that was changed now that she had come to understand the motives of the man next to her. "No, I will not, but you may walk with me to my front door. Do you intend to call on Aurelia?" Her heart was dancing.

He looked down at her, his eyes narrowing slightly. "On all the Kittling ladies," he returned.

"Nonsense. It has hardly escaped my notice that you have taken a fancy to my beautiful sibling and for that I do not blame you, although I must say you have treated me quite shabbily." Here, she pretended to pout, then looked up at him and smiled.

"Good God," he murmured. "I have never seen you like this before. What the devil—I mean, I beg your pardon, what are you doing?"

"Why, if memory serves, I am attempting to flirt with you."

He stopped her suddenly. "What has changed that you would take this tone with me when you have been so opposed to the business before?"

There was fire in her heart that was not so much romantic in nature as wicked. "I have decided, my lord, to change everything as of this moment. Gone are all the rules I have lived by and I now mean to establish new ones of my own. The first shall be that if I wish to flirt with a gentleman, I shall do so." She saw someone walking in a westerly direction and recognized Mr. Brixham. "And here is your friend."

She released his arm, and waved gaily to Brixham. Mr. Brixham waited for a curricle to pass by before crossing the street to the square.

"What do you mean to do now?" Gaventry inquired softly. "Oh, no! You are not to make Brix your mark."

She smiled coquettishly. "Whyever not?" She then strolled away from him, swaying her skirts in the manner she had seen so many young ladies before her do. She trusted this would have the proper effect. "How do you go on, Mr. Brixham? I trust you have come to call as well, for here is Gaventry just arrived."

"Indeed, I have and I must say that is a charming bonnet you are wearing this morning."

"Do you like it? My poor old hat, which I had worn to Lansdown, needed refurbishing badly. I thought this shade of pink silk would suit me. What do you think?"

"Quite to perfection."

She glanced back at Gaventry, who she was happy to discover appeared as though he had been stunned by a bolt of lightning. She then took Brixham's arm and led him toward her town house. "I know Aurelia, Meg and Charlotte have been waiting for you this age. You have become quite a favorite with our family."

"Indeed?" he cried, appearing quite pleased.

"You can have no notion."

"Which leads me to ask—do you think Miss Kittling will play for us today?"

"She has been speaking of nothing else all morning, Mr. Brixham. She told me just after breakfast that she had been practicing the Mozart because she knew it was a favorite of yours."

Mr. Brixham grinned, a faint hue showing beneath his freckles. She understood quite well that although he deferred to his friend he was completely besotted by Aurrie.

She once more turned to Gaventry. "Come, my lord!" she called to him. "I have another arm." She set her arm akimbo, and Brixham waited with her until he had joined them.

"So you have," Gaventry said, presenting his for her to take. She did so, gave his arm a squeeze, and when he looked down at her, she winked.

Gaventry was shocked by Miss Sarah's conduct and wondered what could possibly have happened to have altered her behavior. Not that he was complaining, precisely, since the thought of Sarah Kittling desiring to engage in a serious flirtation appealed to him mightily. However, he was quite curious as to what had brought about so striking an alteration in her. As he considered her, in particular the manner in which she had been reading and pondering the letter now tucked into her pocket, he knew instinctively that whatever was contained within was the key to her present rather wild demeanor.

A dangerous part of him began to be aroused. He had seen precisely where she had placed the letter, and if he was sufficiently clever during the next few minutes he could contrive to retrieve it without her knowing he had done so.

A moment later, inspiration struck, and just before he stepped on the curb, he pretended to stumble, dropped carefully to the pavement and pulled her onto him. Immediately, he began to slide his hand where it should not be. Since they had all been joined together, Brixham also took a tumble. Both Miss Sarah and Brix began to exclaim, all the while immediately trying to right themselves, but Gaventry cried, "My leg is twisted, Miss Sarah! It hurts like the devil. Do not move."

She froze, having risen off him a trifle. Brixham caught her elbow and steadied her.

His fingers touched the letter and formed a small vise about the letter. He shifted his leg in a theatrical manner. "There. All is well. You may rise."

Brixham helped lift her, and as these movements were accomplished the letter slid from her pocket; he palmed it carefully, and as he rose, slipped it into his own pocket.

"Are you all right?" she asked, deeply concerned.

"Yes, yes, the stupidest thing! How mortified I am! To have taken a tumble right in front of your house. But what of you? Did I injure you in any manner?"

"No, not at all."

"And you, Brixham?"

"Perfectly fit, thank you."

"Excellent," he said, at the same time, swiping some of the dirt from his breeches, coat, elbows, and back.

As Miss Sarah and Brix entered the town house, he turned his back to them, quickly removed the letter from his pocket, read the contents, and then palmed the missive once more.

So Miss Sarah knew that he knew! Though he had command of his countenance, he could scarcely contain the joy he felt upon having received this knowledge. What fun he could have entirely at her expense. Oh, but there were occasions when life could be utterly delightful.

As he crossed the threshold, he let the letter fall to the tiled entrance. Upon handing his hat and his gloves to the maid, he pretended to glance down. "Miss Sarah? Is that the letter you were reading earlier? I believe it may have just dropped from your pocket?"

He watched in some amusement as her complexion paled quite ominously, her eyes opened to the size of teacup saucers, and she scrambled to pick it up. "Yes," she cried. "Only, how did it get there, when I was so . . . careful?"

"The fall," he said, taking her by the elbow and guiding her into the drawing room. "I daresay it happened when I fell and took you down with me. Miss Sarah, I do apologize. Generally,

I am not so clumsy. Is there anything I might do to redeem myself?"

She eyed him as one still stunned and dismayed. "No, no, I thank you. Truly I am perfectly well. There was no harm done, nothing to atone for."

*At least not yet*, he thought wickedly.

"Ah, Miss Meg, Mrs. Mears and the lovely Miss Kittling." He advanced into the room, so utterly happy, so ready to do the pretty, so fully prepared to continue his assault on the eldest sister's heart. Although, now, glancing back at Miss Sarah, who was once more replacing the letter in her pocket and frowning all the while, he believed Bath had just become a great deal more interesting. One thing he had just learned to a certainty, Miss Sarah knew quite well that her sister was the authoress of *A Rogue's Tale*.

# Seven

Later, as Sarah reclined upon her bed, she reviewed the earlier incident of the letter on the tile, and she wondered if it was possible that Gaventry had somehow staged the fall and without her smallest awareness, stolen the letter from her, read it, then dropped it in the entrance hall. But this seemed entirely improbable. How could he have done so? He would have had to have been a magician, for she never once felt as though he were touching her inappropriately. However, the entire business had happened so quickly, and then she had become frightened that he had hurt himself when he had proclaimed that his leg was twisted, that all her thoughts were centered upon his well-being.

No, there was only one conclusion she could draw—the letter had become dislodged within her pocket during the tumble, and once inside the town house, it had slipped onto the floor. It was as simple as that. Besides, nothing in his countenance the remainder of the afternoon had caused her to believe he might have read the contents of Mr. Bertram's letter. He had not changed his conduct even one whit—his attention had been all for Aurelia.

She, for her part, had flirted with Mr. Brixham, but Gaventry had failed to take notice. Later, however, when she had sidled up to Gaventry while Aurelia was playing the pianoforte, he had responded to her own flirtatious advances.

"You winked at me," he had whispered. "Earlier, when you took up my arm just before crossing the street to your home."

"Yes, my lord, so I did," she had responded, smiling saucily up at him.

"I liked it very much."

"Did you?"

"Indeed, exceedingly, although I give you fair warning that if you continue in this manner, I shall not hesitate to take extreme advantage of you."

"How my heart is fluttering," she responded, batting her lashes and moving away once more.

She had turned slightly to watch him over her shoulder and had had all the satisfaction of seeing his gaze follow after her. He looked her up and down slowly and deliberately, a purposeful smile coming to rest on his lips. His appreciation was so blatant that for all her belief she was up to snuff, she suddenly found herself blushing. She had an uneasy impression in this moment that she ought to be very careful in the execution of her games, since he was used to playing while she was not.

Now, as she tapped the letter to her chin, and through the window watched clouds rolling across the sky, she felt a renewed sense of excitement about present possibilities. Could she learn to play his games, and that so well, that perhaps this time he might lose his heart? More so, what was there in this challenge that so appealed to her?

She turned onto her side, her gaze still fixed beyond the window at the lovely sunshine, and realized that something in her had changed, though she did not quite understand just what it was. She no longer felt like the same person. For the first time in years she felt free, even unencumbered, perhaps even happy.

Gaventry's arrival in Bath had accomplished this, she thought. Yet what a strange irony this was, since she had stolen all the gossip about him and shaped a plot for her first novel from the essentials of that gossip. He ought to have been the last man to have been the cause of her present liberation, not the first.

Yet, just how was it that she felt free? Even this was not clear to her, save that something about being near Gaventry caused her to think differently about everything. Even some of her guilt attached to the writing of the novel had seemed to fade over the past sennight. Of course, it helped very much that she had grown to understand, because of Mr. Bertram's letter, that Gaventry had come to Bath not to take the waters, or enjoy the pleasures to be found in the city, but with a purpose which involved her sister, whom he believed to be the authoress of *A Rogue's Tale.* For that reason, she had every hope that the next few days, and perhaps weeks, would prove to be some of the most interesting, even exciting, of her life.

Over the next week, Sarah came to believe that she and Gaventry had begun dancing about one another like two boxers in a sparring match. She had chanced to see such an exhibition about two years past, quite by happenstance, when she had taken a very long walk in the direction of Bristol. A match had been underway at the outskirts of a village betwixt the towns and she had been able to view, for a few minutes, the exchange of hits the opponents showered on each other. What struck her most, however, was the manner in which, between flurries of punches, each of the boxers would dance about on their feet, moving as lithely as two well-muscled men could move, in order to avoid being caught on their heels and knocked backward with the next hit. Really, it had been an interesting lesson for her.

Those images, however, became reflective of her relationship with Gaventry over the next several days. Since he was pursuing Aurelia, and therefore his attention was not focused upon her, she was able to surprise him again and again with what she came to a view as flush hits, as she dedicated herself to disturbing his attempts to flirt with her sister.

Several times she had foiled his intention of walking out alone with Aurrie by pretending to happen upon them and then insinuating herself into their outing. More often than not, and much to her satisfaction, she was also able to position herself between them. This, of course, was made quite simple by Aurelia, who was happy to relinquish her place, since she, like Meg and like Charlotte, was convinced that she was in love with Gaventry. This of course was nonsense. Her conduct, however, over the ensuing week tended to prove rather than not, that indeed, she had formed a *tendre* for him. After all, she could hardly tell her family what she was about, for then she would have to confess the truth, that she was the authoress of *A Rogue's Tale*. It was expedient for her purposes, therefore, to keep them thinking that she was in love with Gaventry.

Of course, the whole business of keeping watch over where his lordship was and in just what way he was attempting to fix his interest with Aurelia would have been exceedingly difficult had it not been for the fact that the viscount enjoyed gaming. When the majority of the ladies of his acquaintance, including those living in Queen Square, had long since been abed, he went in search of the nocturnal pleasures most gentlemen preferred; the company of men gathered around either a table of whist or billiards and enjoying a bottle of brandy or port as well as the discourse so specific to men. That he went alone to such places of gaming was evident in the fact that while he never appeared in the entrance hall of the Kittling home before nuncheon, Mr. Brixham was more often than not waiting to escort whichever of their number was desirous of going to the Pump Room that morning, an hour usually set at ten o'clock.

Indeed, Mr. Brixham had become as a brother to the ladies, and so congenial was his society that Sarah wished she might invite him to take a room in Queen Square throughout the year that they might always have him close at hand. Aurelia, in particular, seemed fond of his companionship, and more often than not the pair of them would dawdle behind the others while walking to the Pump Room. Sarah understood quite well that Mr. Brixham had favored her from the first, but though she watched Aurrie closely, she had never been able to detect a peculiar interest on her part.

On Thursday, a full week after Sarah had received Mr. Bertram's letter, Gaventry surprised them all by arriving with Mr. Brixham to escort all the ladies to the Pump Room. Sarah was immediately set on guard by the offering of flowers he brought and placed in Aurelia's arms. Aurelia lifted a beaming expression to him and thanked him sweetly. "For if you must know, pink roses are my favorite."

"I do know," he responded, his gaze fixed to hers in his penetrating manner. He then tapped the tip of her nose, "for you told me as much at the theater Saturday last."

"So I did!" she cried. "And you remembered!"

"Of course I remembered."

"Lord Gaventry, you are quite the kindest gentleman of my acquaintance. Again, I thank you."

Sarah, who had been standing nearby and awaiting the appropriate moment to disrupt Gaventry's assault on her sister's sensibilities, watched a rather cloaked expression descend over his features.

"That you would call me kind is more a reflection of your generous nature than any accurate description of my own." Sarah could not have agreed more.

A faint frown knit poor Aurelia's brow. "Th—thank you." Sarah could see that her sister was unable to make sense of his remark.

Gaventry then smiled warmly upon Aurrie, a circumstance which caused Sarah's traitorous heart to skip at least two beats and for her to wish yet again that he was not quite so handsome when he smiled. He tried again. "That you would think me kind makes you nothing short of an angel."

Aurelia's frown disappeared and she smiled anew, comprehension clearly dawning.

Mr. Brixham stepped around Gaventry's shadow and nodded. "She is an angel. Have I not said so a hundred times!"

"No, no I am not," Aurelia cried, a blush blooming on her perfect cheeks. "I assure you I am no such thing. You have but to ask my sisters and they will be happy to tell you the truth."

When Gaventry appeared ready to step quite close to her in a move Sarah had seen him initiate several times, she stepped between them. "Actually, my dearest Aurrie," she began, bumping Gaventry slightly. She smiled up at him and begged his pardon, then again addressed her sister. "You will not find either our sister or our cousin prepared to argue the point in the least. You were always an angel. Even Mama said so from the time you were born. But come, let us find a vase for your flowers." She took the roses from her carefully and hooking Aurelia's elbow, drew her away from the wolf by the door.

"Oh, yes," Aurelia responded, easily diverted. "At once. For if we are very careful they will last a sennight."

As they made their way down the hall, Sarah glanced back at Gaventry and found that a crooked smile was on his lips and a knowing light in his eye. He nodded to her, something he did frequently when she succeeded in separating them. She could not be certain, but she rather thought he admired her for it.

She only wondered just how she was to keep him from stealing Aurrie away during their walk to the Pump Room, something he was quite capable of doing. If he succeeded, she doubted they would see either of them again anytime before nuncheon.

Once the entire party was walking in a southerly direction, it was Charlotte, however, who engaged Gaventry in conversation, and that so thoroughly that once on Milsom Street he lifted his head and after glancing around, exclaimed, "Where the deuce . . . er, I mean, where is Miss Kittling?"

Meg shrugged. "She was with Mr. Brixham a moment ago. I suspect they have merely gone off in another direction. She often does, you know."

"With Brixham?"

"Yes," Meg responded. "They have become very great friends."

Sarah glanced up at him and saw a concerned light enter

his eye. "Indeed, Lord Gaventry, we have all begun to think of him quite as dear as a brother might be."

"Indeed," he murmured.

"Or even a cousin," she added.

Gaventry glanced at her apace, his lips twitching appreciatively. He, however, did not address her, but asked of Charlotte, "And does he call every morning?"

"Very nearly," Charlotte said. She then addressed Meg. "Would you offer me your arm, Meggie? I believe I have the smallest pebble in my sandal. Yes, yes, Sally, do go on with Gaventry. We will not be but a moment or two."

There was nothing to be done. Sarah doubted quite sincerely that there was such a pebble but to protest would only cause a degree of embarrassment to all, so she turned to Gaventry. "Shall we?" she inquired, if archly.

He offered his arm, which she took, wishing he had instead merely gestured for them to proceed. She did not like touching Gaventry, not in the least, since she liked it so well as she did. She knew that very soon her thoughts would become a jumble of wishing and wanting, with nowhere to go.

She glanced up at him and seeing that he was still frowning a trifle, she said, "You need not be blue-devilled that your prey has slipped from your grasp. Brixham will see her safely escorted to the Pump Room and then you may begin again."

"My prey?" he inquired with a falsely innocent lifting of one brow.

"Oh, do stubble it, my lord. You are intent on winning Aurrie's heart. Everyone speaks of it so there is no need to deny your purposes, especially to me."

"But why do you call her *my prey*? I do not understand."

"What a whisker! You understand very well or do you mean to tell me that you have in truth tumbled in love with her and are intent on declaring yourself before the end of May?"

He appeared to ponder this, lifting his gaze skyward. "Such notions as you give me," he murmured.

"Gammon," she retorted. "As though you will ever take a wife. You are the sort of man, even if you are well-shod and titled, and could afford a hundred wives, who will live his days a bachelor. Tell me I have not spoken the truth."

"I shall tell you immediately," he retorted. "I like your notion excessively of taking a hundred wives."

Sarah shook her head at him. "You have confirmed my opinion. You will never marry."

"In that, you are quite wrong, Miss Sarah Kittling. The right sort of woman could tempt me quite easily to the altar."

"I do not believe you," she said boldly.

At that, he looked down at her, his eyes narrowed and almost cold. "You would question my truthfulness?"

She ignored his attempt to appear harsh and forbidding. "What I question are your motives and your self-knowledge, both of which I believe to be sadly lacking. Only tell me why you have made Aurelia your object? She cannot possibly be in your usual style. Tell me that!" She was testing him and enjoying every moment of it. She watched his profile as she moved beside him, her arm still wrapped about his in what felt to be a very comfortable manner. She did not find it in the least difficult, for instance, matching his stride.

Gaventry glanced at the beauty beside him, with her fawn eyes and quite wicked smile staring back at him in what he could only describe as a completely challenging manner. A current of appreciation ran through him like the swift flow of water in a rapid stream. He liked Miss Sarah very much, especially from the time she read Mr. Bertram's letter. Gone was all her former and quite evident apprehension in his presence, and in its place was a boldness that seemed to fill an odd little empty well deep in his soul. Yes, that was how he felt, that something about her satisfied his soul.

He schooled his features, however, as he looked away, lifting his gaze to the verdant hills of Bath rising in every direction from the streets near the Colonnade. He did not think it at all prudent that Sally Kittling should know even the smallest bit just how much pleasure he found in her society. Indeed, he often wondered, had his present pursuit of Miss Kittling not been his object, whether or not he would have sought out Miss Sarah's company instead. He supposed he would never know, but over the past sennight he had come to look forward not to his next assault on beautiful Aurelia's heart, but on just what his next encounter with Sarah would entail. She had not disappointed him today.

Only where the devil was Brixham and what was he doing with Miss Kittling? The knowledge that his friend had been refusing the usual late evening pleasures so that he might call in the morning in Queen Square disturbed him. He wondered if it was possible he was forming an attachment to any of the ladies, in particular to the very one he meant to bring down. That was a conversation he meant to have in the very near future.

"Now why are you looking thunderous! Do you know, Gaventry, you quite put me in mind of a fierce summer storm, so quickly can it descend on the unwary!"

"Were you always such a fanciful young lady?" he inquired, looking down at her and again seeing a wonderfully challenging expression in her eyes. How pretty she was today in a pale blue walking dress of patterned silk, a bonnet to match, and a white parasol, which she maneuvered to keep the sun away from her face.

"Always!" she returned. "Have I not told you as much?"

"Ah, yes, the winter plays in Hampshire!"

"Yes, at the very least the winter plays!"

She then laughed, and in that moment he found himself caught yet again by her. How was it possible that he could be entranced by the sound of laughter, but so he was. He found a powerful feeling expanding in his chest, something he often felt when he had been in her presence for several minutes, together with only their banter to attend to. Did she know how her laughter and her sparring words held him captive? Did she know how her soft brown beauty appealed so mightily to him or how with a few expressive glances he wanted nothing more than to steal her away, take her in his arms and kiss her as he had at Queen Square and in the library at his godmother's house?

Quite without thinking, he covered her hand with his own and gave it a squeeze. When quiet descended on the lady beside him, he glanced down and knew he had erred. Good God, what had he been thinking to have touched her so intimately, as though they were at the very least betrothed, for covering her hand was no less significant a gesture. He could only wonder what the deuce she was thinking.

Sarah tried to draw in a deep breath but found the air, so necessary to the calming of her suddenly racing heart, barely passing her throat. They had been getting along so famously, and she had been making progress in her scheme to keep him away from Aurelia. However, the moment his hand covered hers, with her arm still wrapped about his, she felt certain she was like to faint.

This was the ever-present truth she tried to keep hidden from herself, that even though she desired it otherwise, her heart was haplessly susceptible to Gaventry. She may have been attempting to protect her sister by keeping him from her side as often as she could, but it would seem the unfortunate result was more often than not that she felt the moorings of her heart slipping away one by one. One thing she knew for certain, had she been alone with him in this moment, instead of walking beneath the Colonnade near the Pump Room, she would have been completely amenable to the notion of allowing him a third kiss!

"What are you thinking, Miss Sally?" he queried, his voice a whisper as he leaned down to her. "May I guess your thoughts?"

"I should think it unlikely, but you have my permission to try."

"You are thinking I am a roguish fellow deserving of a set-down."

She giggled. "Yes, that was it," she returned.

"No, no, this I will not allow. No whiskers. I insist on guessing your thoughts and you have already given me permission."

From the corner of her eye, she saw her sister and Brixham emerge from a shop directly across from the Pump Room. She withdrew her arm from his and drawing to a stop just beyond the Colonnade, moved to position Gaventry's back to them. "Very well," she murmured. "You have found me out. Pray attempt a second guess, but I shall only allow you three."

He narrowed his eyes. "Then I shall need to be very careful in my conjectures."

She shifted her parasol to keep the sun from finding her face.

He took a small step toward her so that they were standing very close together. She could smell the faint scent of his shaving soap, and she felt dizzy suddenly. She resisted the urge to lift a hand to his cheek. Such errant thoughts! Ridiculous, horrid, disloyal thoughts!

He leaned next to her ear and whispered, "Is it that you are distressed that I would flirt with your sister and you at the same time?"

His breath, which struck her cheek, caused a spate of gooseflesh to race down her side. When he drew back to await her response, she lifted her gaze to his face. She wished she had not done so. The blue of his eyes was devastatingly sharp on this clear May morning, and once more she understood why so many ladies lost their hearts to him. There was something more, however, a confidence in him that also appealed to the feminine heart. How she wished it were not so!

She tried to find a flippant response, but could not. She merely shook her head rather dumbly.

He huffed a sigh. "What could your thoughts have been?" he wondered aloud. He then grinned. "I have it! You were thinking you wished for another kiss!"

She knew he did not believe she had thought any such thing, that he was only teasing her and had said as much merely to get a rise from her. Only now what was she to do? She had already established the rules for this exchange and to break them would be to dishonor herself, yet to reveal the truth was beyond thinking. What was she to do?

His grin began from gentle to a knowing smile, and a look of pure devilment overcame his features. "Good God," he whispered. "Can this be true?"

She turned on her heel and moved past him. In a manner she hoped sounded relatively disinterested, she responded, "Of course it is true."

He caught up with her quickly and snagged her elbow, drawing her to a stop. "*Of course it is true?* My dear Miss Sally, you should have told me much sooner. I promise you I am fully capable of obliging you on that score any time you desire it. You have but to say the word."

She turned to face him fully. "Then I tell you I desire it now. Kiss me now." She did not know why she had said something so outrageous, but so she had. What was it about Gaventry that prompted such deviltry in her?

A look came over his countenance like nothing she had ever before seen, and she realized she had erred. She knew if she did not act quickly, he would oblige her, indeed. She learned in this moment never to underestimate what a rogue might actually do when given the slightest encouragement. They were standing very near to the Pump Room, where every manner of person was moving in and out of the building.

Once more, she drew away from him, only so quickly that this time he could not catch her so easily. "I should not have said it," she whispered as he joined her again. "It was a very foolish thing to say. I was only curious to see whether you would sink us both in scandal if I did. You must know that I would not for the world disgrace my family by doing anything so . . . so wicked and vile."

"Not *vile*, surely!"

By now they were at the entrance and she looked up at

him, her heart losing yet another of its moorings. "No," she murmured. "Never that . . . but still quite wicked!"

He followed her into the Pump Room. The tall-ceilinged chamber was alive with chatter. Sarah began greeting her friends, as did Gaventry. She thought, she hoped, that he would soon quit her side, but apparently he was not yet finished with her, for he followed her across the entire length of the chamber.

"You should go away," she whispered when they were once again alone. "You are causing all manner of gossip and do but look, there is your godmother, waving you to come to her. Mrs. Catesby's eldest married daughter is in town and undoubtedly wishes to make your acquaintance."

He did not glance her direction. "Yes, I know. I have been ignoring her."

At that, Sarah smiled, if falteringly. "I must apologize, then."

"For what?"

"For teasing you so, when I have no intention of allowing another kiss and . . . and particularly when I meant nothing by it. "

"But you meant a great deal."

"In what possible manner?"

He drew her further apart from the crowds and lowered his voice. "Because you like kissing me and that means a great deal. Deny right now that you wish to kiss me again."

"That I never shall," she responded frankly. Once more, she smiled before continuing. "I was never happier than when in your arms."

Her words had a strange effect, for he seemed utterly stunned. A moment more and he was frowning slightly. "You are a most unusual, enigmatic lady."

"Because I have spoken the truth to you?"

"Yes. I cannot think of another who would have."

"Pray, do not ascribe a virtue to me because of it. I suppose I merely believe that if I am honest in this respect, I can be in others as well. For instance, though I might desire to kiss you again, it is the last thing on earth I truly wish for."

"Why?" he pressed her.

"Gaventry, must we have this conversation here? Now?"

"Better in public, I think, or we would not be conversing at all."

His expression, almost leering, made her gasp. "What a wretch you are! I am done with you."

She turned to go, but he stayed her by catching her elbow again. There was nothing more for her to do but stop, turn to him, and offer a heavy sigh. "What is it, tormentor?"

"I must have a dance this evening at the Assembly Rooms. Two, preferably, but I must insist on the first."

Here she taunted him. "But, Gaventry," she said with mock sweetness. "If I wait for you to be my first partner, I daresay I shall be waiting for *hours*."

His expression grew challenging once more. "I shall await you at seven in the entrance hall."

"We shall see," she responded.

"No," he returned sharply. "Your first dance."

Sarah felt another mooring snap briskly away from her heart. Rogue to the last. "My first, then," she agreed.

His smile held one of so much satisfaction that she ground her teeth. He bowed to her and moved away. "Abominable man," she whispered, but loud enough for him to hear. A chuckle returned to her.

Sarah watched him go and was not surprised, though she was a little dismayed that he immediately sought out Aurelia. He was abominable in the truest sense of the word for she knew, *she knew*, he meant evil for her family. Yet she was drawn to him, admired him, and longed for his embraces. The effects of roguishness on a weak, female heart, she thought unhappily.

As she watched him secure Aurrie's attention to himself, she observed her sister closely. Was Aurelia suffering as she was, longing for him to embrace her, to kiss her, wishing he would leave Bath but dreading the moment he did, wondering if her existence would ever know a mite of happiness once he was gone? In truth, she could not know the musings of her sister's heart. In this, Aurelia had shown, over the past fortnight, more restraint and proper modesty than she had, but did this mean her heart was any less engaged by Gaventry's practiced flirtations and warm attentiveness?

She decided she must discover, if she could, the exact nature of her sister's heart. So it was that she scratched on her sister's door an hour before dinner, when all the ladies of the house were reclining in anticipation of dancing at the Upper Rooms that night. Aurrie bid her enter, which Sarah did very quietly, neither wanting to awaken Meg or Charlotte, who shared an adjoining room, or to alert them that she wished to converse privately with Aurrie. Meg, for one, would want to know instantly what was afoot.

Aurrie rested on her bed, a shawl covering her, an arm settled on a pillow above her head. "What is it?" she asked somewhat sleepily.

"I thought we might have a comfortable cose while the others slept. Do you mind?"

Aurelia shook her head. "I should like it above all things for there is something I feel I must tell you."

Sarah took up a seat on the edge of Aurelia's bed, her heart sinking. "What would that be?"

"I . . . I am not certain how to tell you for it has all happened so suddenly. He has been so wonderfully attentive to me, always seeing to my comfort, and he is the easiest gentleman in the world with whom to converse."

Sarah felt all the blood drain from her face, and had she not been sitting down, surely she would have fainted. It would seem her suspicions were true after all.

Aurrie took quick hold of her hand. "I can see that I have given you a shock. Did you not suspect, even a little, that I was forming an attachment?"

Sarah nodded slowly. "I suppose I did, at least a little, for who could not help but love such a man? But it is all so sudden. Are you certain you are not merely experiencing the first throes of a calf love since you have known him less than three weeks?"

Aurelia shifted her gaze from Sarah's and her expression became beatific. "I have never been so certain of anything in my entire life." She sighed blissfully, then once more met Sarah's gaze. "But is it not surprising? I never thought to tumble in love. One day I knew that you would, and Meggie, as well, but not I. Oh, Sarah, do be happy for me. I . . . I would be so miserable if you told me you did not approve."

How could she possibly tell her anything else or even that the man she had grown to love had wished for just this—to have won her heart that he might break it. Seeing the anxious concern on her sister's face, Sarah rose from her place on the bed, and, still holding Aurrie's hand, looked down at her. "Aurelia, I have had but one wish for you since times out of mind, that you would be happy. If this love has brought you happiness, then I could wish for nothing more."

Aurrie's expression softened. "I knew I might rely upon you."

"You always can." She paused, then continued. "I do have a suggestion, however."

"What is it?"

"That you say nothing of this to Meg or Charlotte."

"Oh, I would never say anything to Meg for she would tease me forever. As for Charlotte," she said, rising up on her elbow, "I would not mind telling her but if you think I should not then I will not."

"At least wait a few more weeks until you are absolutely certain, but there is one more thing, something I hope you will promise me."

"Anything dearest Sally," she responded, smiling sweetly.

"Only that you conduct yourself with great circumspection so that no one will have the least cause to gossip about you. This is of the utmost importance. Will you promise me that?"

"Yes! Indeed, yes! I would never wish to disgrace my family on any score!"

Sarah smiled, if falteringly. "Thank you. Such discretion will serve you, and our family, very well. You may trust me in this."

She kissed her sister on the cheek, bid her to sleep if she could before the assembly, and quietly quit the room. She felt dizzy as she made a slow return to her chamber at the front of the house. She had tried so hard to keep Gaventry from accomplishing his heinous deed, but he had succeeded despite her strenuous efforts.

Well, it was one thing for Aurelia to have tumbled in love with him, but quite another that she would permit him to hurt her. As she lay down on her bed, she began conjuring her own manner in which she might right what was quickly becoming a truly dreadful wrong. The notion did cross her mind more than once that she ought to confess to her family not just her authorship, but her publisher's belief that Aurelia had penned *A Rogue's Tale*, as well as the precise reason Gaventry had come to Bath in the first place. This she quickly dismissed. Things had not come to such a pass that they could still not be undone, not if she was very clever where Gaventry was concerned.

To this purpose, she spent the next hour pondering a score of ways in which she could begin avenging Aurrie's poor heart this very evening. When at last she had conceived of and dismissed a great number of schemes, inspiration struck. The idea that had presented itself was as bold as it was scandalous but would certainly serve quite well, of that she was utterly convinced, in keeping Gaventry separated from Aurelia. To that purpose, she rose from her bed, settled her portable writing desk on her dressing table, and penned a small, discreet missive. After sealing it and plunging it deeply into the pocket of the gown she would be wearing at the assemblies, she rang for her maid to begin the process of making her presentable for the evening.

* * *

Later, when Sarah arrived at the Assembly Rooms, she found Gaventry precisely where he had said he would be. Of course he was surrounded by a bevy of adoring beauties, all fluttering their fans and their lashes, but the moment he saw her a wicked gleam entered his eye, a smile curled his lips, and an expression of intense self-satisfaction overtook every handsome feature. So much so, in truth, that Sarah found herself suddenly out of reason cross with him. He was a very bad man, intent on hurting Aurelia. This knowledge altered her temper completely. She had little thought beyond how wretchedly he was intending to use her sister, and so it was that whatever passionate sentiments she usually experienced in his presence faded to a dim memory. Her thoughts, her purposes, were all for protecting dear Aurelia.

"You are out of spirits," he murmured, as he led her to the ballroom. "You must tell me why."

"I cannot," she returned uneasily. "The matter is one of some delicacy involving my family. To speak would be to betray a confidence and that I shall not do."

"Then you must not tell me."

"As I have said." She smiled up at him, but her cheeks felt stiff and his response was nothing short of a frown.

As she began going down the dance, she realized that this would not do. She could not possibly accomplish her objectives if she remained cool and distant toward him. No, she must coax her thinking in another direction entirely if she was to win the battle, only for some reason she was not at all interested in waging war.

She caught sight of Aurelia, who was going down the first dance with Mr. Brixham, and her heart felt very low, indeed. Aurelia was in love with Lord Gaventry, and Gaventry meant to hurt her.

"Come, come, Miss Sarah," he murmured kindly as the

dance drew them together. "This will not do. I have never seen you so blue-deviled."

She made the worst mistake imaginable by meeting his gaze. There was so much surprising sympathy in his expression that she felt, in almost a completely physical sense, the very last of the moorings which had secured her heart to a safe harbor break completely. She knew she had been set adrift in a current so powerful that there was nothing to do but let the tide take her away.

The movements of the dance separated them, but when together again, he whispered, "Indeed, I am grievously concerned. Are you become ill, perchance?"

As the tender, concerned strains of his queries penetrated her ears, a blinding insight pierced her with such force that for several seconds she simply could not breathe. When the dance brought them together, and her arm was linked with his, she gazed into his eyes and understanding, perfect and true, at last flowed in every vein. She was not angry that Gaventry had seduced Aurrie's heart. She was angry that Aurelia had tumbled in love with a man whom she had come to believe belonged to her exclusively. No one was to have, to love, to belong to Gaventry but herself!

The dance parted them again, and she moved by practice into the next several turns, but all the while her mind was caught up in trying to determine what precisely had happened to her, or perhaps more accurately, when? If only she were not at an assembly, where her conduct was visible to every manner of scrutiny and gossip. How much she longed to be alone so that she might ponder deeply the precise state of her heart.

However, she was not alone and she was dancing with Lord Gaventry. She could not continue in this absurd manner of shock and dismay. What fodder for the gossips were she to do so! No, she must take command of herself. She drew in a deep breath and forced a smile, then another and another and another until her cheeks no longer felt frozen and her mind began to become untangled.

Her ability to converse with Gaventry and others in the set improved. One glance about the chamber and she knew a great many matrons were frowning her down, clucking their tongues, and shaking their heads. In so critical a social setting, she certainly did not have the luxury of indulging her thoughts or feelings. There would be ample time for that once she returned later that evening to Queen Square. For the present, she must keep her wits about her, not just for Aurelia's sake but for her own, now, as well.

Once the dance ended, Gaventry turned her over to another gentleman desirous of dancing with her. Even this small separation helped her to gather her wits further although the sight of his broad shoulders moving away from her did not in the least make her content. She suddenly felt jealous of every lady whom he would partner that evening, or with whom he would converse, or who would receive his smiles. She wanted him for herself, a sentiment so new to her that she simply did not know how to manage so powerful a desire. However, above even these sorts of sensations there rose the largest concern of all which framed itself in her mind as a truly wretched question, which was whether or not a confirmed rogue could ever truly love anyone.

# Eight

After going down two more sets, and aware during the latter that neither Aurelia nor Gaventry was dancing, Sarah made her way to the octagonal entrance hall and began searching for them. She was not surprised, as she peeked into the long chamber in which refreshments would soon be served, to see them conversing together at the far end.

She decided not to intervene herself, but instead sought about for the best way by which to disturb Gaventry's continued assault on her sister's heart. She withdrew, sensing that it was not yet time to make use of the note secreted in the pocket of her skirt. As she considered several possibilities for disrupting the tête-à-tête, she saw Mr. Brixham emerge from the ballroom, the perfect solution to her present dilemma. Gaventry would hardly refuse to relinquish her sister to his bosom bow.

She lifted her fan and waved to him. He nodded in recognition, smiled in his very friendly manner, and began a halting progress toward her as he greeted friends along the way. During that time, Sarah had more than one gentleman pause and ask for a future dance, so that by the time Mr. Brixham was bidding her a pleasant good evening, she found herself engaged for the next several sets.

"And how do you go on, Miss Sarah?" he asked. "I must say, you look quite lovely with your hair covered in peach-colored flowers. Very pretty."

"Thank you," she responded, taking his measure. "I

chanced to see you earlier dancing with my sister. Have you gone down but one set with her?"

He nodded. "Only one, though I must confess I am hoping for a second." He glanced around, then continued. "Are your sisters enjoying the ball? I do not see them in this moment so I must presume they have both been fully engaged by other partners."

"It is a very odd circumstance, but I have not spoken with either of them since we first arrived so I cannot say whether or not they have given away all their dances. But it is so early in the evening I daresay they must each have a few left which puts me in mind of something I wish to ask you."

"And what would that be?" he queried, his gaze now fixed on her as he smiled. Such a nice smile, Sarah mused. She could only wish, however hopeless such a thought was at this juncture, that Aurelia had chosen to love such a man as Mr. Brixham. She felt certain, by everything she knew about him as well as the kindness and warmth present in his expression, that he would be the sort of man who could gently safeguard any tender young woman's heart.

She withheld a sigh and said, "Actually, it is more of a favor than anything else."

"You have but to speak the word. I am yours to command."

She drew him away from listening ears, and in a low voice said, "It has to do with my sister, I fear, Aurelia."

Something in her tone must have startled him, for he paled instantly. "Good God!" he whispered. "Whatever is the matter? Has she been taken ill? Do you wish me to go to her at once, to escort all of you home? Do tell me."

She was quite taken aback and laid a quieting hand on his arm. "No, no, it is nothing like that, I promise you," she assured him. "And, indeed, I had no intention of alarming you."

"What is it, then?"

She paused, but only for a moment, then responded, "I have become concerned that Lord Gaventry has become too particular in his attentions to her." Once the words left her mouth, she realized that no gentleman would be better suited to help her in this difficult situation than Mr. Brixham. She understood perfectly well that he had a *tendre* for Aurrie, and what better person to enlist in her campaign against the vengeful rogue than a man who would not want Aurelia's heart injured by any man, much less by his good friend. "I was therefore hoping that you might be able to protect her, as it were."

He seemed to struggle with himself, but for what reason she was not at all certain. The line of his mouth grew quite grim, and his nostrils flared. For the barest second she wondered if he meant to do something quite rash, like challenge Gaventry to a duel. For that reason, she hastened to say, "Mr. Brixham, I did not intend to overset you by telling you as much, merely to alert you to what I feel to be an important concern." For the first time she began to wonder if he knew of his friend's intentions.

He met her gaze directly and with some force stated, "Lord Gaventry and I have been friends for a very long time, but he can be ridiculously stubborn about . . . about many things."

She was a little surprised by this outburst, and even if he knew that Gaventry's flirtations with Aurelia were not without a dark purpose, she still did not quite understand the source of his venom, although a new thought entirely occurred to her. "Mr. Brixham, is it possible you think he is in love with Aurelia?"

At that Mr. Brixham smiled. "No, I have no concerns on that score."

"Nor do I. He is the sort of man who can love no woman, at least that is what I think."

An odd smile twisted Mr. Brixham's lips. "And why is that?"

"I think it is simple, really. He is a rogue amongst rogues whose heart is never touched. Have you, for instance, ever known him to be in love?"

"Actually, I have known him to be in love twice, but the first time, the lady used him dreadfully."

"Miss Fulbourne, of course. How I have grown to detest

her! However, you have confirmed my opinion exactly since I have seen his bitterness on more than one occasion which means he is determined never to love again." She then wondered who the other lady might have been. "And the second?"

He shook his head. "I do not feel I can speak of her, at least not at the present."

She nodded in complete understanding. "I approve of your discretion." He then chuckled, but she did not comprehend in the least why. She queried, "And you believe as I do, that he is not in love with Aurrie?"

"Not even in the slightest. I have known Gaven for ages and there is nothing in the way he either speaks of her or attends to her that suggests that his heart is engaged."

Worse and worse, she thought, feeling frantic suddenly. She again wondered if Mr. Brixham was at all privy to Gaventry's intentions, whether he understood that the viscount was intent on hurting Aurelia, but she did not feel she could possibly pose such a question, particularly since it drew so closely to the subject of her authorship. "I hope I do not offend you by saying that I fear for my sister. Mr. Brixham, you must see that something should be done at once before Lord Gaventry succeeds in winning Aurelia's heart."

"And you have such a fear?" he asked, a little stunned.

"Yes. I had not meant to tell you but something she told me late this afternoon has convinced me she is already half in love with him."

"I beg your pardon?" he queried, paling once more.

"I can see that I have given you a shock."

"Indeed, you have. But are you certain?"

"Quite certain I am afraid for she told me as much."

He seemed stunned. "She told you?"

Sarah nodded.

"May I ask just when she informed you of these sentiments?"

"This afternoon." She felt very uncomfortable having revealed to some degree Aurelia's confidences, but she was desperate and felt certain she might be able to rely on Brixham.

"I see," he grew silent for a long moment, then continued, "And she actually spoke of Gaventry by name?"

Sarah nodded, then tried to recall if Aurrie had used his name. Realizing she had not, she responded slowly, "No, now that I think on it, I suppose she did not but I had no doubt she was speaking of him. Our entire conversation was solely about Gaventry."

"No doubt at all?"

She shook her head. "So you see, you must help me. You must do me this one favor. You must help me to keep Gaventry away from Aurelia by claiming her hand for as many dances together as you dare and by . . . by taking her in for refreshments. Will you do that for me?"

He smiled warmly. "You may rely upon me," he said. "And . . . and I would say that you should not be overly concerned for your sister. I . . . I have reason to believe she may not be so much in love with Gaventry as you suppose."

"How good you are, Mr. Brixham, to be trying to relieve my worries. Even though I am not so sanguine as you, I have every confidence that with but a little push we will be able to spare her a great deal of suffering. Go now. The last I saw of her, she was standing with Gaventry at the far end of the tearoom."

He assured her that he would do all in his power to make certain of Aurelia's happiness. He then bowed and moved past her.

Sarah was smiling happily when Charlotte approached her. "Such an intense conversation you were having with Mr. Brixham just now, and I was not the only one to have noticed. What on earth is going forward?"

Sarah smiled and hooked her cousin's arm. "Nothing to signify. Merely, I am helping to avert a disaster."

"Oh dear," she murmured, but not without a great deal of amusement in her voice. "A disaster, truly?"

"Yes, but you may rely on me to see the whole business resolved tidily and without the smallest repercussion."

Charlotte regarded her with a curious frown. "What are you about, Sally?" she asked.

Again, she smiled. "You must trust me but a little."

Charlotte then leaned close to her and whispered, "I must ask—are you aware that Aurelia has tumbled in love at long last?"

"So you know then?" she queried, quite shocked.

"Yes, as it happens, I do. I have suspected it from the first for there was something in the manner in which he engaged her so readily in conversation that I knew your sister would respond to him."

Sarah's spirits sank further. It was one thing for Aurelia to confess to a love that might be a moonling sort of sentiment, but quite another to have Charlotte holding to the same opinion. "So you believe Aurelia to be truly in love, for her heart to be completely engaged?"

Charlotte nodded.

"I must confess that I hoped it was otherwise."

"Why? Do you mean because of his rakish associations?"

"At the very least."

"I see," Charlotte murmured. "Do you have any objection beyond this concern were he to attempt to fix his interest with her?"

Sarah thought for a moment about Lord Gaventry. How could she possibly tell Charlotte of the depths of her suspicions about his motives in pursuing Aurrie in the first place. Instead, she addressed the more obvious aspect of the situation. "You cannot really believe him to be serious?" she asked.

Charlotte frowned. "I suppose I do. Indeed, his attentions have been most marked."

"Well of course they have been," she whispered urgently. "He has intended from the first to win her heart."

"Yes, I believe that much was true. Ah, well, I suppose we are speaking at cross-purposes and all will be resolved happily in the end."

"I hope what you say is true."

At that moment, Mr. Brixham strolled across the entrance

hall with Aurelia on his arm. Sarah said, "At least we may rely upon Mr. Brixham."

Charlotte frowned. "But, Sally . . ." She stopped suddenly and turned to regard her in her open manner. "That is, of course we can depend upon Mr. Brixham."

"If you must know," Sarah confided, "I have asked him to squire Aurelia about, at least for the present time. If what I suspect is true concerning Lord Gaventry, he will very soon reveal his hapless motives and then, as you have said, all will be resolved. My only distress, and it is a very great one, is that Aurrie will have her heart completely broken." She sighed heavily.

"But not if you can help it?" Charlotte offered.

"Precisely so. I love Aurrie, and I do not mean to see her crushed if I can possibly prevent it."

At that, Charlotte pressed her lips tightly together, but after struggling with herself released a peal of laughter.

"Why are you so amused? I promise you there is very little in this situation that is in the least entertaining." She wished at this moment that she might be able to reveal all to Charlotte, including her authorship, but she simply could not. She realized she was growing weary of carrying such heavy burdens.

Charlotte, still chuckling, responded. "I must disagree completely with you, Sally. There is a great deal in this situation to make me laugh. No, I beg you, do not try again to explain your concerns. Ah, but there is Gaventry. Perhaps you should attempt to engage his interest yourself and thereby detach him from Aurrie's side."

"In that, at least, we are certainly of a mind!" she cried.

Charlotte began laughing heartily once more for reasons Sarah could not in the least comprehend. However, she did not have time to probe precisely what it was that amused her about Aurelia's dire predicament, particularly when Gaventry was looking at her in that horridly rakish way of his and winking at her.

"I shall leave you now," Charlotte whispered, "for it would seem Gaventry is intent not just on possessing Aurrie's heart."

"He is a truly wretched man," Sarah whispered from behind her fan. This comment, which she had thought her cousin might understand, merely set her off again. Sarah frowned her down which caused Charlotte to beg pardon and move away. Sarah then turned her attention wholly upon Gaventry, casting him a blinding smile as he approached her. He bowed and asked for the next dance, which she happily gave to him.

"I see that you are recovered from your fit of the dismals earlier," he commented, offering her his arm.

"Quite," she responded. "I do beg your pardon for my previous conduct, but I had suffered something of a shock and, yes, I did require this hour or more to regain my bearings. But I promise you I am fully restored and you shall find me much more conversant than during our last dance together."

So it was that she flirted madly with Gaventry, not caring if she set up the backs of a dozen Bath tabbies, not when Aurrie's heart was in such supreme jeopardy. He responded in kind, and she could see he was enjoying himself prodigiously. In truth, she was as well. To behave so carelessly was a quite heady experience, so that by the time the dance ended she was laughing heartily with him.

"I am feeling quite overheated," she said, fanning herself rapidly. Glancing about, she could tell by the general movement of the crowds that refreshments would very soon be announced. Because she had her own plans, she continued. "I believe I shall move to the entrance if you do not mind."

"Not in the least. Do you require an escort?" She could see that he, too, was glancing about the ballroom and that his gaze had quickly become fixed on Aurelia, who was walking with Mr. Brixham.

Understanding perfectly well that he was once more intent on his own prey, she responded, "No, it is not at all necessary, but thank you."

He bowed to her, afterward moving away quickly, undoubtedly with the hope of taking Aurelia in to refreshments. At least in that she had already thwarted his plans. Once in the entrance hall, however, she reached into the pocket of her gown and withdrew the message she had composed for precisely this moment. She sought out a servant and bid him deliver it to Lord Gaventry, as discreetly as possible. The shilling she placed in the palm of his hand brought a smile to his lips.

"Aye, miss," he murmured and disappeared into the throng that was pushing toward the tearoom.

For herself, she returned to the entrance and retrieved her hooded cloak. A moment more, she stepped out-of-doors, ignoring the clusters of sedan chairs and servants milling about. She made her way quickly in a southerly direction to the alleyway she had specified in her note. She had not gone far when she noticed that more than one set of gentlemen was walking about, and more than one of each number was quite foxed. She suddenly felt all the value of the strictness of the rules by which proper young ladies conducted themselves. Her present vulnerability prompted her to take up a rock in her right hand, but instead of retracing her steps she continued boldly on her way. Whatever the dangers of the situation, they could not be any greater than the one Gaventry posed to poor Aurrie's heart.


Gaventry turned away from Brixham and Miss Kittling and broke the seal to the missive a manservant had just delivered to him. He read the contents with a feeling very much like shock coursing through him. There was no signature, only the initials, S. K. He was in no doubt, however, that the note was by the hand of Miss Sarah, though he thought the contents provocative in the extreme!

He read the body of the message again: "If you are desirous of the kiss I all but promised you in the Pump Room, you may find me in the alley behind Gay Street."

*The alley behind Gay Street. Good God!*

He glanced at Aurelia, who was still holding Brixham's arm and whose invitation to go in to refreshments she had already accepted. He considered the dilemma before him. In actuality, there would be little possibility at all of separating Miss Kittling from Brix, at least for now, and therefore no real chance of advancing his purposes. At the same time, the promise of a kiss was precisely what he had been desiring since his last dance with Miss Sarah.

She may have begun the evening in a dull state, but she had finished with so much flirtatious charm that there was but one response he thought in the least rational. He made his apologies to Brix and Miss Kittling, and said that he was required to attend to an urgent matter and would return to the assemblies in a few minutes.

"Is everything all right?" Brixham asked, frowning.

Gaventry grinned. "Indeed, perfectly well, thank you."

Brix rolled his eyes and returned his attention to Miss Kittling.

Gaventry set his boots in a westerly direction. He could not keep from smiling. Bath was proving to be a far more enjoyable city to visit than he could have ever thought possible. He knew quite well that Miss Sarah was very suspicious of his attentions toward her sister and that she was playing her own game for the strict purpose of keeping him separated from Aurelia, a game he was more than willing to play. And now a kiss was as good as his.

When he neared the alley, a faint scuffling sound reached his ears. As he turned the corner he could see a lady struggling in the arms of a man. Another burly fellow was sprawled on the pavement, leaning up on his elbow and touching his head gingerly. Gaventry was sprinting in the direction of the fray before the thought had even formed in his head that he was watching another man take the kiss promised to him.

Within two seconds, his hand was grabbing the man's col-

lar as well as the seat of his breeches. A moment more and
Sarah's assailant was tumbling beside his compatriot.

He then slid his arm about her waist to support her lest her
knees give way.

"Oh, thank heavens!" she cried.

"'Ere now, gov,'" the second man drawled, his speech thick.
"We wuz havin' a spot of fun with the wench, is all. Ain't no
'arm in that."

"You have accosted a lady," he returned sternly.

"That ain't no lady!" the man rubbing his head cried.
"More like a cat wif clubs fer claws." He touched his forehead anew, which Gaventry could see, by the light spilling
from the houses nearby, was swollen, split, and seeping with
blood.

"You have accosted my wife," he said, hoping in telling such
a fabrication that the men would take him more seriously.

"Eh?" was the first shocked response.

"Eh?" was the scholarly second one.

"The pair of you had best be gone within a handful of
seconds or I shan't answer for my actions."

Never had two inebriated fellows moved more quickly, although the injured fellow ran at an uneven gait, all the while
moaning. A moment more and Gaventry was left alone with
Miss Sarah.

"And what of you?" he cried, turning to her, holding her
chin at such an angle that the light might catch her face and
reveal injury. No swelling was visible, nor cuts, nor scrapes,
only a warm smile which served to brighten her countenance.

"Did you see what a facer I landed that terrible creature?"
she cried, her eyes sparkling as if with lightning.

Gaventry was stunned. "Indeed, yes, but how the devil did
you manage it?"

She showed him the rock, which was still clutched in her
hand. "I picked it up when I first turned down the alley, having seen these two in particular. Being fairly certain they were

the sort of cretins who would not hesitate to take advantage of a solitary female, I thought to arm myself as best I might."

"As events proved, you were very right to have done so, but you cannot know how relieved I am that you were not hurt, or worse, *far* worse."

"Yes, yes, I know," she returned, "but I beg you will not come the crab for I have not had such fun in ages."

"Fun?" he exclaimed. Once more, he turned her face into the light and examined her. "I begin to think you must have sustained an injury to your head to be speaking in so nonsensical a fashion."

She dropped the rock, and it clattered on the pavement below. "I am perfectly well. Indeed, more than well! I feel as though I could fly!"

He was fully aware of what she was experiencing, the strange euphoria after a successful fight. Something of what she was feeling transferred itself to him and he suddenly grabbed her about the waist, hoisted her into the air, and began whirling her round and round.

Her squeals of pure delight could be heard down the alley and did not cease until a voice from one of the houses called out, begging them to be quiet. Only then did he lower her to the ground. As she slid through the circle of his arms, however, he did not let her go, nor was he surprised that her arms became fastened about his neck in a most obliging manner.

"How happy I am that you have come to me," she whispered against his lips.

He needed no further encouragement and kissed her hard on the mouth. She moaned, leaning in to him, and gave kiss for kiss.

There had been precious few times in Gaventry's life when he had experienced the joy that now sank into his bones. When he had seen Sarah struggling in the arms of another man, he had been certain that her sensibilities would have been so deeply violated by the man's heinous assault that she would have been reduced to tears, hysterics, and possibly a little swooning by the time he reached her. Instead, given the fact that she had rendered one of her assailants helpless with a blow to the head, she had exulted in their joint thwarting of the enemy. Her excitement, even her rapture at vanquishing the drunken fools, had become instantly for him a boundless thrill. He realized, as her kisses became as passionate as his own, that he had never known a lady like Sarah Kittling. She surprised him and pleased him. More often than not, he absolutely delighted in her company. Presently, he wished to devour her completely.

Sarah had never felt so thoroughly alive in her entire existence. This was what she was made for, kissing and doing battle and kissing a little more, not setting stitches in a sampler or playing the pianoforte or experimenting with the use of the watercolors. She leaned in to Gaventry as he kissed her more deeply still, her tongue tasting the soft recesses of his mouth, a sensation that turned all her thoughts to porridge. She could no longer think, only feel, and what she felt was a profound desire to belong to Gaventry as only his wife would, with her heart, her mind, and her body. She wanted the event of the past few minutes to be the usual course of her daily activities and for kissing and other things to be the joy of her evenings. He held her so tightly. She could feel the length of him through the thin silk of her gown. He was well-muscled as all men who loved sport were wont to be. He was all that any woman could desire.

"Gaven," she murmured breathlessly, "take me away."

He kissed her fiercely again, but after a moment drew back. "Where do you wish to go?"

She looked into his eyes. "Paris, Rome, Istanbul, Calcutta, the south China Sea—I do not care!"

A smile touched his lips. "You are ripe for adventure."

"Yes."

He kissed her again and again. Tonight, this was her adventure, the exploration of thoughts never before realized, of desires never before understood, of deep kisses filled with so much promise that tears seeped joyously from her eyes.

"I never understood myself before tonight," she said.

"You are so different," he whispered, his lips trailing kisses over her ear and down her cheek and along her neck.

She ached in her soul, a piercing sensation which she knew would never allow her to continue on her present dull course in Bath. Her chest was tight with a sensation of wonder, hope, and fear all bound together. What if after tonight nothing changed . . . ever? How could she bear it?

She unwrapped her arms from about his neck and slid her hands to rest against his chest. How much of what she was feeling had to do with this man, or had he merely been the force that revealed the truth of her deepest thoughts to herself?

"What thoughts now, Sarah?" he whispered.

She shook her head. She truly did not know what to say. "I only wish that I might hold onto this moment forever."

He kissed her lightly on the lips, a kiss that once more ignited every passionate sensation. So it was that a minute passed and then another and another until the stars began to shift their positions and warn her that her absence from the assemblies would soon be noted.

"We should return," she murmured at last.

He nodded, a frown descending over his face. "Indeed, we should for I greatly fear that were we to remain here very much longer I believe I might behave as badly as our two recent friends were intending to."

She was not so innocent that she did not fully comprehend his meaning. So it was that she took his arm, and together they began walking the gentle ascent to the Assembly Rooms.

Sarah was not surprised that very soon a silence fell between them. Certainly her thoughts required reflection and scrutiny. She had much to ponder, not least of which was the startling realization that her jealousy where Aurelia was concerned reflected nothing but the deepest desires where Gaventry was concerned. What his feelings and thoughts were she could only guess, but she believed it likely he, too, was trying to fully comprehend all that had just happened.

For his part, Gaventry found himself between opposing forces, a place he rarely experienced. On the one hand, part of what had just happened felt reminiscent of younger days when he had been a relative innocent and such sensations were prompting him to cast all caution to the wind, to ignore his experiences of the past several years, and court Sarah in earnest, as was proper. How he longed to recapture such a simpler mode of existence, how he longed to believe that life was full of honor and justice, that a woman could love with purity and dignity.

On the other hand, he was no longer a naive lad still green behind the ears. His youthful ideals had long since vanished. He glanced down at the lady beside him, her face now obscured by the hood of her cloak. He wondered how much he could in truth trust her. After all, she came from a family in which her elder sister had invaded the stuff of his life and written a despicable novel. If this was the sort of character common among the Kittlings, wherein lay Sarah's defect? Was he willing to spend even a portion of the next few days or even weeks in discovering whether she was as unworthy as her sister, merely because a few kisses had prompted him to long for his innocence? To these last ruminations he had but one response—he thought not!

He could only hope that Miss Sarah was not so foolish as to think that a few kisses meant anything of significance.

Sarah sensed the change in Gaventry by the time they had reached Alfred Street, which was hardly any distance at all! She knew that there was an undercurrent of bitterness in his thinking that tended to color all his reflections. So it was when at last they crossed the portals of the Assembly Rooms, having stolen in at an appropriate moment when no one was standing about to note their return and thereby report their absence, she decided to part quickly from him. He bowed formally to her, and she could not help but notice that a familiar wariness had entered his eyes yet again. She suspected he had already set his mind on his former objectives.

She decided therefore to follow after him, discreetly of

course, to see what it was he meant to do next. This, she knew, would determine the precise meaning of the last half hour in his company and what, if anything, she could expect of him of a romantic nature in the future. He went from chamber to chamber until he found Aurelia, who was located in the recesses of the tearoom, laughing at something Mr. Brixham was saying to her. A moment more, and he was leading her sister in the direction of the ballroom.

Sarah's heart sank. The kiss, the extraordinary experience of having vanquished two drunkards together, the gentle exchange of words between them had meant nothing to Gaventry, or so it would seem. His purposes had not changed in the slightest. He meant to do harm to Aurrie no matter how many kisses she allowed him. She began to understand by this just how angry he was that *A Rogue's Tale* had ever been put into print.

She refused, however, to permit these truths to overset her. Gaventry may have had his purposes, but so did she. With that, she waited until the dance had ended and, feigning a severe headache, forced her sister to escort her home. Gaventry, who had watched her performance, wore a curiously knowing smile, which once more caused her to suspect that he had read Mr. Bertram's letter after all and therefore knew that she knew that he believed Aurelia had written the wretched novel.

Just before taking her leave, however, she told Aurelia there was something she needed to ask Lord Gaventry, in private. Her sister nodded. "Yes, of course, speak to him."

She drew near him and whispered, "You shan't succeed with her."

"Oh, but I shall," he whispered in return. "Indeed, I believe I already have."

Since she knew this to be true, she met his gaze directly and stated, "I cannot permit you to hurt her."

"That is not in your power. You ought to have warned her against writing that absurd novel."

Sarah's heart was suddenly beating quite violently in her chest. She felt the strongest impulse to tell him the truth, that Aurelia was not the authoress at all, that she was. However, the words would not rise from what she soon realized was her painfully constricted throat. For the past two years, from the time she had conceived of the notion of writing *A Rogue's Tale*, she had somehow managed to keep the endeavor a complete secret. So long had she protected her identity that she found she could not say what truly needed to be said. Gaventry, of all people, had a right to know precisely to whom he should be expressing his venom and disgust. With Aurelia waiting for her, finally she said, "My lord, would you call on me tomorrow? I wish very much to discuss this matter with you. I have long suspected you knew the truth, but would you please do me this favor and call on me?"

Hesitation was writ in every feature as he stared back at her. She smiled softly, of a sudden. "I would promise another kiss?"

Lightning shot through his eyes, and he laughed suddenly. "Very well. I believe I may never have quite understood you, Miss Sarah."

"Will ten o'clock suit you?"

"Will not your sisters and cousin be at the Pump Room?" She nodded.

"Very well."

"Tomorrow then. Good night." With that, she turned on her heel.

On the following morning, Sarah paced the drawing room. The hour wanted but five minutes. Her sisters and Charlotte had left for the Pump Room a quarter hour past and would not return until after eleven. She doubted her conversation with Gaventry would require that much time. After all, precisely how many minutes would it take to confess the truth to him?

She knew the time had come for telling him that she and not Aurelia was the authoress of *A Rogue's Tale*. She plopped down on the sofa by the window and dropped her head in her hands. How much she was dreading this confession, more than she had ever thought possible. Yet it must be done. Aurelia must be spared. Indeed, the moment she had learned that Gaventry believed her sister to be the authoress, she ought to have addressed the matter. Perhaps it was habit that had kept her silent, or perhaps she had hoped he might just go away and leave her family in peace. Now, however, there was another reason why she so dreaded telling him—his anger at the writing of the novel would now be directed solely at her. Whatever small hope she might have been harboring that love could blossom between them would very soon come to an end.

"I am very late," Gaventry stated. He stood before his godmother, who had called unexpectedly at his town house, insisting on speaking with him.

"You will be later still if you do not listen to me."

"There can be nothing you wish to tell me of the Kittling ladies that can interest me overly much. I have been in their company nearly three weeks now and I believe I have an excellent comprehension of each of the ladies, their virtues and flaws combined."

Lady Haslingfield compressed her lips and her large bosom rose and fell in nothing short of an irritated sigh. She had already taken up a seat near the window. "Sit down, Gaven!" she commanded.

He ground his teeth, but remained where he stood.

She narrowed her eyes, but began again, only in softer tones. "I beg you will sit down and hear what it is I have to say. I know you think me a ridiculously interfering goat of a female, but I truly have your very best interests at heart. I would not be here did I not think that Miss Sarah would make an excellent match for you."

He had begun to think so himself of late, but thus far had succeeded in repressing such impossible thoughts. He had long since given up even the smallest hope that love could ever be real and lasting. He also had no intention of aligning himself with a lady whose sister had written a story based on his life. However, he could not help but smile. "A goat of a female?"

She smiled as well. "You see—I can read your thoughts exactly."

With that, he seated himself, flipping back the tails of his coat and removing his hat, for he had, indeed, been ready to leave his house just when she was announced. "So, tell me what it is you have to say, but I hope you do not have expectations of altering my rather fixed opinions on this subject."

"As fixed as having disappeared with her from the assemblies last night? My dear friend Mrs. Catesby saw you strolling with a hooded lady while refreshments were being served. Upon waiting to see who the lady was, she expressed great shock that it was Miss Sarah Kittling. What possessed either of you to leave the assemblies as you did?"

He decided to be quite frank with her. "An assignation, of course. I see I have shocked you, but it was her notion, not mine. Once the invitation was proffered, however, I found I could not refuse."

An arrested expression took hold of her face. "You are serious, then?"

"Quite."

She spoke more to herself when she said, "I wonder what would have driven her to such a course of action." She lifted her gaze to him. "Why did she do so? She was never so careless of propriety before your arrival. What do you make of it?"

"She wished me to leave the assembly for a time undoubtedly."

"But why? It makes no sense at all. What are you not telling me?"

"I believe you should pose that question to Miss Sarah. I am convinced she has the answer for you."

"Does it have anything, perchance, to do with her silly novel?"

"*Her* silly novel?" he queried, wondering if he had heard her correctly.

"Yes, for if you must know, she is the authoress of *A Rogue's Tale*."

Gaventry felt as though a sudden strong wind had just slammed into his face and chest. Of course it was true, it had to be true. Sarah had already confessed to being a playwright, and her sister Aurelia could scarcely converse in more than two or three sentences at a time. She could hardly have written so many paragraphs, one after the other. He had questioned it from the first. But Sarah! *His* Sarah?

"Now I see that *I* have given *you* a shock. Surely you knew or suspected. Why else then did you come to Bath but to exact some sort of punishment on the author?"

"I was told by her publisher that Miss Aurelia Kittling was the author, not Miss Sarah."

"Oh," she responded, chuckling slightly. "Well if that does not muddy the waters, I do not know what would. But how amusing. So all this time, when I have seen you dangling after Aurelia, it was because you thought her the authoress! Charming! Utterly charming."

"There is nothing *charming* about any of it, Godmother."

"Oh, do come off your high ropes, Gaven. You are never so unattractive as when you are gazing down at the rest of us from the cross of your wounded pride."

"When I am what?" he cried.

"You heard me distinctly," she returned impatiently. "Only tell me what you mean to do."

With that, he knew he had had quite a sufficient dose of her impertinent meddling. He rose to his feet, smoothed his hat with his gloved hand, and settled it on his head. "I intend to keep my promise to call on Miss Sarah at this hour. I am already late, so I beg you will forgive me, but I must go . . . now."

She rose, albeit reluctantly, and walked on her firm tread to the door. "Don't be a fool, Gaven. Life is very, very short. You have already wasted seven years of the time allotted you and all because of that stupid, beastly Fulbourne chit. Try not to waste any more by punishing a perfectly amiable, respectable girl because of it."

"Amiable?" he cried, following her from the house. "Respectable?"

"Pray lower your voice. Do you wish your neighbors to hear us squabbling on the drive?"

"I do not give a fig for the neighbors."

"Walk me to the corner, then. I am returning home and we can part at the top of the street. You may, therefore, at your leisure, give me the dressing down which I can see writ in every feature, godson. Only lower your voice, if you please!"

He ground his teeth anew. Lady Haslingfield was by far one of the most trying creatures of his acquaintance. "I only wish to know how you can ascribe even the smallest virtue to Miss Sarah, when she has taken a mountain of gossip, shaped a story around it, agreed to have it published, earned profits from it, and all at my expense."

"What of her expense?"

"What the deuce do you mean?"

"Have you any notion what her sufferings have been and why a lady, whom I know you to admire excessively, would be so lowered in situation as to be driven to concoct that story in the first place? Have you never asked yourself that question?"

"I do not think it matters, not one whit."

"That is because you were born a man of substance. What do you have? Eight thousand a year?"

"Ten, but that is immaterial."

"Spoken like someone who has never been deprived of a thing. I know what it is to have nothing. When Haslingfield offered for me, my family was impoverished gentry stock and not a day has gone by that I have not thanked the heavens for this good fortune of being free of such worldly worries and fears as to wonder where the next tuppence would come from to pay the butcher or the grocer, the chandler, or the farm wife. I suppose most people have to experience these things to really understand them, but I thought you at least had more sense. You know, Gaven, perhaps I am wrong after all. From the beginning, I blamed Miss Fulbourne for having ruined you but now it occurs to me that you always were a trifle spoilt, thinking you could have what you wanted when it pleased you. I daresay you were never given the cut direct and exiled from society as you have led everyone to believe! No. I think you have been throwing a rather violent tantrum for seven years and that is why you have been unwelcome in London's drawing rooms for that same length of time."

Gaventry seethed. Had his godmother been a man, so help him he would have planted her a leveler. "You go too far," he muttered.

"High time, I believe, that someone did. Good day." She did not look at him, but continued down Brock Street, which led to her town house in the Circus.

He turned quickly away, heading in the direction of the Gravel Walks. He was grateful they had parted company when they had, for he feared he would have said a great many truly dreadful things to her had he remained beside her even a second longer. He lengthened his stride. So, Sarah was the authoress after all and she had allowed him these many days and more, since receiving her letter from Mr. Bertram, to keep him uninformed as to the truth of her identity. Well, well, it would seem her day of reckoning had come. One thing he knew for certain, this was one meeting with Sarah Kittling that would not end in a kiss!

# Nine

Sarah saw Gaventry approaching from across Queen Square. He was late, but walked quickly, as though atoning for his tardiness. His gaze was fixed on the stone path in front of him, but she could see a sufficient portion of his expression to determine that he was more solemn than she had ever before known him to be.

*He knows.*

Something akin to relief and fear, plaited together, ran through her. She would not have to speak a word of her transgression, he would give her a dressing down the moment he entered the chamber. The closer he drew to her town house, therefore, the more she found she was able to relax, and instead of fretting over what might happen next, she was able merely to look at him.

She understood clearly that the flirtation that had been an ongoing delight for the past three weeks was now at an end. Perhaps it was for that reason that she felt able to allow herself to feel quite fully the rather startling depths of her sentiments for the man whose life she had put into print. She doubted she would ever see him in any setting without feeling, just as she did now, that the world looked different to her the moment he came into view.

When he crossed the street, she decided she would not stand on even the smallest ceremony with him, not when the dreaded moment had come. She left her place on the sofa and hurried to the front door, which she opened. He had just arrived at the end of the walk and paused to look up at her. She smiled, but though he met her gaze firmly, he did not smile in return, nor had she expected him to.

As he drew close, she knew a sudden desire to give him the already promised kiss, for she was certain there would be no such tender embrace later, and so in full view of whoever might chance to pass by, she took his lapels in hand and pressed her lips fully to his. But only for a brief second or two.

"That will not happen again," he said.

"I have every certainty, my lord," she began somberly, though a smile which she knew must have appeared wicked played on her lips, "that it shall not, which was perhaps why I kissed you in the first place."

He scowled at her as he passed into the entrance hall.

"I trust you will forgive the informality," she said, taking his hat and allowing him a moment to remove his gloves and toss them into the well, "but I saw you coming and thought it would be best not to disturb the servants."

"Indeed?" he retorted sharply.

"Allow me to ask you this—who told you?"

His expression of anger and distrust deepened. "My godmother."

She moved into the drawing room and once more seated herself on the sofa, but this time she drew her legs up beneath her. She watched him take a seat across from her, his countenance unyielding. A hunger took hold of her heart, deep and painful, a longing to return to last night when suddenly the world had held every possibility. How strange to think that scarcely little more than twelve hours had passed before such hoped-for possibilities had diminished again to nothing. "Your godmother always seems happiest when she is being of service. I ought to thank her, really, though I was never quite certain if she knew the truth."

"Why would you thank her?" he asked, the handsome lines of his face appearing as though sculpted in stone.

"You have known me well over these past several weeks. Cannot you guess?"

"I am not inclined to play at games this morning."

"No, I imagine you would not be so I shall tell you. From the moment I first set pen to paper—no, that would not be entirely accurate, for I did take pleasure initially in the thought of conjuring up a great deal of idiocy in the form of a novel. But after a few days, I began to think of you, though I had never of course met you. I wondered how you would feel having had a story written of much of the gossip told about you. I began to believe that you would not like it and as events have proved, you did not. I daresay there has not been a day since those first few innocent ones in which I have not regretted the writing of *A Rogue's Tale*. Do you recall the first day we met and you approached me in Queen Square?"

He nodded.

"I was suffering from an attack of conscience even then. I remember it distinctly for I thought nothing could have been more astounding than that I had just been kissed, and that so wondrously, by the very man I had betrayed and who had just been dominating my thoughts. Really, it was quite extraordinary."

Gaventry stared hard at the female curled up on the sofa before him, and all he could think was, *I wish she had not kissed me.*

He had been shocked that she had done so and that in full view of anyone who had chanced by at that moment. She was a strange and unusual creature. And she was tucked up on the sofa as though they had been friends for years and had never allowed propriety or ceremony to disturb their comfort.

*I wish she had not kissed me.*

What he had thought was going to be a simple matter—a severe dressing down, a promise to take his revenge in whatever manner appealed to him, a boxing of her ears, and anything else that might occur to him when he saw her—now seemed quite complicated. He had not expected a confession, not like this, not in so easy a manner that she might as well have been buttering her bread as admitting to so grievous an affront to his dignity and pride.

"How did you dare?" he asked at last.

She sighed deeply. "I only dared because our family was in such a fix. My uncle, who had command of our annuity, quite foolishly tried to enlarge it on the Exchange. He lost everything of ours and a great portion of his. My sisters and I have little family left to us and therefore no one who could offer us even the smallest assistance. I refused to tell either Aurelia or Meg of our troubles, nor Charlotte, for they would certainly have offered to take up some form of employment to resolve our troubles and that I could not allow. I was, I am, still hopeful that at least Aurelia might make a suitable match.

"Regardless," she continued, "I do not know precisely how it happened, but gossip about you had been rife for so long that I thought, I hoped, it would serve as a basis for a novel that might just sustain us in Bath a little longer, long enough to see one or the other of my sisters wed. Or even my cousin, Charlotte, should love chance upon her again. However, a twelve-month has passed and we are as we have ever been, a rather love-forsaken lot, I fear." She smiled, but it was a very sad smile at best.

He recalled Lady Haslingfield's admonition to mind. *I suppose most people have to live these things to really understand them, but I thought you at least had more sense.* However, he refused to allow this to be even the smallest justification. "I can appreciate your difficulty, Miss Sarah, but I think your means of saving your family at my expense quite abominable."

"Then we are of a mind," she returned. She was silent for a long moment, then said, "You may read me the Riot Act, my lord, or anything else you might desire. I would only ask that you would give up your pursuit of Aurrie since she is a complete innocent. Indeed, none of my family knows of my authorship. Will you do at least that much? You may take your revenge on me in whatever manner you think fitting, but please, I beg you, spare my sister."

He narrowed his eyes, watching her carefully. He could think of several quite satisfying manners in which he might avenge himself. He had known her but a few weeks, yet during that time he felt certain he had come to know her quite well. It would be simple enough to switch from one sister to the other, to exact the proper form of punishment on Miss Sarah rather than on her elder sister. However, another deeper, more gratifying retribution made itself known to his mind. He crossed his arms over his chest. "So, I may take my revenge on you in whatever manner I desire."

"I have said so." He watched a blush steal up her cheeks, and he understood that her thoughts were hardly maidenly in nature.

He laughed. "You intrigue me. However, I believe I shall hold to my original design. It does not matter to me which of the Kittling sisters suffers now and if she is wounded, it appears I would cause you injury as well. Indeed, I believe you have made the task even more satisfying than I previously believed it could be."

At that, she leaped from the sofa. "Oh, but you cannot!" she cried. "You do not know how cruel you would be using Aurelia, particularly when—" She broke off.

He rose to his feet as well. He saw no need to prolong the interview. "Particularly when what?" he asked, but a suspicion darted into his head. "She is in love with me."

Her sudden expression of dismay gave him the answer he sought.

"She told you as much?" he asked, wanting to understand her response perfectly.

Sarah nodded.

"Well, well. I did not expect to be made happy this morning, but so I have been."

She crossed the distance between them swiftly and once more took hold of his lapels. "Do not do this thing, Gaventry, I beg of you! What can you really gain by doing harm to someone so sweet, so pure, so completely innocent? 'Tis I who have given offense, your punishment should be directed at me!"

The tears in her eyes gave him pause, but only for a moment. He had for so long been the brunt of society's harsh, hypocritical censure that he quickly and quite easily hardened his heart against the lady clutching at his coat so tightly. He took her hands in his, meaning to disengage her, but the moment he touched her and once more looked into her dewy brown eyes, another sensation overcame him entirely. This was the lady he had kissed, what was it, oh, yes, three times now. Three extraordinary occasions which he believed would be burned forever into his memory.

He had kissed a great number of women, but what was it about this one, who had used him so ill, that always seemed to set his senses reeling? Even now, as angry and bitter as he was, his fingers began to move over hers and a familiar sensation of passion began to rise within him. He should release her. Nothing good could come of doing what was suddenly in his mind to do. He realized the lady leaning into him was trembling, almost violently.

"Kiss me, Gaven, one last time," she whispered, lifting her face to his and tilting her head just so. At the same time, her fingers slid from his grasp and up his chest.

He should spurn such an outrageous advance. He should take her shoulders, give her a hard shake, and cast her aside. He should . . .

Sarah felt the change in him occur so abruptly that for a fraction of a second she was certain he meant to do her some manner of harm. Instead, however, his arms surrounded her in a grip so fierce she could not draw breath, and his eyes blazed with a myriad of thoughts. His bitterness was clear, but there was something more. The next moment, his lips were on hers, demanding punishment for her wickedness, bruising her sorely yet igniting within her so savage a need that instead of recoiling, she slipped her hands and then her arms fully about his neck. There was nothing that could be considered maidenly about the kiss that ensued, yet nothing she believed she would ever regret. She understood at last just how deeply, how fully, she had tumbled in love with the man set on destroying her family. She belonged to him with every part of her soul. How had this happened, and that so quickly, so thoroughly, as to overturn her life completely? Regardless, and no matter what happened next, she was changed, now and forever.

"What do you mean?" Aurelia asked, a distressed frown between her brows. "Are you telling us that you are the lady who wrote *A Rogue's Tale*?"

"Yes."

Meg stared at her. She did not appear in the least sad as Aurrie did. Rather, she had set her chin at a familiar mulish angle, and her lips were clamped shut. She would not meet Sarah's gaze and she was tapping a foot quite firmly, her arms crossed over her chest. "How is this possible?" Meg cried at last. "You never breathed a word of it, this year and more! And I! Not to know! It is . . . it is most *lowering*!"

Sarah would have laughed at Meg's response had she not felt so downhearted. "So, you do not mind that I am the authoress only that you did not know of it?"

"Precisely!" she exclaimed in clipped accents.

Charlotte's thoughts were less clear. Her gaze was fixed out the window. Finally, she queried, "Why did you wait until now to tell us? Why did you tell us at all? And is this really how we have been living this past twelve-month?"

Sarah drew in a deep breath and told them of their uncle's misdeeds. He was also Charlotte's uncle, so she was allowed to be as incensed as both Aurelia and Meggie.

"But I do not understand," Meg cried, uncrossing her arms and sliding to the edge of her chair. "Are you saying that you have borne this misfortune all by yourself these two years past?"

Sarah nodded. "It seemed the only practical measure to

take," she explained. "Had I told all of you about the reversal of our fortunes, what do you think would have ensued? We would all have been forced to take up some manner of employment as governesses, perhaps, or as companions, and before the cat could lick her ear we would be cast to the four corners of England without the smallest ability to protest."

"But you did not even give us a chance," Meg complained. "I think it very badly done, very badly, indeed!"

Aurrie's eyes filled with tears. "I wish that I could feel as Meg does," she whispered, "but I could never have been a governess for I do not understand things as I ought and I should have despised being a companion like poor"—she sniffed—"poor, poor Miss Whittle!"

A silence fell over the chamber. Sarah thought of Miss Whittle's birdlike countenance and nervous demeanor. As companion to Lady Haslingfield, she was often referred to as "her ladyship's broom."

At the mention of Miss Whittle, even Meg's outrage at not having been consulted diminished visibly. She once more sat back in her seat.

Charlotte, having a few more years of living within the scope of her experience, was more prosaic. "Undoubtedly, you were right, and I for one would not have liked to have been separated from any of you for even though I am but a cousin, I do think of you as my sisters."

The ladies assured her that her sentiments were reciprocated completely, after which Charlotte asked again, "But why now, Sally? Why do you tell us now?"

"Because of Gaventry." Here she looked at Aurelia, who was dabbing at her eyes with a lace kerchief. She seemed not to hear her, or was uninterested or perhaps did not understand that there might be a hidden meaning.

"Does he know?" Meg asked, her eyes widening with shock.

"Know what?" Aurelia asked, sniffing again.

Meg rolled her eyes. "That Sally wrote that book about him."

"Oh," Aurelia murmured. "Yes, does he, Sally?"

Sarah nodded. "It would seem he has known since before he arrived in Bath. You see, he wrote to my publisher and demanded, on threat of legal recourse, to know who the authoress of *A Rogue's Tale* was."

"And he told him, without consulting you?" Charlotte asked, clearly shocked.

Sarah nodded. "I believe he feared Gaventry's influence."

"As well he might, I suppose," Charlotte said.

The drawing room was silent for a very long time. What her sisters' and cousin's thoughts might be she was not certain, but for herself she was trying to determine whether or not she should tell them of Gaventry's true intention of doing some manner of harm to Aurrie. After a moment, she rather thought she would be unwise to confide in volatile Meg, who was just as likely to confront Gaventry as not, and as for Aurelia, she did not see in what possible manner it would benefit her to be told that the man she loved was intent on injuring her. No, the only person she dared confide in was Charlotte.

After nuncheon, Sarah took Charlotte to the park in the center of Queen Square, ostensibly to enjoy the fine spring weather, but once they were alone she immediately explained her purposes. "For I most expressly wished to lay my, that is *our*, true difficulty before you."

"Then you did not tell us all," she responded quietly. "I feared as much. You appeared a great deal more distressed afterward and kept biting your lip."

"Was I doing so? I cannot recall but then I am not in the least surprised. It is worse, much worse than my sisters can know." Since she felt quite oddly as though she would very soon become a watering pot, she drew in a deep breath before continuing.

"Gaventry means to hurt Aurelia and I believe he intends to do more than just break her heart."

"I do not understand. Why is he intent on hurting Aurelia?"

Sarah felt reluctant to confide the complete truth in Charlotte

just yet. She therefore stated a portion of it. "Because he knows
it is the surest way of breaking my heart and that is something,
I promise you, he is intent on doing."

"Because you wrote the novel."

"Precisely."

Charlotte frowned and shook her head as they strolled in
the direction of Gay Street. To the right, one of Mrs. Catesby's
serving maids was scolding her mistress's pug dog, who was
in turn growling at her. There were several persons about, either sitting on benches or conversing in small groups. For that
reason, Sarah worked at keeping her expression disinterested.

Charlotte queried, "And he means to do harm to Aurelia
by winning her affections and then what? I must say, I do
not understand what he hopes to achieve."

"I suspect he believes it will be a very great punishment to
cause her to fall in love with him, which as you know he already has, perhaps even woo her to the altar, then refuse to
marry her.

Charlotte was very quiet and when Sarah glanced at her
there was an odd little smile on her lips. "Do you doubt what
I am saying?"

"It is not so much that I doubt you, Sally, but rather that I
think you may be confused on one or two points."

Since they passed by a neighbor, Sarah smiled politely and
inclined her head. She sighed. "I wish I were, truly I do. But
Aurrie confessed she was in love with him. I spoke with her
at length and there could be no doubt of her affection for him,
indeed, of her love. She appeared more than smitten, completely and utterly attached."

At that, Charlotte stopped her midstride by taking hold of
her elbow. She turned to face her. "And again I would ask
you, are you certain she was referring to Gaventry?"

"Of course. He was the only gentleman we were discussing
at the time. I recall it most particularly. Charlotte, is there
something you know but are not telling me?"

"Actually, there is, but now is not the time. I feel it much more important that we discuss our present difficulty regarding Lord Gaventry. There is one point I wish you would clarify for me. If Gaventry knew you were the authoress of *A Rogue's Tale* from the first, why then did he make Aurelia his object when he came to Bath? That makes no sense to me."

Sarah sighed. "Because he believed she was the authoress." She then explained that even her publisher thought as much and that she had made such an arrangement in order to keep the funds coming to the same bank, under Aurelia's name as they always had. "My whole purpose was to keep my identity a secret."

Charlotte regarded her in a very penetrating manner as they continued to walk the circumference of the small square. "I think I understand. So you told Mr. Bertram you were Aurelia for legal purposes, so that any monies you received were in her name, which were then sent directly to the bank."

"Just so," she said. "As long as the household monies were managed in Aurrie's name then no one would question the source of the income. Do you see? If Uncle's money had stopped and I had suddenly begun receiving an income I would have had to explain a great many things. Everything was managed at the bank."

"Very clever, Sally, I must say. No wonder you were able to keep this business a secret for so long. And our uncle never questioned our continuing on in Bath?"

At that, Sarah smiled. "He was so deeply ashamed at having lost our annuity that he accepted readily my excuse that I had been for years setting aside a significant portion of our quarterly allowance as a safeguard against future troubles and that we would be able to continue on in Bath indefinitely."

"And he believed you?" Charlotte asked, stunned.

Sarah found even she could smile in this moment. "I daresay for our sakes he wanted to believe me."

"Good God. I begin to think I have never known you. I applaud both your discretion and ability to dissemble."

"Now you are being facetious. I suppose I ought to be

relieved that the truth is come out, but there is more, something so dreadful I truly fear to speak the words aloud. No one knows of this but Mr. Bertram."

"Oh dear," Charlotte murmured. "Sally, here is Mrs. Catesby. Pray do not look so somber or she will report it to Lady Haslingfield."

As Mrs. Catesby approached, Sarah purposefully brightened her countenance. "How do you do, ma'am? What a pretty bonnet. Is it new?"

"Quite new," Mrs. Catesby cried. "Do you like it, indeed? Lucretia thought it was too young for me."

Charlotte shook her head. "Not in the least. I daresay Lady Haslingfield was jealous that you found it first."

At that, Mrs. Catesby trilled her laughter. "I believe you may be very right." Her gaze drifted past them. "Oh, there is my useless maid scolding Pug again. I do beg your pardon, but I must attend to my little dog before that dreadful creature begins beating him again."

"Of course," Charlotte said.

"Good day," Sarah offered. Mrs. Catesby hurried away.

"Now, quickly, Sally, before we are interrupted again. What is your terrible news?"

"Only that I have written a sequel and copies of the novel are due to arrive at our local bookseller's any day now. Gaventry knows nothing of it and I greatly fear that whatever anger he may be experiencing now will swell tenfold and then we will be in the basket."

At that, Sarah could see that Charlotte was staring at her. "May I ask precisely when you wrote either of these novels?"

"In odd bits of time when the house was asleep. I kept the pages in my old trunk, the one in the bottom of the wardrobe. When I was ready to send it to London, I waited until you had all gone to the Pump Room."

Charlotte smiled and nodded. "That would explain the increase in the chandler's bill. Cook complained more than once to me that she thought one of the maids was stealing candles."

"How well I know it. Of course, eventually I confessed that I was often up late at night, unable to sleep, and was using them myself. I do not think she ever quite believed me. Candles, however, have been one of my greater expenses, that and paper and ink."

"So you are a master of words," she mused. "Really, it is most astonishing and quite wonderful. I cannot tell you how much I enjoyed reading *A Rogue's Tale*. I only wish that we might be able to boast of your accomplishments, for I am quite proud of you, regardless of the subject of the story. Add to that, that your efforts have kept us out of dun territory, truly I am grateful to you."

At that, Sarah, who had always thought so meanly of her efforts, said, "Dear Charlotte, how you have warmed my heart. The guilt I have endured is beyond expression, but to have you compliment me so sincerely and offer such gratitude truly makes me feel that whatever I have suffered has been worthwhile after all."

At that, Charlotte took her arm. "My dear Sally, you have saved us all these months and many more to come. You have made our lives possible. How could I be anything other than deeply grateful, which I am. There is only one question I would put to you at this point and I hope you will not think it too probing or invasive."

"I cannot imagine what you intend to ask that could be either of these things. Pray, what do you wish to know?"

"Only this, are you in love with Lord Gaventry?"

The question stopped Sarah's heart for a beat or two. She had not been prepared for it, thinking that Charlotte meant to ask her something about her latest story. So it was that a feeling of acute anguish suddenly swept over her at the knowledge that she had already lost what she had not even possessed. The knowledge that her sister was also in love with him only added to her sense of desolation. "More than I can say," she murmured, her throat aching.

Charlotte nudged her. "Do turn your parasol to cover your

face, for I can see Lady Riseley coming from your direction and if I am not mistaken, dearest, you appear ready to weep."

"I am," she whispered, lifting and angling her parasol to keep her face from being seen by another of Lady Haslingfield's friends.

"Oh dear," Charlotte murmured, tucking her arm about Sarah's. "I knew you had formed a *tendre* for him, but I had no notion that your sentiments had deepened so completely. How long have you felt this way?"

"From the first, I vow it is so. When he kissed me, then kissed me again and again."

"Sarah Kittling!" Charlotte cried, clearly shocked. "How many times has he taken liberties with you?"

"Four," she murmured in a small voice.

"Oh, my dear Sally," Charlotte murmured.

There was such sympathy in her voice that Sarah could barely restrain the tears that rose to her eyes. "Not that it matters, not in the least, for he could never love me, not when I am the authoress of *A Rogue's Tale*. Only what is to be done to protect Aurelia?"

"And you truly believe her to be in jeopardy?"

"Of course. Have I not said so? Have I not revealed to you that she is in love with him? How much more vulnerable can a lady be, I ask you?"

Charlotte regarded her kindly. "Not one whit, of that I am certain. I remember what it was to be in love. I know that you are aware of my exceeding dislike of horses, so only imagine how much I was in love with Captain Mears that I would have married a gentleman belonging to a cavalry regiment."

"It would seem we share this in common—we both fell in love with men for whom it was an irony to be in love."

"Such great ironies. There is the stuff of a real novel." She chuckled.

"I am not amused, not in the least."

Charlotte patted her arm. "So let me see if I understand you. You are in love with Gaventry, he may or may not be in

love with Aurelia, you are persuaded he could never be in
love with you since he now knows you wrote *A Rogue's Tale,*
and you are convinced he means to hurt Aurelia because he
initially believed that she was the authoress."

"Yes, you have the right of it."

"This is all very complicated," Charlotte said. They had
reached the far side of the square, and her cousin stopped and
faced the house. A curious frown descended over her brow.

"What do you think we should do?" Sarah asked.

"I . . . I cannot say. I suppose I would like to ponder the
situation before offering advice, only, Sally, is that not
Gaventry's curricle?"

She turned slightly and regarded their town house. "Yes, I
believe it is." At that moment, he appeared in the doorway
with Aurelia, who in turn was carrying a bandbox.

"Oh, no!" Sarah cried, and immediately began running
across the square. To little avail, for by the time she had
reached the street, Gaventry was drawing his team away from
the curb.

"Wish me well," Aurrie cried, waving to her gaily, "for I am
to be married!"

Sarah was completely and utterly aghast. "No!" she cried
out. "Gaventry, do not do this wicked thing!"

Gaventry ignored her completely, but there was a thoroughly
satisfied smile on his lips.

"Aurelia, come back! Come back! You do not know what
you are doing?"

She was weeping by the time Charlotte reached her, which
was at the same moment that the curricle left the square.

"Oh, Charlotte, what are we to do? If only we had an
elder brother who could give chase and see that her honor
was protected!"

"We may not have such a man living in our home but I
know of one who will, I believe, not only desire to help us but
who will know precisely what Gaventry means to do with
your sister."

At that, Sarah dried her tears. "Brixham!" she cried. "Yes, of course, and he was always so kind to us, even to Aurelia. He will want to help us."

"Of that I am utterly convinced!"

Fifteen minutes later, after a brisk walk to the Royal Crescent, Sarah watched as Brixham paled ominously. She had just told him of the abduction but was a little surprised that the man before her was so obviously overset by it. She had expected concern, even a certain shock at having learned that his friend could be so very bad, but not this! Mr. Brixham had turned as white as chalk and appeared ready to swoon. She was not surprised when he dropped into a chair and gasped several times for air.

Charlotte hurried forward and actually placed her vial of smelling salts beneath his nose. "I do apologize, Mr. Brixham. I should perhaps have warned my cousin that you are in love with Aurelia. I daresay had she known she would have been gentler in her recounting of what happened."

Mr. Brixham took the salts and shook his head. "I knew Gaven was intent on hurting my dear Aurelia, and I had meant to tell him that our hearts were given to one another but—"

"Oh, Mr. Brixham, you are mistaken," Sarah said, kneeling before him. "You are quite wrong, I fear. I do not mean to hurt you further, but I must remind you that Aurelia told me she was in love with Lord Gaventry."

"You said as much at the assemblies but 'tis you I fear who is laboring under a misapprehension. I knew of your error last night when you asked me to escort Aurelia in to refreshments. Perhaps I should have corrected you then, but I did not feel at liberty to do so. Aurelia and I are betrothed."

Sarah frowned, sitting back on her heels. "But she told me most particularly that she was in love with Gaventry. I had been fretting over Gaventry's conduct as I told you, knowing that he meant to hurt my sister, and so I went to speak with her. That is when she told me that she was in love with him."

"But did she actually speak his name?" Mr. Brixham asked, taking another whiff of the pungent odor and wincing at the sharpness of the smell. "As I recall, you said she did not."

Sarah thought very hard about her conversation with Aurelia but could not recall her having used Gaventry's name. "I remember her saying that he was wonderful and attentive, always seeing to her comfort and that he was quite easy to converse with. I believe that would describe to perfection her relationship with Gaventry."

"And me," he said softly.

Sarah stared hard at him, and finally enlightenment dawned. "Yes, of course! And you! I see it now! Good heavens, how very blind I was thinking that she meant Gaventry when she was always disappearing with you at least nearly as often as she was with Gaventry." She turned suddenly to Charlotte. "And you knew last night! That was why you laughed so heartily."

Charlotte smiled, if falteringly. "Yes. That is why I was laughing, only I am not laughing now."

Sarah reverted her attention to Mr. Brixham. "So she is in love with you and you are absolutely certain of it? You are truly betrothed?"

Mr. Brixham nodded.

"Oh, but this is wonderful!" she cried, but her spirits immediately fell. "And horrible! Mr. Brixham, I believe I made everything worse! I was so convinced she was in love with him that I told Gaventry as much, which was why I believe he felt so confident in abducting her as he just has. Only, how did he persuade her to go with him?"

Mr. Brixham gave the vial back to Charlotte and rose from the chair. "Your dear sister is a very trusting creature and I believe it possible she misunderstood his intentions."

"But she said she was leaving to be married! She shouted

as much to me when Gaventry was giving his horses the office to start!"

He took her hand. "Miss Sarah, your sister and I are betrothed. I think it possible Aurelia misunderstood what Gaventry was about, perhaps thinking when he spoke of an elopement, or whatever words he used with her, she thought he was referring to me. You know how easily she becomes confused."

Tears filled her eyes. "Yes, I do, which is what makes it all so very bad of Gaventry. She is so innocent, good and kind, but she will not know that he is intent on hurting her!"

"We will follow after them. Never fear! I know my friend. He will reconsider his actions at some point and we will meet them on the road as they are heading back to Bath. Mark my words! All will be well!"

Several hours later, well into Gloucestershire and nearing the Shropshire border, Gaventry stared at the simpleton beside him. "What the deuce do you mean?"

Aurelia Kittling chewed on her lip a little more. "I mean, where is Mr. Brixham? Why is he not here? I thought we were to be married. Is he perhaps following in his Stanhope?" She then lowered the window of the post-chaise and stuck her head out, trying to see behind the coach. Evening was settling heavily in the west country. "All I see is a cloud of dust. I wish these roads were paved as Bath is."

"Oh, dear God, what have I done," he murmured. Tugging on Miss Kittling's wool pelisse, he drew her back into the coach. "Now you must tell me about Brix, that is, Mr. Brixham. Why did you think you were wedding him and not me?"

"Well, for one thing," she responded, appearing quite pensive, "I do not love you, but Sally does. Why do you not ask her to marry you if you wish to wed someone? For I believe she is in love with you although she pretends she is not, which leads me to say that she feels very badly about having written that novel about you. Were you not quite vexed with her?"

"Exceedingly so."

"It is no wonder," she said. "I daresay you are the sort of man who would never like to have his life put into the pages of a book, would you?"

"Certainly not, only we have wandered from the point. Tell me of Mr. Brixham."

"I love him," she stated simply. "But you must know that if you asked me to elope with him."

"But I did not," he countered. "I asked if you would enjoy eloping with a gentleman who thought you an angel."

"Well, yes, but that would be Mr. Brixham, would it not, since he is forever telling me that I am an angel, *his* angel?"

This much was true, Gaventry thought with dismay. How many times had he heard Brix refer to Miss Kittling as an angel. No wonder she had packed her bandbox with such speed and had jumped into his curricle as though she had been waiting to do so her entire life.

An unhappy thought occurred to him. "Miss Kittling, I would ask you a question. Are you perchance *betrothed* to Mr. Brixham?"

"Why, yes, of course? I should not have agreed to go with you otherwise. What did you think?"

Gaventry groaned and wondered just how soon he might return to Bath and whether or not he could avert what would quickly become a dreadful scandal once returned. At the next posting inn, therefore, he gave instructions to the postboy that they would be returning forthwith to Bath, then settled into a surprisingly fine dinner of boiled chicken, peas, fresh bread, and a fine spice cake served with the landlady's homemade currant wine. Since he had already told Miss Kittling a very fine whisker about Brixham obviously having become confused about their plans, and that they were returning to Bath, Miss Kittling relaxed and became a rather delightful dinner partner. What she lacked in intelligence, she made up for in cheerfulness, kindness, and charm. She spoke to everyone in the dining room and held an irritable baby on her lap, who soon calmed down under her gentle coaxing.

So it was that, an hour or so later after he had just assisted her in climbing aboard the post chaise, a hand grabbed him at the shoulder and pulled him backward. A fist swung at his face, but because he was a student of Jackson's in London, he ducked, the body careened into him, he threw his now-stumbling assailant backward and with a hard right leveled him to the gravel drive at his feet.

"Gaven, what are you doing?" Sarah Kittling called to him from a nearby coach. "I hope you have not just killed Mr. Brixham!"

# Ten

Gaventry peered at the prostrate form of a man, scarcely recognizable in the darkening gloom of the May evening, until he finally realized that he had indeed struck down his dearest friend, Mr. Brixham.

"What a monster you are!" Sarah cried as she descended the coach and crossed to him. "Why could you not restrain yourself even a little?"

He stared at her in some shock. "He attacked me from behind," he offered by way of explanation. "And if you have not noticed, it is very dark here in the courtyard. How was I to know?"

Aurelia, who had climbed down from her coach, was kneeling beside her beloved. "Mr. Brixham, oh, my darling, please wake up." A groan was the only response.

"Come, we must get him inside," Sarah said. "I shall fetch a manservant."

"It won't be necessary," Gaventry said. He reached down and pulling Brix up by the arm, slung him over his shoulder and within a few seconds was laying him down on a padded bench in a private parlor.

A moment more, and Brixham's eyes fluttered open. "Is that you, Gaven? Good God, you have a fist like a sledgehammer." He touched his jaw gingerly with his fingers, then scowled. "And what the deuce were you doing eloping with my betrothed anyway?"

"I did not know you were engaged to Miss Kittling," he

said. "Which leads me to say you have been very sly with me all the while you knew what I was about. Why did you say nothing? Why did you not at least give me a hint?"

"I was going to, as soon as you returned from your drive and if you will remember, just before you left I said I had something of great import to discuss with you. How was I to know you were intent on abducting Miss Kittling even then?" He groaned again and once more felt his now-swelling jaw. "Damme, if I will not be sore for weeks, see if I won't."

"Sarah," Miss Kittling murmured, "what did Mr. Brixham mean, *abducting Miss Kittling*? I think he must be very confused."

"Undoubtedly. Perhaps you should ask him to explain everything to you. I shall fetch some brandy."

"Yes, brandy will do," Gaventry said. He made the profound mistake of meeting Sarah's gaze and received a look so scathing as to leave him in no doubt of her present sentiments toward him. Not that he gave a flying fig what she thought, vixen that she was, authoress of that deuced novel, his nemesis! No, he did not care one whit what she thought!

He then caught Aurelia's gaze and saw a look of such disappointment that he suddenly felt to be the worst criminal in all the world. Somehow her brain had managed to make sense of the meaning of her present circumstances. "You . . . you were abducting me?" she queried in a small voice. "But you were always so kind to me. Whyever would you want to hurt me?"

Gaventry had never felt so guilt-stricken in his entire existence. He could easily manage Brixham attacking him or Sarah regarding him as though he were a worse creature than a rabid dog, but there was something in Miss Kittling's angelic countenance coupled with the simplicity of her mind and the purity of her heart which slew his conscience completely.

"Yes, Gaven," Mr. Brixham said, rising up on one elbow.

"Pray explain to my betrothed just why you would wish to do her injury."

"Do stubble it," he said, throwing himself into a chair by the fireplace.

He knew he should apologize to Miss Kittling, but he was frustrated and angry, mostly, he realized, with himself. He could not, however, bring himself to look into Miss Kittling's wounded eyes one more time.

This, however, proved to be an impossibility, for in scarcely an instant more Miss Kittling was kneeling before him. He was shocked and would have immediately begged her to rise, but she whispered, "You must forgive her. You must! She loves you so. You can have no notion. I . . . I do not always understand things, but I can see that I was not your object. You wanted to hurt Sally, did you not? And you must have known that you could not hurt her more than if you hurt someone she loved. I see that now. But, indeed, Lord Gaventry, you are the one being hurt, not me, not even Sally. 'Tis only you."

He looked into dewy, pleading blue eyes and thought, just as Brixham had said a dozen times, that Miss Aurelia Kittling was an angel. Her understanding came in fits and starts, but more often than not she seemed able to penetrate to the core of his character and sufferings. He found himself so deeply touched that something within him began giving way, like a dam no longer able to hold back the flood waters. "Oh, God," he murmured, "to have sunk so low."

He leaned forward, settling his elbows on his knees, and buried his face in his hands.

Sarah arrived at the doorway with brandy in hand and was so stunned by the sight before her that she nearly dropped the glass. Aurrie was petting Gaventry's head and murmuring something to him in what appeared to be a very comforting manner. What had transpired since she quit the parlor she could only imagine, but never in a thousand years would she have expected this tender scene. Except . . . Aurelia had such gifts, such sweet powers, that in general only her family understood her. Now, it would seem, Gaventry was beginning to comprehend her as well.

She moved at last from her frozen position in the doorway and took the brandy to Mr. Brixham. She found him sitting up, his jaw red and swollen, but his eyes were filled with happiness. Finding herself undone, she handed him the brandy and without knowing what to say, simply sat down next to him. He then possessed himself of her hand and gave it a warm squeeze.

After a moment, Gaventry leaned back in his chair and smiled down at Aurelia. He caressed her face with both hands and kissed her forehead. "You are an angel," he murmured.

"Indeed, I am no such thing!" she protested.

Brixham squeezed Sarah's hand again and whispered. "She is *my* angel."

"So she is," Sarah returned. "And you are to be my brother. We have always wanted a brother, Meg and I, and now we shall have one."

The part of her, however, that was always counting the contents of the household coffer suddenly replaced every sentiment. She lowered her voice. "You must know that I stand as a mother to Aurelia in some ways and I must know, before the banns are to be read in church, if, that is, if you are able—"

"Perfectly able," he responded, releasing her hand and giving it a reassuring pat. "I may not be as plump in the pocket as my friend here, but I have a snug property in Devonshire and a very pretty house. My housekeeper is a bit of a tyrant, however. But why are you weeping, Miss Sarah?"

Sarah felt her throat constrict further. "Because I know now that my sister will be the happiest lady imaginable in your care." She searched her pocket for a kerchief and once finding it, began dabbing at her eyes.

He pursed his lips together mightily. "It means a great deal to me to hear you say as much."

If he cleared his throat several times and blinked heartily

at the ceiling, she paid no mind. Instead, she hooked her arm
about his and for a very long moment, remained beside him.

When at last Aurelia rose from the carpeted floor and
moved to sit on the other side of Brixham, Sarah released her
soon-to-be brother-in-law and crossed the room to the dia-
mond-paned window overlooking the innyard. A mail coach
had just drawn up and passengers spilled from the top of the
coach and the doorway like birds descending to a field of
newly sewn seed.

The evening gloom had turned to night. Aurelia may have
found it in her heart to forgive Gaventry, but Sarah was not
certain she ever would.

A half hour later, Sarah boarded the post chaise Mr. Brixham had originally hired to follow in Gaventry's wake and
took up a seat beside her sister. The viscount and Mr. Brixham
were to travel together. The discussion about just how the
party should return to Bath was a brief one involving but a single object, to minimize the gossip that surely had rung through
the streets of Bath following Aurelia's fine declaration that she
was to be married when she and Gaventry had first quit
Queen's Square. Gaventry, deeply subdued in Sarah's opinion,
said he would beg his godmother's assistance in making matters right, which he felt certain, given her fondness for the
Kittling ladies, she would do quite readily, particularly when
she learned that Brixham was betrothed to the eldest.

Several hours later, Sarah climbed between the sheets, exhausted to the bone. Aurelia was not less so, since the greater
part of the day and evening had been spent traveling.

She awoke the following morning to a stillness in the house
that was both exceedingly pleasant and a little alarming. At
the same time, she knew something had awakened her, but
she could not imagine what. Why was the square so quiet and
where was her family? A moment later, several shouts and a
scattering of applause resounded to her window. The front
door slammed, and running feet were heard on the stairs. She
was not surprised when Meg, breathless, threw open her door.

"You will never guess!" she cried. "But a very small troup of actors and jugglers, magicians, and even a Gypsy prepared to tell all our fortunes, is come to the square! You must hurry for there is such acrobatics as I have never before seen!"

Aurelia stumbled sleepily into the chamber, rubbing her eyes. "What is it, Meggie?"

Meg pushed past her. "Tell her, Sally, for I must return at once!" Her feet were once more pounding down the stairs.

Sarah had already slipped from her bed and though standing discreetly to one side of the window since she was dressed in her mobcap and nightclothes, she held the curtain back for her sister. "Come and see for yourself."

Aurelia, also as discreetly as possibly in order to not be seen from the window, glanced down into the square. "A fair, here in Queen's Square! How delightful! Look at the dog doing tricks. I have never seen a creature jump so high!"

Sarah smiled. After the difficulties of the day before, she found she wanted nothing more than to take part in the festivities below. "We must dress at once," she cried. She was about to move away when a tall figure moved into view.

Gaventry.

Her smile vanished. Brixham was with him, and together they were watching a juggler tossing several oranges into an ever-broadening circle above his head. She still felt as she had last night, that his conduct had been unforgivable. She was grateful he had not attempted to apologize to her, for she believed had he done so, she would have rung a peal over his head that could have been heard in London.

"There is my Mr. Brixham," Aurelia said, almost reverently. "Does he not look handsome in his brown coat?"

"Indeed, he does," Sarah responded. "I think brown suits his ruddy-colored hair."

"I could not agree more. Oh, Sally, I never thought to love. I am more blessed than I can say."

Sarah set aside her own discontent and slipped her arm

around her sister's waist. "Yes, you are but I have never known a lady to be more worthy of love than you."

"Do you know in all these years I have thought the very same of you?"

"No," Sarah returned, letting the curtain fall back into place. "You cannot be serious. I am not nearly so sweet-tempered as you, so deserving in every way."

Aurrie regarded her thoughtfully for a long moment. "I . . . I always wished I was more like you, so clever, so willing to sacrifice yourself for our sakes, or did you think we never noticed that your gowns were usually cut from cheaper cloth or that you sported less ribbons on your bonnets than either myself or Meg? And I shall never forget the time that you gave Charlotte your favorite reticule when hers had worn thin. Sarah, I shall confess something. I always thought I should have given her one of mine for I had three. Three! So, you see how very bad I am, not an angel in the least. I fear I am very selfish, indeed!"

Sarah embraced her suddenly. "If the worst that can be said of you, my darling Aurelia, is that you did not give up a reticule when you might have, then you are safe from being condemned by even the best of any of our friends and acquaintances. But go, now! Summon Betsy to do your hair first for I daresay Mr. Brixham will call in but a scant few minutes."

"Oh, yes, you are very right. I shall do so at once." She scurried away, but returned immediately to give Sarah a kiss on her cheek, then hurried away once more.

Sarah was left to dress herself at a more leisurely pace. Though she wanted to attend the gaieties in the square, she was not anxious to see Gaventry again. She could only wonder why he had come to Queen Square at all. Surely he must know he was not in the least welcome.

Gaventry watched the acrobats, jugglers, and the dark eyes of a Gypsy fortune-teller with only a small portion of his attention. The greater part was fixed on the door to Sarah's town house, wondering when she would emerge, for he had something of a very particular nature he wished to tell her today.

The journey last night from the Shropshire border back to the seven hills of Bath had been sobering in the extreme. He had of course apologized to Brixham for having been so mulishly set on his own course that he had been incapable of seeing that his good friend had fallen in love at last with a lady whose reputation he had meant to destroy. His pride had suffered a different sort of blow this time, for he had always considered himself a man of perception and discernment. To have not known that Brixham, who was always escorting Miss Kittling hither and yon, had serious intentions of his own was lowering in the extreme.

Brixham, in his usual good-natured manner, however, had told him to forget his blunder, that for himself he could only be grateful that Gaventry's pique over *A Rogue's Tale* had been the cause of his journey to Bath and thereby his path to Miss Kittling and love. Gaventry felt humbled by his friend's gracious spirit and for the remainder of the trip had set himself to examining, even scrutinizing, much of his life from the time Miss Fulbourne had used him so wretchedly. He allowed himself to be chastened as he had never been before, not only by these circumstances but equally as much by Lady Haslingfield's parting words to him earlier that day, to the effect that he was a thoughtless, spoiled man who had not had a proper thought in his head for a very long time.

At last returning to his home in the Royal Crescent, he had climbed between the sheets exhausted and determined to make matters right between himself and Sarah. He did not know precisely how this was to be achieved or even what it was he would say to her to express his regret over all that had transpired, but having resolved in his mind to do so had given him a profoundly restful sleep.

He had awakened this morning set on his course and prepared to speak with her, only why had she not left her house?

The door opened at last, but only Miss Aurelia Kittling

emerged, looking as she always did, like an angel. Brix went to her at once and quickly possessed himself of her hand. Gaventry greeted her warmly, and she responded with her usual sweetness, assuring him that *Sally* was intent on attending the small, impromptu fair and would surely be leaving the house very soon. "Would you be so good, Lord Gaventry, as to attend to her?" she asked. "For my cousin is gone and Meggie I can see is having her fortune read by a Gypsy. Sally would not like to be alone, this morning, of that I am certain."

Gaventry was a little surprised, even more so when Miss Kittling winked at him.

"Of course I shall," he returned.

"I knew I might rely upon you." In a lower voice, she whispered, "And for all her protests otherwise, try to remember that she is quite violently in love with you."

With that, she allowed Brix to guide her in the direction of a man riding an extraordinarily tall hobbyhorse.

Gaventry watched them go, oddly content at the sight of his friend having found a match at last. At the same time, he felt a little stunned by Miss Kittling's revelation as to the state of her sister's heart. So Sarah was violently in love with him. A familiar, powerful sensation gripped his chest. She loved him. He turned toward her house and saw a lady moving in the upper window, probably the woman herself, but what did it mean that she loved him?

Lady Haslingfield had thought her an excellent match for him, but why had she thought as much? Because she had written that deuced novel or perhaps because whenever she but came into the realm of his vision, he could scarcely look at anyone else? He did not know.

He recalled the beginnings of his relationship with her, the very first encounter here, in Queen Square, when he had chanced upon her and had kissed her. He marveled to think that she had been in truth the very woman he had come to Bath to destroy. A sudden breeze tugged at his hat and whipped the tails of his coat. Fate at work again, perhaps, he thought, his gaze still fixed on the window above. Fate seemed to have been involved in his affairs at the outset to completely undo him in every possible sense, for here he was unwilling to take the revenge he had been so determined on from the time he had read *A Rogue's Tale*.

The real question that rose to his mind in this moment, however, was whether or not he was in love with Sarah Kittling.

As though somehow comprehending that he was thinking about her, she came to the window and looked at him. By habit, he lifted his hat and bowed slightly. She waved in response, but not even a hint of a smile touched her lips. She then disappeared from the window.

He crossed the street quickly and rapped softly on the door. He did not have long to wait. She opened the door herself just as she had, good God, was it only yesterday? "I believe we have much to discuss," he said.

"Then perhaps you had best come in," she responded, stepping aside.

As before, he handed her his hat and dropped the gloves within. She settled his hat on the narrow table by the door, then led him into the drawing room. There was a frost in her demeanor that had never been there before. It would seem he had succeeded after all in causing her injury. She sat down in a straight-backed chair near the fireplace.

When he did not take up a seat, she glanced up at him. "Will you not sit down?"

"Not when you are so angry with me," he responded, wondering just how she would respond. He supposed he hoped she might smile, but she merely sighed.

"Then I suppose you will have to stand," she said, "and that for a very long while unless what you wish to say to me is of short duration."

"It is not," he returned. "So I shall sit."

"As you please."

He drew a chair close to her, directly in front of her in fact, which so startled her that she flinched. "What are you about?" she whispered.

Before Gaventry even knew himself what he intended to do or say to her, he had possessed himself of one of her hands. He then understood precisely what it was that he wished her to know, something very few people knew. There was no help for it, he must tell her what had really happened so many years ago. "I was deeply in love with Arabella Fulbourne, so much so that had she said night was day I would have believed her. I would have believed anything she told me. I do not know what manner of charms she possessed that had so blinded me to her true character, perhaps it was just my youth, but so I was.

"I courted her with such dedication that all my friends laughed at me for making such a cake of myself, but I did not care. She was the lady I loved and the woman I would make my wife, the mistress of my home, the mother of my children. I had begged her to marry me a dozen times. She made half-promises, toying with my affections, something I did not in the least comprehend at the time, so seriously was I besotted with her, and in my blindness I did not see the trap she was setting for me.

"There was another man she desired, perhaps with as much fervor as I desired her, for she would have done anything to snare him." He paused, the memories inflicting the sharpest of pains in his chest. Anger roiled in him, sudden and fierce.

"Stewkley," she murmured, her complexion having paled.

He nodded. "His was a rank higher than mine, his worth in her eyes a hundredfold no doubt. But there was something more that I did not comprehend about either of them. There was a baseness to their characters that I have to this day found unmatched, even among those who would drink wine from skulls."

"What did they do?" she asked, her brow pinched with concern.

"I was led by way of a desperate missive written in her

pretty hand to a brothel near one of the east gaming hells. Stewkely was holding her captive, or so she had written."

"What?" Sarah cried. "What do you mean?"

"It was a game, a very deep one, in which a lady might win an earl. They had been in league, you see. He had wanted to see me crushed and when I arrived, alone, but ready to vanquish a man whom I knew to be inferior in both strength or ability with sword or pistol, I was set upon by four men, not one of whom was the earl.

"I awoke with a headache such as I had never known before. I was bruised in every imaginable part of my body, my leg sprained. Three days and nights had passed during which time I had lain unconscious. One of the women who worked in the brothel informed me that I had been attacked by thugs hired by Stewkely and beaten to the point of death. She had cared for me during that time, being an avaricious if not kind creature, since she understood I was well-shod and would reward her handsomely for her succor. She also told me that both Miss Fulbourne and Stewkely had laughed over the incident and drank a glass of gin to my recovery."

Sarah gave his hand a squeeze. "But to what purpose? I do not understand."

"Sport. Nothing more, nor less. The, er, lady who saved me said that it was a game they had played many times before, with lesser connected gentlemen previously, green young men just arrived in London from the country. Apparently, it had been Miss Fulbourne's notion, once I took up a prominent place in her court, to pit their skill against my youth and foolishness.

"What Stewkely did not know was that there was another lady present to witness the event, one of London's most prominent hostesses, Miss Fulbourne's aunt. This lady I count as equally vile as her niece, for she watched the whole of the incident for the sole purpose of being afterward enabled to blackmail Stewkely into wedding Miss Fulbourne."

"This lady knew that you were nearly killed, but she did nothing to help you?" she asked, clearly shocked.

"Not to my knowledge. Afterward, I believe it was she who devised the damning gossip about me to the effect that I had lured Arabella into the brothel that night and that Stewkely had been summoned to save her."

Sarah had listened to this recounting with a growing horror that made her feel quite ill. Her anger had dissipated the moment he had spoken of having been beaten and left for dead. Somehow the difficulties of her own life, the frustrations of her poverty and living in Bath, paled in comparison to Gaventry's story of loving a woman but being so violently betrayed by her. She now understood the source of his bitterness and why he had shunned society so completely.

She was not certain where to begin. Finally, she said, "I would never have guessed that anything so vile could have occurred."

"That is because your mind cannot conceive of such evils. The most Widenhall did in your novel was to elope with Lucinda, which was what she had planned all along at Daventry's expense."

"Yes, that was the worst I could contrive. The truth is so horrible that I feel utterly sick at heart. Does anyone else know?"

"Brixham," he said quietly.

"Of course. No truer friend could any man have." She was silent for a moment before saying, "I suspect Lady Haslingfield also knows something of what happened."

"You may be right."

Sarah smiled, if faintly. "Or she may not care overly much. She is quite protective of her role in Bath society and holds a very poor opinion of London's beau monde. It may have been enough that you were her godson."

He smiled also. "Regardless, we at least hold the same opinion of London society. That much we have in common."

Sarah regarded him thoughtfully. She was still so shocked

by what he had told her that she did not know what more to say to him.

"My dearest Sarah," he said suddenly, his voice husky with emotion as he leaned toward her, "will you ever forgive me for having made your family the object of my vengeance? I was not thinking at all properly, not until your sister showered me with such love, pity, and forgiveness. All changed for me in that moment, but can you forgive me?"

Sarah looked into his clear blue eyes, now lit with remorse and filled with a deeper sentiment that she could not quite comprehend. For the longest moment, she felt as though her heart would simply stop beating. Somewhere in the midst of his having related the accounting of that fateful event of seven years past, her anger had, indeed, disappeared. She understood so very much about him now, certainly the reasons for his bitterness. Was he bitter still, though?

"Of course I will," she murmured, tears filling her eyes. "Will you, that is, how will you ever forgive me for what I have done?"

He took possession of her other hand and holding both very tightly, responded, "There can be no excuse for what I did. Your reasons for having written your novel, however, were at least in part honorable—you meant only good, even salvation, for your family. While I—" He broke off, unable to complete his thought.

"While you were responding as anyone would, with outrage!" she exclaimed. "I should never have written *A Rogue's Tale.*" The realization that very soon the sequel would be at the bookseller's made her shudder inwardly.

"Perhaps you should not have, but I hope that we both can forget the past."

"I am certain I can forgive you but not so certain I will ever be able to forgive myself."

"Then I must help you." With that, he leaned closer still and placed a tender kiss on her lips.

When Gaventry drew back, understanding dawned in his

mind as though a rising sun, struggling to redeem the night, had just cleared a tall mountain. The love he felt for Sarah Kittling pierced bone and marrow. He loved her, full and deeply, now and forever. He loved her. He loved as he had never loved. Certainly the sentiments that now possessed him were in no way comparable to the naive infatuation he had felt for Arabella. No, this was a profound sentiment that spoke of the foundations of the earth, of the far reaches of heaven, of the depth and beauty of the stars in the sky. He loved her.

"I love you," he said. Once more, he leaned forward and kissed her. This time, he felt her lips tremble beneath his. He drew back and lifted her to her feet, at nearly the same moment catching her up in his arms. "I love you so very much. How dear you are become to me in but a handful of weeks."

The expression on her face of disbelieving wonder, the way her arm crept around his neck, the manner in which she touched his lips lightly with her fingers, bespoke her sentiments and he was not surprised when she kissed him hard on the mouth in return. The kiss that followed took him on a long, long journey to places he had never been before, to the deepest recesses of his heart, where so much bitterness had once resided, but no longer, to the innocence of his youth which he had long believed lost to him forever, to what now became a mounting wave of affection that rose to heights he could never before have imagined. He could not hold her tightly enough nor did he believe there were sufficient words with which to express all that was within him of devotion, passion, of enduring love. He wanted her beside him always.

"Marry me?" he whispered against her lips, the words, though surprising him, felt as perfect as any two words could ever have been.

Sarah heard his proposal asked with such simplicity, and could not for a moment doubt his sincerity. "Oh, Gaventry," she murmured, placing kisses on his lips one after another. "I should like nothing better for I believe I tumbled in love with you the moment I first saw you."

The kiss that followed, coupled with Gaventry's declaration, affected Sarah strangely. She felt as though she had just climbed to the top of the highest mountain and was now dizzy with exhilaration. Was Gaventry spinning her in circles? Would her heart ever stop racing? Why could she not feel her feet? What did any of it matter? Gaventry was kissing her, he had asked her to become his wife, she loved and she was loved. His lips became a fire that set her soul to burning brightly.

"I never thought this would happen," he whispered against her cheek.

"Nor I," she returned, kissing him anew. How she loved him. How dear, how critical to her happiness, he had become in such a short while. How much she wished, as she had wished on several previous occasions, that she might hold him and kiss him forever. She said as much.

A chuckle returned to her. "Then perhaps we ought to consider marriage by special license."

"Yes, indeed, we should," she responded, again settling her lips on his. With such a license they could be married within three days and she could keep her arms wrapped about him for as long as she wished . . . except . . .

The worst bolt of fear suddenly shot through her and with such a powerful emotion, she fairly flew away from him. "I forgot!" she exclaimed.

"Good God, whatever is the matter?"

*A Rogue's Revenge*. But how could she tell him the terrible truth now that all was settled between them? Now that love was confessed and marriage promised?

"You look very ill," he said, immediately taking her hands and leading her back to the chair she had been sitting in earlier.

She sat down blindly. There would be no marriage, of that she was certain. Her first novel was one thing, but the second? Surely, Gaventry would be angered beyond reason? Surely the love he was presently expressing to her would disintegrate, and why wouldn't it, for she had used him badly . . . again.

He sat down as well, still holding her hands. "Sarah, please speak to me, please tell me what it is that has given you such a shock. What were you thinking that took the bloom from your cheeks and the light from your eyes? Is it possible you just realized you were mistaken in your affections?"

She saw the frown between his eyes and knew she could not remain mute forever. "No, no! Indeed, it is no such thing. I love you." She squeezed his hands and added, "My darling, I believe I love you to the point of madness."

"Then what is it?"

How could she tell him? She closed her eyes and sought about in her head for the right words, but all that returned to her was a powerful warning that once he knew he would leave her forever. That was something she could not face, not just yet, not when their professed love was so new and so very wonderful. "There is something I must tell you, something that might make you wish that you had not offered for me. Indeed, I believe it is so very bad that you will desire to be released from our betrothal once you know."

With that he began to smile and then to laugh. She did not think what she had said in the least amusing. "Why do you laugh?" she asked, offended.

"Because though I have known you only a few weeks, your notion of having done something that would be *so very bad* that I would no longer wish to marry you, is undoubtedly of such little consequence that I can only laugh. Do you not see? There is nothing you can have done that would alter how I feel about you, nor could it dim in the slightest my desire to make you my wife."

She felt the weight of his sincerity and began to relax, but still the words would not come to make this new confession. She therefore rose to her feet and smiled. "I shall choose to believe you, and though there is something of great importance that I must tell you I beg you to allow me to wait until I am ready to do so, in perhaps a day or so."

"Of course," he said. "What do you say then, that we cross

to the square? I should like to have you on my arm for a time so that my intentions toward you might be marked by all."

Sarah felt certain she was making a mistake in not speaking, but she chose to ignore the warning bells that resounded in her head. "I should be delighted."

She put her bonnet on and he, his hat and gloves. Leaving the town house, she walked beside him, her arm tucked around his very tightly. The circumstance of their having emerged together, and without even one of her sisters or Charlotte to lend them a proper countenance, was noted by more than one gabblemonger.

"Do you see how many matrons are staring at us and whispering?" he queried softly.

"How could I not notice when there have even been a few gasps. I suppose you will be required to marry me now."

"And do but look," he added, giving her hand a squeeze. "There is my godmother descending on us like a ship-of-the-line. I pity her companion. Look how Miss Whittle runs to keep pace."

Sarah smiled, for he was very right, and with a white veil lifting off Lady Haslingfield's bonnet, she did seem to be in full mast.

"How do you go on, Godmother?" he asked congenially as she drew near.

She did not speak but glanced from one to the other several times. "It is all settled!" she cried. "I can see it in your eyes, the pair of you! But this is wonderful!"

Sarah glanced up at Gaventry and could not keep from smiling, something he did in return. "Yes, it is, my lady," she said softly.

"This is most excellent but I can see as I look around that there are several of my friends shaking their heads and frowning. What have the pair of you done now?"

"Something shameful. We were alone together in the drawing room of Miss Sarah's home."

"Oh, dear. Well, I can see that you have set the tabbies to

gossiping, but do not fear, I know very well how to deal with such impertinence, only you will see that the banns are read for the next four Sundays and do not think for a moment of either eloping or settling on one of these absurd special license marriages. I shall give the wedding breakfast, which will lend a proper tone to your marriage, and that will be the end of it. Oh, and there is one more thing before I take my leave." Here she stopped and stared very hard at Sarah. "You ought to take Gaventry to Milsom Street for something very interesting is on display in one of the windows. Presently, there are very few people about because of the fair, but it will not remain so much longer."

Sarah felt the blood drain from her face. "Is it something of a *roguish* nature, my lady?"

At that, an amused smile twisted her lips. "Indeed, very much so but now I see we have both shocked your betrothed, so do go at once and then return to me here that we might set a proper date for your nuptials."

She moved on, with Miss Whittle bobbing beside her.

Gaventry leaned down. "What mystery is this?" he inquired as Sarah inclined her head, gesturing in the direction of Milsom Street.

"I had hoped to be spared telling you now, but it would seem fate will not have it otherwise."

"I wish you would not speak in circles. Tell me now."

She shook her head, but felt her spirits dropping with every second that passed. "No, it will be better for you to see for yourself and then, as I have said before, I will release you from our betrothal if you wish for it."

"That will be a very difficult thing to do at this juncture since I know that by now a great number of personages, many of elevated consequence, have just been invited to a wedding breakfast to which you and I will be required, undoubtedly on pain of death, to attend."

She could only laugh, but her amusement vanished quickly. All she could think now was that her second novel had arrived at the booksellers and that she must answer for it to the man she loved. She tried to keep her spirits calm, but visions of a terrible future rose in her head, horrible images in which she had become a confirmed spinster, dandling Aurelia's and Brixham's children on her knee, and forced to listen to stories of how Gaventry went to London, found himself a proper young lady to wed, and now had dozens of children of his own. By the time she reached Milsom Street, tears stung her eyes.

The bookseller was not far as they turned in a northerly direction.

She glanced up at Gaventry and noticed that he was looking up and down the street. "For the life of me," he said, "I cannot see anything that would put you in such a quake."

Two shops more.

"You will understand in but a moment."

How many steps to the bookseller? Fifteen, perhaps? She began to understand how a criminal might feel approaching Tyburn Tree where a noose awaited. Her heart was pounding in her chest so loudly that she heard the steady beats in her ears.

Ten steps to go.

She felt sick and wondered if she would now truly disgrace herself by casting up her accounts or possibly even by swooning.

Five steps. She could see the window of the store and her book was on display, with a small card beneath which said, BY THE AUTHOR OF A ROGUE'S TALE.

"Oh, Gaventry! Pray forgive me!" And with that she could no longer restrain her suffering and promptly burst into tears.

"What?" he cried. "What is it?"

She leveled a finger at the traitorous book. She buried her nose in her kerchief but all the while she peered at him above a fluff of wadded lace. Her heart ached beyond words. He would never forgive her! Never!

He moved closer and she could see he was reading the card

beneath the book and then the actual title of the book, *A Rogue's Revenge*, in beautiful gilt.

He turned to stare at her, his mouth slightly agape. "You wrote this?"

She nodded and a fresh layer of tears flooded her eyes and seeped into the rumpled kerchief. "You see how bad I am?" she wailed, wiping her eyes and blowing her nose.

He then appeared to be searching his memory. "This looks like the size and quality of the book I picked up from the paving stones in Queen Square on the first day I met you."

She nodded. "It was. I had just received a copy from Mr. Bertram."

"Good God," he murmured. He seemed utterly astounded. "Does the story involve a ridiculous hero who comes to Bath intent on hurting the author of the first novel?"

"Of course not," she said. "It is more that the hero, who learned the real villain of the piece was His Grace, the Duke of Widenhall, slays him."

He narrowed his gaze. "Swords or pistols?"

"Swords, naturally, because it is so much more interesting to describe than a simple shot with a pistol."

"Of course." He wore an expression as though this made perfect sense to him.

"Are you not angry?" she asked, her tears drying, now that the bridge had been crossed.

He turned to her. "Livid," he cried, taking a step toward her.

She backed up and blew her nose again. She would have immediately started apologizing and begging forgiveness, but he was not done. "Outraged!" he exclaimed, taking another step toward her.

Again she backed up.

"Furious!" he continued, taking yet another step.

She backed up once more.

"Incensed! Irate! Mad as fire!" He shook a fist in her face.

"And so you should be," she cried, taking a few more steps backward, for indeed he seemed somewhat deranged of the moment. "I . . . I am so sorry. Indeed, this was why I told you earlier that I doubted you would truly wish to marry me."

He kept approaching her and she kept walking backward until finally he caught her arm and held her still. "So you wrote another deuced novel," he cried, glaring at her.

"Yes." There was no use trying to justify what she had done.

"You will need to write a third, I imagine, also about revenge."

"What do you mean?" He was out of his wits, she could see that now.

"Only that there will naturally need to be another sequel, something to the effect that Daventry discovers that two novels have been written about his exploits, how he falls violently in love with the authoress but is so angry that she has written the books in the first place that he plots a very, very wicked revenge upon her."

"What does he do?" she asked, frightened to hear his answer, for images of strangling the authoress and throwing her into the River Avon came sharply to mind.

"There is only one thing he truly can do that will in the smallest way force the authoress to atone for her wretched, heinous impertinence in writing stories about him."

"If you are thinking he should murder her," she said, lifting her chin, "you must know that so honorable a man would never do anything so horrible. Indeed, though he might think it he would soon realize that he would probably hang for the crime itself once it became known that she was the authoress and he was actually seen threatening her in public, on, er, Milsom Street, for instance!"

He narrowed his gaze at her again. "Is that how you intend to write it?"

"Yes. He would never actually slay the woman he loves."

"I quite agree. No, he concocts an even worse punishment for such a terrible betrayal."

Sarah tried to think of something that was as horrid as

murder but could not and again she rather suspected that the sight of the sequel had somehow addled his mind. "What in your opinion then could possibly be worse than murder?"

He smiled. Yes, it was a smile. His expression softened. "Having to live with him the rest of her years as his wife. That would be sufficient punishment, indeed!"

She was stunned. Perhaps she could have mistaken the meaning of what he had just said, but it was not in the smallest way possible to misconstrue the deep tenderness that had taken hold of his eyes.

"Silly chit," he whispered, slipping his arms about her in full view of the numerous people and carriages who were about at this time of day. "I do not give a fig if you wrote a dozen novels about me and they all appeared in that window in the next few seconds. I have fallen desperately in love with you and I will marry you."

Sarah could not believe what he was saying. "You are not serious," she cried. "You cannot be. I think you must be ill."

"I have never been more serious in my entire life. I was a fool coming to Bath for the reasons that I did, but I shall be a fool no longer." With that, he settled his lips on hers and in the sweetest manner possible, gave proof of the depth of his sentiments.

Only after some few minutes, in which several ladies had gathered close and were clearing their throats ominously, did he finally draw back.

Sarah, realizing that she had actually permitted Gaventry to kiss her in public, felt her cheeks begin to burn. As she let her arms slide away from around his neck, she turned to find Lady Riseley and Mrs. Catesby staring at them. They then began sending others away who had stopped to observe the shocking conduct of one of London's most notorious rogues.

Mrs. Catesby said, "Your godmother sent us to find you. She wishes to speak with you at once about your *wedding breakfast*."

With these words, she confirmed their betrothal, which

caused a number of the passersby to nod in understanding at the spectacle she and Gaventry had just made of themselves. For herself, Sarah was happy to be going and had never left Milsom Street so quickly in her entire life.

Halfway to Queen Square, she glanced up at Gaventry, still unable to credit that he was truly able to forgive her. "But are you certain?" she asked quietly, lest the ladies in front of them could overhear her. "You will not perhaps regret our marriage some weeks, months, or years hence when you consider what I have done?"

He held her arm tightly and patted her hand. "No, not at all. You must understand, I am convinced that marrying me will be sufficient penance."

"Will you not be serious?" she whispered.

He met her gaze. "I love you, Sarah. Did you not consider the possibility that had you not written that novel, we might never have met? Just how well in this moment do you think I can bear that thought? I had no reason to come to Bath, no interest, except for your novel."

"I am not certain how sound your reasoning is, but I confess I take great comfort in it."

The remainder of the journey back to Queen Square, where a large crowd of revelers had now gathered, had been a quiet one. The ladies, acting as a vanguard, guided Sarah and Gaventry to Lady Haslingfield, where she was told by Mrs. Catesby precisely what had transpired in Queen Square.

She was rightly incensed and addressed Gaventry. "I hope you do not mean to settle in Bath!" she exclaimed. "For I vow it will require six weeks of strenuous work to undo this folly! And you, Miss Sarah! I had thought you would have had a great deal more sense than to make such an exhibition of yourself on Milsom Street. Milsom Street!! Well, well, there is nothing to be done now. You had best not attend the Pump Room anytime during these next several days and please, the pair of you, do attend church each Sunday that the banns are read for this will aid me in my efforts to undo this damage. Oh, what a dreadful thing, kissing in public! But you must heed my warnings, or . . ."

Lady Haslingfield continued to speak, but Sarah stopped listening. She glanced up at Gaventry, and when he met her gaze she suspected he was no longer listening to the pontifications of his godmother either. On and on, her wisdom waxed as she poured forth each plan, each lecture about discretion and dignity, each upbraiding for their very bad conduct. Throughout, Sarah looked into Gaventry's eyes and he into hers. She let him feel the strength of her love for him, which she was certain he had begun to feel in earnest. He took a small step toward her, and everything but him seemed to fade away completely. She smiled and took a step in his direction. He reached for her, but the next moment the spell was entirely broken when Lady Haslingfield forced herself between them. "Good God!" she cried. "Have you heard, nay, have you not understood a thing I have been trying to tell you?"

Sarah turned to stare at her blankly, uncertain what just had happened. Gaventry shrugged.

Lady Haslingfield rolled her eyes. "I think you must consider a special license after all, and a protracted honeymoon anywhere but in Bath!"

"As you wish, Godmother," he said.

"At least try not to kiss her again in public! Well, I am done with you, the pair of you!" She then led her entourage in the direction of several dogs who were performing tricks.

"Perhaps we could walk about," Sarah suggested.

"That will not do, not by half."

Sarah thought for a moment, then smiled. "There is a very private courtyard just beyond the kitchens."

"That will do very well, indeed!"

Sarah spent the next hour with Gaventry taking his kisses at leisure and beginning the delightful process of planning just how the next few days would see them wed, and where they should honeymoon.

Sometime later, when the family was gathered together in the blue drawing room, Sarah sat beside Gaventry, who in turn was telling Meg of his travels in the West Indies. Meg listened enraptured and proclaimed that above all else she wished to travel just as Gaventry had, to the ends of the earth if possible. Charlotte listened as well, smiling all the while, her needle plying the fabric stretched within her tambour frame as more of the roses came to life beneath her skilled fingers. Aurelia played the pianoforte with her usual brilliance while Brixham leaned over the instrument and gazed adoringly into her face. Sarah glanced from one visage to the next and thought there could be no greater happiness than this, to be in the midst of family and friends, to know love and to be loved, and perhaps above all, to be forgiven.

# More Regency Romance
# From Zebra